I0757897

HOPE EMERGES

BOOK 5 OF THE NATURE'S FURY SERIES

Respect isn't always earned. Sometimes it's demanded.

A.E. FAULKNER

INDIEOWL
PRESS

4700 Millenia Blvd.
Ste #175-90776
Orlando, FL 32839

info@indieowlpress.com
www.indieowlpress.com

HOPE EMERGES

Cover design by Michelle Preast
Indie Book Cover Designs / Michelle-Preast.com

Interior layout by Vanessa Anderson
at NightOwlFreelance.com

Manufactured in the United States of America

Paperback ISBN-13: 978-1-949193-10-7

Scott, Landon, and Aidan – characters come and go, but I'm thankful to have you as permanent fixtures in my life. Thanks for being by my side through this series! I look forward to many more adventures to come.

"And I will punish the world for their evil, and the wicked for their iniquity; and I will cause the arrogancy of the proud to cease, and will lay low the haughtiness of the terrible."
— *Isaiah 13:11*

Contents

Contents

Contents

HOPE EMERGES

Chapter 1

Every minute of every hour we're down here, the biting chill seeps deeper into my bones. Humans are not meant to live underground, shrouded in darkness. While the solid rock acts as a protective barrier from the poisoned air outside, on some days, it feels more like an impenetrable prison wall.

The dim beam of our lanterns and flashlights creeps into the corners and sweeps across the path. But in the two weeks we've been here, the lack of natural light dampens the mood, a sullen emptiness swelling within the cavern.

We all have jobs to do. Everyone other than Jeff, that is. His condition hasn't improved. The day Riley, Aidan, Jeff and I arrived here, we were carrying loads of supplies down a flight of steps carved from the rock. Riley and I brought our dog, Snickers, with us and the rat terrier could not contain his excitement while Jeff was attempting to navigate the slippery steps with his arms overloaded. He lost his balance and tumbled into the unforgiving abyss. What followed was a literal explosion caused by what he was carrying when he fell and the tunnel collapsed, injuring Jeff and separating Aidan, Riley, and me from the others.

The next day, with help from Jeff's brother Matt, we broke through the barrier of stone and rubble. The significance of Jeff's injuries, however, quickly doused the initial euphoria of our success. He has not regained feeling below his waist, and no one here has any medical experience.

Aidan's dad stays busy organizing and keeping track of everything that isn't made of stone. It's almost obsessive. I can't criticize, though. He created a schedule to ensure a balance of duties—and privacy for bathing. It works.

The youngest cave dwellers are Aidan's teenage sisters Jessa and Kaylee, who spend a lot of time together in their "room." They aren't physically active beyond necessity, and they respond to every conversation attempt with disinterest. Even when they're helping wash clothes or prepare meals, they slide into a trance-like state. I recognize it from the first few days after Riley and I arrived at our aunt's trailer.

Time was an immeasurable entity, as we wavered between disbelief and denial. Granted, we had just lost our parents in a horrific car crash, so maybe I'm not the best judge of what they're going through. I do sense a sadness born of loss, though.

Their family is together right now, though. Safe. I can't imagine that's something most teenagers would consider, let alone appreciate. When your family reduces by half in an instant, like us, that type of loss is an emotional blunt force trauma. *And who knows how many others have been forced to face the same type of sorrow right now.*

And, as trivial as it may seem, I understand the void left when a certain handheld device no longer connects you to the outside world. For them, that connection has been completely severed. Regardless of whether cell phone towers still stand above ground, all this rock does a great job of blocking any viable signal, which only adds to their lack of freedom. Riley and I have already grown accustomed to being disconnected from everyone. After everything we've faced this summer, it's a minor inconvenience.

Other than Aidan's family, Jeff and his parents round out the rest of our little community. We briefly met Jeff's brother, Matt, but he's a police officer and he was sent to provide support closer to Yellowstone's impact zone. I worry about his safety. Without him, I'm not sure how we would have ever reached the others through the collapsed tunnel. While he dutifully accepted his obligation, he left behind a fractured family.

His parents spend most of their time by Jeff's side. Their worry is palpable. It's not just evident in their furrowed brows and slumped shoulders. Anxiety clouds the chilled air. These are not the same people who fluidly helped set up the space when Riley and I first arrived. Shadows lurk in bags beneath their tired eyes and worry lines crease their foreheads and jawlines.

I often wonder if Riley and I are part of the reason they've withdrawn. Though it's not been said, I sense that they blame us for their son's injury. They'd be completely right to feel that way, but it still stings when they avoid eye contact or acknowledge us with a barely-discernible nod.

Jeff doesn't join us for meals anymore. He eats in his "room." Sitting upright for more than a few minutes leaves him feeling nauseous. Although we try to spend time with him, he mostly wants to be alone. His parents stay by his side as much as possible, yet I sense that time is mostly shared in silence. With each day, the traces of hope that previously flashed in his eyes extinguish. I recognize the despair that lives within his soul, blistering any sense of contentment. It's been a reliable companion of mine since the only world I ever knew fell apart.

Lately, when Jeff's parents emerge from their seclusion for meals, the conversation steers toward the government communes—and the medical services they must provide. The rest of us shovel food into our mouths with exaggerated effort while focusing on our plates. Inevitably, voices rise, tension lacing each word until an argument flares.

Aidan's dad, Scott, is dead set against leaving the protective environment that cradles our small group right now. Besides potentially exposing our hiding place, he reminds us of the harsh consequences of breathing ash. Until it clears, those miniscule, jagged shards can invade your eyes and nose, gifting you with a lifetime of respiratory problems.

Besides that, he reiterates Matt's warning about the communes: supposedly, they're like warehouses where food is rationed, and privacy is an unaffordable luxury. At least down here, we have control over what we do and how we do it.

So far, the disagreements have fizzled out before they've gone too far. But I sense the brewing dissent is on the verge of boiling over.

Chapter 2

Our first few days weren't so bad. A few moments even felt like a mini-adventure. When we weren't tasked with chores, Riley, Snickers, and I would explore the openings and tunnels, as if we were following the carved paths of a giant ant farm. Those brief escapes offered a chance to clear our minds and focus only on our senses, temporarily banishing reality to oblivion.

Initially, we let our rat terrier's nose lead the way. Until we realized every crevice looks the same, and the likelihood of getting lost grew exponentially the farther Snickers drew us into the cave system.

It took little convincing when we invited Aidan to join us on our explorations. He's been coming to Couturier Caverns since he was a kid. Indulging his interest, the family became regulars here, and eventually friended the owners. That relationship paved the way for our ability to hole up here since Yellowstone erupted.

Although he invites the others to join us, they never do. It's probably better this way, because Riley and I make a new, captivated audience for Aidan. The others have probably heard his touristy commentary more times than they can count.

Each time we set off to visit a new section of the cavern, guilt slithers through me. Jeff should be with us. The old Jeff would have cracked jokes at every corner, pointing out questionably shaped formations or challenging Aidan's in-depth knowledge.

But the longer his legs don't work, the more I fear they won't bear weight ever again. I understand his parents' growing determination to take action.

Although our physical distance from the others is a welcome escape from the problems clouding our little community, the reprieve is always too short. By the time our excursions end, wisps of sadness chase each step. There aren't enough distractions to help forget our challenges.

During these times, I narrow my focus solely on Aidan, embracing every description and story that passes through his lips. He's our own personal tour guide, and he's memorized every crack, mineral deposit, and formation. I had visited this place in elementary school on a field trip. Back then, I had no appreciation for the magnificent displays hiding underground. Honestly, even a few weeks ago, I would have rolled my eyes and silently groaned if I had to listen to Aidan rattle on about stalagmites and stalactites. But somehow all the losses I've faced have also ingrained an appreciation. Not only for the distraction but also for nature's amazing ability to create and destroy with unharnessed power.

Thankfully, he's adapted the explanations for his audience.

Initially, he tried detailing the role limestone and carbon dioxide play in the formation process of caves. When he noticed the effect it had on us—drooping eyelids and uncontrollable yawns—he tried a different strategy. His description of water as a sort of superhero among elements boomeranged our attention back and instilled a new respect for the substance that keeps us hydrated, sustains life forms, and carves paths through solid rock.

Besides the other humans, we're learning to share the cave with its original inhabitants. Aidan points out where bats roost— at least the colonies he knows of. We don't know how many bats actually live throughout the cavern, and I hope to never find out.

Silently we spy glimpses of their crumpled bodies, clustered together in an upside-down slumber. The unspoken deal is that we don't bother them, and they don't bother us. Riley and I don't even dare whisper when we're in "their" territory. I've seen enough movies where an unsuspecting cave visitor stumbles upon a sea of bats. The mouse-like bodies cascade around her while she shrieks, throwing her arms up to prevent the writhing creatures from tangling in her hair. The image alone wills me to tiptoe and hold my breath, as if it will allow us to pass through their territory unnoticed.

The general mood mirrors our surroundings: dampened, heavy, and dark. The cooperative spirit remains, but time seems to wear down our collective hope for the future. Riley and I worry about our aunt. *Is she okay? Does she have enough food? Is she alone and scared?* We have no way to reach her, and the uncertainty of her safety is a weight we carry each day. We never wanted to leave her behind. But just as it was our choice to come here, it was her choice not to join us.

We're safe here, and even though these people aren't our family members, there's a certain comfort that comes with proximity to others experiencing the same unknowns. Still, it doesn't outweigh the fact that so many questions about what's happened, and what's next, remain unanswered.

Riley and I have lived in this area since we were born, but I never would have imagined we'd carve out an existence underground, even if it's only temporary. The house we grew up in is only miles away, but it might as well be on another planet.

Aidan and his dad monitor the ham radio. Right now, it's our only connection to the outside world. A few times I hiked up the long flight of stairs to listen with them. Riley never wants to join me. Most times I think she's right to avoid it altogether. Some of the disembodied voices reek of fear, releasing a cascade of assumptions and rhetorical questions that bloat the air. We have no way of knowing where the messages originate from or how much truth they hold.

"Everything's dying or dead out here. What wasn't burned to a crisp from the eruption looks like it's rotting. If trees and plants die, they'll take us with them. We'll choke on our own desperate gasps for air."

With each passing day, we pick up fewer transmissions. Aidan's dad isn't sure if something's wrong with the radio or if people have more pressing issues to deal with. I'd like to believe it's just a fluke but worry subdues the corners of my mind each time dead air greets our ears.

"You can't tell me scientists didn't see this coming. Someone's damn job is to watch for the ground to shift or an asteroid to fall from the sky. What I want to know is who knew and why they didn't warn anyone!"

No good news reaches our ears. Each time I listen, I understand Riley's avoidance, silently promising myself that this is the last time I'll join Aidan and his dad for this ritual. Yet, each time, curiosity conquers my resolve.

"They're looking for survivors in what they call 'the kill zone.' But what about the rest of us in the ash zones? The National Guard says we have to evacuate, but what'll happen to my house if I leave it behind? And what about our pets? We can't leave them to fend for themselves."

Aidan suggests we try to send a message out in hopes someone will reply, but we aren't even sure we have whatever equipment is needed for that, let alone how to do it. And even if we could "send a message," no one of authority seems to be broadcasting. At least not that we've picked up:

"Why weren't we better prepared? I'm in northwest Oklahoma and the ash smothered nearly every living thing here. If the plants and trees die, what does that do to oxygen levels? If cattle and other farm animals die, what does that do to the food supply

chain? Is this what climate change does?"

Most times, Aidan's dad switches the radio off in frustration, complaining about the lack of useful information. "These people aren't sharing anything that can help us," Scott mutters. "It's all just complaining and opinions. And questions that no one seems to have the answers to."

"You're right," Aidan agrees. "But it's not like we can just look up the news online. Right now, there is no verified source of reliable information. And even if there was another public broadcast, can we trust what the president says? I mean, with all these cover-ups, we don't even know if something else is brewing out there right now!"

Whatever we hear or say stays in this confined space. It's an unspoken agreement among the three of us. No one wants to upset the others—and besides, we really don't have much to share. There are only a handful of people out there that I would trust to tell me the truth. And that's if they're even still alive.

Chapter 3

As his mood shifts, Jeff breaks his silence. First when he's alone with Aidan, but soon after, when Riley and I join them. Conversations are slow to start, and defiant hesitation looms in his eyes. The playful remarks and expressions I associate with him are just a memory. Initially, it was as if the shock of his injury and current state left his mind as numb as his body. But now a bitterness awakens, spurred by a personal injustice.

No matter how the conversation starts, it always seems to swing back to the government. And how we were all kept in the dark about impending natural disasters. Not just the earthquake that started this whole mess, but more recently, Yellowstone's eruption.

It's unfathomable to consider how much our lives have changed in less than a year. Not that long ago, Riley and I were typical teenagers. High school days droned on, complemented by extracurricular activities—track distance running for me and musical productions for Riley.

But the recent chain of events had other plans for us. Circumstances steered us toward those we now live with, dropping us on the same converging path.

If it hadn't been for an unexpected earthquake along the East Coast, Riley and I never would have met Aidan, Jeff, and their friends. And beyond that, if we never knew that Yellowstone was preparing to blow its stack, we would have parted ways. Aidan and Jeff would be home with their families, probably counting down the days until they would return to their college campus for fall semester.

There's no point in allowing my mind to drift, lost in what could have been, but has very little chance of ever being again. Tension wafts through the chilled air as Jeff shares what must have been dominating his thoughts since the accident. Bitterness laces each word when he insists we tell the world—what's left of it—that the U.S. government exposed its own citizens to an impending disaster and can't be trusted to rebuild, leaving anarchy as the only way to fix all that's wrong.

His words are rife with passion and fueled by anger. Seeing him this way is almost worse than when he barely communicated at all. I understand the resentment and desire for retribution, but there's no realistic answer. We're powerless. With each recycled discussion, Riley, Aidan, and I cautiously glance at each other, unsure of how to maintain a conversation without stoking—or completely extinguishing—the fire growing within him.

Jeff denounces every argument we have, although it doesn't make them any less true. We have no proof. We're just a bunch of kids with no credibility. And we have no means to get a message out to whoever will listen. We've got a ham radio that we barely know how to use. Even if we made some sort of broadcast, we probably wouldn't reach many people.

Besides, does anyone even care right now? What would it change? If people are out there struggling to survive, what good would it do to tell them we should have been warned? Sure, some deaths and suffering could have been prevented, but that fact won't lessen their pain and loss now. Time isn't a two-way continuum. Nothing can erase the destruction and devastation that remains.

And even if people heard that kind of message, would they truly act on it? I can't imagine anyone is able to retaliate, especially when the government and military are supposed to be helping survivors. Who's going to turn that away on principle?

It's not like anyone could have stopped the earthquake from jolting our little piece of Earth off its axis or plugged Yellowstone's opening, trapping the lethal lava and ash inside. A warning would have saved my parents. It could have changed everything for me and Riley. But nothing will bring them back, so I shake the thought away before it drags me into a downward spiral of despair.

It feels like wasted energy to discuss the "what ifs" or "should haves," yet it's the only thing Jeff wants to talk about. It must occupy his every thought. The more time we spend with him, the more convinced I am that his parents are right. He needs medical attention. And this dank, dark environment is depressing even for those of us who are healthy, but right now he's trapped in his body and his mind. And neither are pleasant places.

Each day, Riley and I retreat to our "room" after completing our daily chore rotation. While the work isn't hard, it's also not fun. We all wash our own clothes, hanging them in designated drying areas. I initially thought the fire pit I saw in the pile of supplies was for campfire stories and s'mores. I was way off.

Aidan's dad set it up in a section of the caverns with flowing air, taking advantage of the natural ventilation. That's the only place we're allowed to light it. Otherwise, the smoke would consume our air or our clothes would never dry in the humidity and darkness.

The cave isn't sealed. There's a larger opening at the lowest point, where the rock floor meets water. Aidan's taken us down there a few times on our unofficial tours. Four boats, each about the length of a tractor trailer bed, gently sway on the interior portion of the freshwater lake. They float idle, awaiting tourists that may never return.

Beneath the surface is another story. A flurry of brown bodies dart through the dusky green water. Aidan says they're trout, and they are our backup plan if the food reserves fall short. Somewhere in the vast supplies are fishing poles, which I hope to never use. I don't even want to know what the plan is for bait, so I don't ask.

After a lifetime of consuming food that came into our home in a carton, box, or bag, the thought of catching, killing, and cooking one of these slimy creatures twists my stomach into knots. Besides that, I've never had a taste for seafood. I don't bother mentioning these details to Aidan, but Riley throws me a side-eye whenever he talks about the fish. Thankfully, she withholds my secret. We already owe Aidan and his family the world for taking us in. The last thing I want to do is appear ungrateful by criticizing a potential food source.

Snickers provides a great distraction whenever we're near the water. He's well aware of the creatures swimming just below the surface, and he's eager to announce his own presence by barking in the direction of any movement he senses. His yaps echo and bounce off the surrounding rock walls, invoking a canine concert. Whenever someone's ears tire of his vocals, we consider it a signal that it's time to return from our latest exploration.

Thankfully, he listens when we call, satisfied that he's sufficiently terrorized the fish for another day. Since he's grown accustomed to the tunnels and pathways that comprise our daily route, he serves as our compass, scurrying past, his little feet racing back to the main room.

Chapter 4

The days drift past in a blur of monotony. We all take on extra chores so Jeff's parents can spend more time with him. The three of them remain fairly isolated, which only drives a deeper divide between the families.

He's obviously annoyed with me, Riley, and Aidan. Once he realized we weren't willing participants in his mission to broadcast a mounting resentment of the government, he went silent again. His stubbornness clouds the air, projecting an unwelcome aura.

Given the shift in duties, Aidan assumes sole responsibility for monitoring the radio for transmissions. I accompany him as much as possible. The others have taken notice of our budding relationship. Whispers and smug smiles chase our steps when we disappear together.

Riley insists on spending time with Jeff. He doesn't forbid it, but he also doesn't exactly encourage conversation. Even when he won't talk, she sits with him. Sometimes she talks about family memories from long before we met him, other times she just rambles. It gives his parents a chance to socialize with the others, and it gives Riley a purpose other than scrubbing pots.

They aren't usually gone for too long and when they return, whoever's visiting with Jeff leaves them in privacy. After a particularly tense visit with Jeff, the three of us trudge back to the main room.

Aidan rakes a hand through his tousled hair. "I could use a distraction. Wanna go check the radio?" he asks no one in particular. Riley shakes her head no. I shrug and accept his offer. It's not like I've got much else to do.

"Alright," he slaps his hands together, likely glad for the company. "Let's see if anyone's talking about clear skies."

We weave through the tunnels to the main room, passing Aidan's mom and sisters as they arrange plates and utensils for the next meal. "We're gonna check the radio," he mutters as we pass them. "Your dad will appreciate that," his mom says, a grateful smile curving her lips.

Riley turns on her heel and, rather than retreating to our room, offers to help the others with their task. Again, Aidan's mom smiles in gratitude, readily accepting the offer. I call over my shoulder, "Be back soon."

As we approach the steps, I cast one more glance at the others. All four of them scurry about, engrossed in the mundane process of meal preparation. A paranoid part of my mind wonders what they think about my fledgling relationship with Aidan. They must sense that we like each other. But maybe they're caught up in their own thoughts to drift beyond the confines of our current situation.

Although everyone still smiles at each other in passing and at mealtimes, I've noticed that no one's eyes quite crinkle in the corners the way they used to. And their lips don't lift in that familiar upturn as readily. This temporary lifestyle afflicts each of us differently. We've all had to give up, or hopefully just suspend, relationships and modern conveniences. I can't imagine we'd be better off aboveground, but at least we'd know what's happening.

We ascend the steps in silence, the weight of the unknown smothering unnecessary small talk. So far, regular updates from the president have been as scarce as the advanced warnings were before the earthquake. Each time we expect new information, some good news for a change, we're left disappointed.

As soon as we reach the radio, Aidan takes command of our only connection to the outside world, summoning it to life. My stomach drops as the words reach my ears.

"It just keeps getting worse out here. We've got bridges down, power out, and there's no one to fix it. Everyone's at these communes, living like we don't have to worry about tomorrow. Like we can just line up for a meal and bed and not think about the future."

Even in the dim light, Aidan must sense my anxiety. He reaches toward me, palm up. I smile and gratefully accept his unspoken offer of comfort. As he wraps a calloused hand around my own, I relish his warmth and close my eyes, mentally bracing for whatever comes next. With his free hand, he twists the dial in search of another voice.

> *"Yellowstone's got me thinking. Remember that power plant in Japan, maybe ten years ago? An earthquake and tsunami banged the hell out of a reactor…it leaked all over the surrounding area. How do we know that isn't happening here? Once this ash clears up, are we gonna find radioactive nuclear waste in our backyards?"*

I hadn't thought about power plants and the toxic chemicals lurking within their walls. Safety has become a relative term, defined only by the moment.

There's a nuclear generator less than an hour's drive from here. We took a field trip there in middle school. Like Couturier Caverns, I spent more time laughing with my friends than paying attention. I remember the four giant towers, cylinders flaring at the top and bottom, spitting out white plumes of steam. But other than that, my memory's blank.

My fists clench and my stomach twists. There are already enough dangers lurking around every corner, patiently waiting to knock humanity down another notch or two. We don't need one more worry, or to be blindsided by another disaster.

"You wanna shut this off and take a walk?" Aidan asks, his blue eyes piercing mine. He must sense my anxiety. Distance from this doomsday radio sounds perfect.

The air rushes from my lungs, leaving me slightly light-headed, but I manage to squeak out a high-pitched "Sure!" My cheeks flush crimson, but I doubt it's noticeable in the dim light. That's one perk to living underground.

Smiling, he switches the radio off and rises, tugging me along as our fingers entwine. We glide down the steps and sidestep the main room, disappearing into the darkness of a tunnel. It's one of the lesser-used passageways, but I'm sure Aidan knows exactly where it leads.

Chapter 5

I follow his every step. We alternate between walking side-by-side and single-file, depending on the path's width. Monstrous spikes of rock jut from the walls and ceiling at random intervals. *No wonder the group rarely uses this tunnel—it's like the formations stand as a foreboding warning to trespassers.*

No matter how awkwardly we contort our bodies to maneuver through the openings, Aidan never lets go of my hand. Even when I question it.

"I think I'm gonna need my hand back to squeeze through this opening," I say.

"Sorry, I can't do that," Aidan teases. "Do you have any idea what the oils on your skin can do to rock formations?"

"I know, I know, it's terrible," I agree, attempting to avoid a lecture on the subject. "And I promise not to touch anything. I just need my hands…for balance."

"I think, in this case, we're better safe than sorry." I sneer at his back. Even though I can't see his face, I hear the smile in his voice.

"You can't be trusted, and the last thing we want is someone to single-handedly—see what I did there—alter the surface tension and stunt future growth."

I knew it; I knew he couldn't resist injecting some sort of geology lesson into our trip.

"Alright, I get it, enough with the lecture, professor." I huff out a pretend-exasperated breath. He must sense I'm loving every minute of this. Although I had a few boyfriends before, it rarely amounted to more than slapping a label on some boy at school who passed me a note that likely said, "Do you like me?" with lopsided, hand-drawn check boxes for "yes" and "no."

Those days were nothing like this. Maybe it's the extreme experiences Aidan and I have faced together in such a short time period, but I feel a closeness to him I've never felt before.

Releasing my hand, he stops and turns toward me, raising the flashlight to his chin as if he's about to unleash a grisly ghost story.

"Uh oh, did I offend someone?" I can't tell if he's genuinely concerned or just continuing the torment. Using silence as a weapon, I strive to make him squirm. "Okay then, I guess this calls for some humor to lighten the mood."

"No, that's okay, I'm not mad, really." I raise my hands in surrender, but the effort is futile, evidenced by the grin that cracks his cheeks.

"Where do geologists like to relax?" he asks, anticipation radiating off of him with every passing second.

Deciding the direct route is also the fastest, I take the bait. "Where?"

"Rocking chairs!" He barely gets the words out before a guttural laugh erupts from his throat.

I shake my head and cross my arms, unable to even feign amusement.

"Aw, come on, Quinn," he starts, gently grasping the crook of my elbow and tugging me closer. "Even geologists have their faults."

"Uggghhhhhh!" I let my head drop back in a show of aversion to his second attempt at humor. I can't stifle the giggle that escapes though.

When I level my gaze to meet his, the smile fades and his expression turns serious. My skin tingles as he closes the gap between us. Dipping his chin, he gently presses his lips to mine.

Taking my hand prisoner again, Aidan leads us through the rocky corridors to an expansive opening. Darkness swallows the entire room. His flashlight beam is like a flickering candle in the night sky. He guides us from memory. Unsure of my footing, I twist and contort to follow in his footsteps.

My heart flutters, and goosebumps erupt along my arms. The air chills my extremities, but our deepening relationship ignites a warmth that stretches throughout my core. For this moment, the teenage girl inside me revels in the intimate comfort we've created in an otherwise inhospitable environment.

We sidle along the massive wall. Aidan skims the flashlight across it, just below shoulder-level. After a few tentative steps, he stops. His eyebrows wiggle obnoxiously, and a smirk tugs his lips. Raising a hand, he snaps a switch.

"Power's still working down here. For now, at least." He points toward the farthest corner of the room, its rounded surface bathed in colored spotlights. Blue, purple, and green bursts of brilliance mingle in a stunning array, drifting across the naturally rigid curves and crevices.

My jaw drops as a sharp intake of breath reveals my awe. "It's beautiful. It looks like the Northern Lights. Not that I've seen them in real life, but in pictures."

"You said you came here before, on a school field trip. This room is part of every tour, so you must have seen them before." He eyes me with doubt, but my reaction is sincere.

Allowing my eyes to explore every ridge and crack of the lit section, I answer him. "I don't remember it. I guess if I saw it, I didn't appreciate it the way I do now."

"Well, you're in luck then." His goofy smile awakens a happiness that manifests into another escaped giggle. I cross my arms, protesting his proclamation.

"Oh really? And how is that?" I cock my head, pretending to scrutinize the response before he can form it. He leans toward me, playfully jostling my shoulder.

"Well, I can explain everything those spotlights are focused on up there. And, since travel is out of the question right now, and for who knows how long, you can consider this your own personal Aurora Borealis."

"I can't think of anything else I'd rather be doing right now." I rise on my tiptoes and plant a quick kiss on his check. "Thank you," I whisper, "for sharing this with me."

His smile stretches from ear to ear. He wraps a hand around mine and leads me to the center of the room. About a dozen crude wooden benches are wedged along the inclining rock floor, forming a rudimentary form of stadium seating on a much smaller scale. He leads me to the center of the middle row.

We huddle together in the near-dark as Aidan explains each crag and boulder. For the first time since I've met him, I devour his words and commit the knowledge he shares to memory.

Chapter 6

Each passing day eases some burden of the workload. Our tasks become mindless distractions, completed easier and quicker than even a week ago. Scott's preparations and organization tendencies guide us to a constant flow of efficiency.

We curb our trips to the lake when Jeff's dad develops an interest in the tourist boats. Snickers' surround-sound barking would annoy him, and we won't subject him to that ear assault.

Aidan and I stay busy by checking the radio at least four times a day. His dad wants us to vary the times we listen, hoping we'll pick up a useful broadcast—a reliable source that addresses what the air quality is like or an official government announcement. Sometimes Jessa and Kaylee tag along, but most of the time it's just the two of us.

Although we scan for voices and attempt to listen, we're only able to achieve the focus of toddlers. Aidan's mostly to blame, cracking stupid jokes or asking random questions, like my favorite color. Of course, I want to know his answers too, so the conversation quickly snowballs into an ongoing cycle of chatter and chuckles.

Our carelessness reaches a sobering point when we catch a message mid-broadcast. We both instantly recognize the authoritative, sobering voice. President Taves.

...and I know that this is the last thing anyone wants to hear. The last thing we can even fathom facing right now. But as Americans, we will do just that. We will overcome the challenges that await, and we will prevail. Together, as one nation. That is our only hope.

Our numbers have diminished, through no fault of our own. We've lost millions, perhaps even hundreds of millions; our brothers, sisters, parents, neighbors, and loved ones. And I know the pain they leave behind is still a fresh wound. That's why we have to act right now. It's the only way to prevent losing more innocent lives.

If you are hearing this message, I implore you—seek shelter. Our armed forces have set up safety communes in communities throughout the nation. We are committed to providing food and other necessities to all citizens. By entering a commune, you're helping us to know where help is needed most so we can best take care of you.

Stay tuned for future broadcasts. I will address the nation daily until we cross this latest hurdle. Until tomorrow, I wish everyone a safe evening. Good night and God Bless.

Bile rises in my throat as my jaw drops, and my vocal cords shirk their purpose. The questions in my mind remain silent. I'm incapable of forming syllables. *What's he talking about? What did we miss?*

Aidan continues to stare at the radio several minutes after the message ends. Pressing his temples and scrunching his eyes closed, he murmurs a half-statement, half-question. "Maybe they'll repeat the broadcast. Maybe we'll find it if we keep scanning."

I nod dumbly and find my voice, hopefulness waking me from my stupor. "Yes. They've got to repeat it. I'm sure they want as many people to hear it as possible. You don't play something like that once."

"You're right." He runs a hand through his ruffled hair and zeroes every bit of his attention on the radio. Nervously, he tunes from frequency to frequency. Neither one of us admits the truth. *Something else bad is about to happen and we have no idea what. If we had just paid attention to this one task entrusted only to us, we would have heard the entire broadcast.*

I pace the room while Aidan searches for the information we need. Each time I near the steps that lead down to the main room, a tangy aroma tickles my nose. It grows stronger as time passes, and my churning stomach reminds me that a mealtime is approaching.

After what feels like hours, Aidan rises in defeat, throwing his hands out at his sides.

"This is useless, we aren't making any progress." He shakes his head in defeat. "If we aren't back for dinner, someone will come get us."

All I've contributed is an etched path in the dirt from my feet plodding back and forth all this time. It conjures bittersweet memories of running, my stress reliever. Whether it was a track meet or a non-competitive fun run, the rhythmic movement soothed my muscles and cleared my mind. I haven't run since we sealed the door, fully committing to life underground.

While the cave system offers more than enough distance to cover a several-mile run, the dark tunnels contain too many potential hazards. It's not a risk worth taking when we've already established that the group isn't prepared to provide medical treatment should I face an untimely meeting with a hole in the ground or some jagged formation.

"I've got to tell my dad that something's happening." He shakes his head, eyes searching the ceiling in frustration. "And I'm spending the night in here. I'll just keep checking and listening until I find out what it is."

"We don't have to figure this all out ourselves. And you can't stay up all night." I step toward him, planting a palm on his chest. "Besides, Taves said he's going to give updates every day. Let's go tell your dad and promise that we'll listen all day tomorrow, or as long as it takes."

His eyes drop to my hand as he smiles. Sweeping a tousled

brown lock of hair behind my ear, he whispers, "I'm glad you're here. It was an incredibly smart move to leave behind a life of luxury aboveground. Just so you could spend more time with me." Amusement dances in his eyes as he awaits my response.

Okay, I wanted to help, but I can't allow this level of mock arrogance to slide.

I retract my palm and cross my arms before deploying verbal crossfire. "Just so we're clear, you lured me with the promise of food and non-contaminated breathing air. If either of those items were not part of the deal, you'd probably be sitting here alone, daydreaming about me right now."

I'm unable to contain the slight neck sway that accompanies my last words. All the same, I think it reinforces the message.

"You know," he starts. I cock my head to the side, anticipating a comeback. "I think you're right!"

My jaw drops. Before I can finish my next thought, his lips crash into mine. All thought evaporates, along with our words.

Chapter 7

Hand-in-hand, we work our way down the steps to rejoin the others. My stomach flutters as I wonder what they'll think if they notice our entwined fingers. Unwilling to face any perceived scrutiny, which would likely be a product of my paranoid imagination, I focus on our descent.

When we near the bottom, my eyes to dart toward our destination. I'm relieved the others are scurrying around, focused on plates and bowls instead of us. In our absence, they've prepared the place settings and tonight's dinner. Aidan's mom claims it's a beef barbeque; but having helped with food preparation at least once each day, I know that all the fresh meat is gone.

In fact, we've used up all the fresh food. Every preservative-laden meal now originates from a pouch, box, or carton. This alleged barbeque must be some canned concoction doused in sauce. As I focus on not wrinkling my nose, Riley scampers over and grabs my elbow.

"Well, you two took your good old time!" she huffs, throwing a stern, guilt-fueled scowl at me.

"Sorry, we heard the end of a message that sounded important, and we kept trying to find the part we missed." I shrug, painting the most innocent expression over my face that I can muster. She doesn't need to know we were flirting when we should have been scanning.

"Well, I told Jeff's parents that we're eating with him tonight. He needs to spend more time with people his age and you and I are going to cheer him up!"

Being reprimanded doesn't exactly motivate me to spread joy to others, but I'll give it a shot.

"Look, I'm sorry, okay? I'm ready now."

In tolerable silence, we fix a hefty serving for Jeff and then prepare our own plates. Jeff's parents settle at our usual table and throw us a slight wave, probably their exhausted attempt at casting appreciation.

As we pass, Aidan tilts his head in a knowing nod. He'll share our intel, if you can call it that, with the others over dinner. I decide to keep the information to myself for now. I'll tell Riley at bedtime. Jeff doesn't need more to worry about, and this conversation should focus on pleasantries. No need to weigh down the mood with what's coming next, whatever that is.

Genuine happiness surges through me when Jeff greets us. It's the most animated I've seen him since we first entered the cave, and it's a welcome reminder of the person he used to be.

"Ladies, looks like dinner's on you tonight." He flashes a crooked smile that reaches his eyes. I snatch a side-eye glance at Riley, but she doesn't even notice. She's focused on arranging a food tray before him.

She could have told me he's had a colossal attitude adjustment, but I probably wouldn't have believed her anyway. Jeff's moods plunge from vacant to hostile, then rocket back up to enthusiasm at the drop of a flashlight. Whatever's going on, I'm just relieved that he's acting more like himself.

"Hey, it's great to see you," I say.

"Yep," he eyes his plate with healthy interest. "Better take advantage of it while you can cuz I'm outta here soon."

My chest constricts as I freeze the smile on my face with fake enthusiasm. Something else bad is coming. I don't know what, but it might not be safe for him to leave anytime soon.

"Jeff, you can't…right now…" I point toward the way we came, as if that means anything. "Aidan and I…we've been listening to the ham radio…and we heard something today."

They both watch me with mild interest. "And?" Riley coaxes, extending her hand. "Get on with it."

Although they're clearly not worried by my announcement, I shrink under the weight of perceived scrutiny.

"So we heard a message, well, the last part of a message, from President Taves." My eyes jump between them, but my audience still appears unimpressed. "It sounds like something big is about to happen. Something…not good. He's telling everyone to go to one of those safety communes."

Jeff scratches his chin and purses his lips in amusement. "So, you're saying we're supposed to go to a commune, which is what

I want to do. I'm not seeing the problem."

"Quinn, if that's what they're saying, maybe we should all go, not just Jeff and his parents," Riley says, wringing her hands together in a nervous dance.

"But you both know…we can't trust anything Taves says. We already know he lied about Yellowstone, and someone should have warned us about the earthquake." Frustration rushes my veins. No matter what I say, I feel unheard.

Narrowing my gaze on Jeff, I question him, attempting to remove any accusation from my tone. "You've been saying all along how you want to expose the government for what it did, or what it *didn't* do. Why would you want to do what they say now?"

His reaction sharpens like a knife slicing air. "I want out of here. I'm tired of sitting around waiting for my legs to work! Nothing's going to change as long as I'm stuck in this damn bed all day."

Riley sets her food aside and reaches for Jeff's arm. "We completely understand. I mean, not what you're going through, but that you're angry and that things can't stay like this." She throws me a side-eye, a silent provocation to offer support, but my frustration is reaching its breaking point.

"Things may be a total mess up there! Maybe you're even better off down here." I struggle to dial down the building emotion. "How many people are dying right now as we speak, and how many doctors and nurses are already dead? What if you can't even find anyone to help you?"

"Quinn!" Riley shrieks.

"Nah, let her talk," Jeff says coolly. "This is the first thing anyone has said to me since the accident that wasn't a candy-coated pile of dog crap."

"You know, we left our aunt aboveground, and it wasn't easy. We did it because it was the best thing for us in this situation. But whatever, you have to do what's right for you. And if going to a government-controlled commune is the right thing for you, then you should do that."

Riley forces a labored smile. She's probably focused on the candy-coated dog doo comment, taking it personally.

Jeff nods in appreciation for my candor. A soft thudding echoes in the momentary silence.

Our exchange must have attracted a visitor. Snickers wanders into the room. "Look, I just can't with him right now," Jeff says, nodding toward the terrier. "I know it was an accident, but that dog is the last thing I want to see."

"Fair enough," I mumble, then swoop Snickers up and head to the makeshift kitchen.

Riley follows close behind. "Well, that went well."

I shrug.

Chapter 8

Riley takes a detour with Snickers in hopes that he'll do his business in the designated area, while I start stacking the evening's dirty dishes. As I prep the washing area, approaching footfalls echo. *It's way too soon for Riley and Snickers to be back.*

Aidan's mom smiles when she sees me. I return the gesture as she drapes a washcloth over a rope that doubles as a wash line for kitchen towels.

"Thanks for all of your help with cleanup and meals, oh and laundry." Her tone is genuine even though we're just earning our keep. It's only fair that we help as much as we can, considering we weren't on the original invite list.

"Oh, it's no problem," I say. She lingers, as if awaiting another response. When I focus on the mess before me, she nudges my shoulder.

"You know, Aidan says a lot of nice things about you—and your sister. I'm glad you're both here. And I'm glad that Aidan has you in his life. Everything's such a mess right now, but as long as we all take care of each other, we'll find a way out of this somehow."

Another smile tugs at my lips.

"That's a really nice way to think of it," I say. She nods and retreats back to the main room, likely returning the chairs to their ready positions beneath the tables for the next meal.

Before long, Riley returns, and we finish scrubbing the dinner plates and utensils. Aidan pays us a visit. Casually leaning against the wall, he asks, "So, how was Jeff?"

"Really good. Better than I've seen him since we got here," Riley says, shooting me a side-eye glance that screams, *keep your mouth shut.*

He nods, "That's good." Shifting his attention to me, he asks, "Did you tell them?"

"I did, but they don't care. Jeff wants to go." "There wasn't much to tell," Riley says. "You two heard *something* is going to happen, but you don't know what. Or when." She throws her hands in the air. "And people are supposed to go to the safety communes, but we already knew that."

"Why don't we take a walk?" he suggests. "I need to talk to you. Both of you."

Apparently, while Riley and I joined Jeff for dinner, his parents announced their family's decision to leave. As the group was about to discuss how to share enough information at a safety commune to get the help Jeff needs versus what to withhold in order to keep the rest of us hidden, Aidan shared our news.

While Jeff's parents see it as confirmation that they're making the right decision, Aidan's parents feel that staying hidden is the safest for all of us until we can figure out what Taves is talking about.

It's a delicate arrangement, trust dangling over a precipice of loyalty. Neither family would purposely cause the other harm, but each is driven to protect their loved ones and now that common goal has diverged.

We know the change in Jeff's mood is hinging on his family's departure. It's the only thing that's given him any genuine hope since the accident.

Caught between dueling opinions, nothing I can say or do will help. We meander back to the main room, a claustrophobic unease charging each step.

"I almost forgot," Aidan murmurs. "I've got some clothes drying." He tilts his head toward the makeshift laundry area. "I'll grab whatever's done and catch up with you."

"Alright, see you soon," Riley says.

As we near our destination, anxiety spikes along the nape of my neck. Voices crescendo, slithering their way through the cavern until they reach our ears. Tension carves through the chilled air as heated words rip through the enclosure. Male voices, instantly recognizable as the only two other than Aidan and Jeff.

Riley and I attempt to slink into the main room. Though I'm sure they see us, no one even glances our way. Snickers is nowhere to be seen, and that's probably a good thing. He's likely curled up on a bed, napping or dozing off, oblivious to the latest issues we face.

"The last thing we want to do is break the seal on that door," Scott insists, pointing toward the top of the steps. "We all agreed that this was the best place to wait out the ash."

Before he can continue, Jeff's dad responds. "That was when my son could still walk! We can't sit around here and wait anymore. It's not getting any better. He's got to see a doctor!"

Without missing a breath, Scott responds. "No, he needs to see a team of specialists, which you won't find at a government commune. Just think about what you're risking for an outcome that's probably not even possible. This is a new reality we're talking about. If that were my boy in there, I would not put him at the mercy of a pencil-pushing drone calling the shots in a commune. Providing food, shelter, and clothing. Those will be their highest priorities—getting them and not running out of them."

He pauses, his tone softening. "Don't you see? Jeff's stable, and whatever these communes are, I'm betting they aren't surgery centers. I mean, the likelihood of finding someone who knows what to do and has access to whatever medical equipment is needed...how likely is that?"

With those words, Riley and I share a guilt-ridden glance and fade further into the shadows. The last thing we want to do is draw any attention to ourselves when we bear the responsibility for Jeff's accident. If we hadn't brought Snickers with us, this argument wouldn't be happening right now.

Hugging the walls, we slowly continue toward the tunnel leading to our quarters. *I thought they already discussed this over dinner. How many times can they rehash the same argument?*

"And you heard Matt! He said those communes aren't what

they seem." Scott throws his hands in the air. "And now we find out something *new* is coming. What if it's another earthquake or hurricane or worse? If we open that door, we expose *everyone* to whatever poison is floating around outside!"

It feels like we're stomping through a field of land mines. One wrong move could turn the spotlight on us, along with the blame. *Almost there.* Practically tiptoeing the remaining few feet to our escape route, relief shudders through me. But just as quickly, it plummets to my toes. Drawn back to the escalating tension, Snickers skulks from the shadows, emitting a low growl. *Is the tense exchange fueling his behavior?*

Riley lunges, scooping him up and hugging him to her chest, attempting to shush him. She scratches his ears before gliding a flat palm across his back, smoothing the agitated tuft of short fur. If he'll just stay quiet, we can disappear into the tunnel and escape to our room.

"So you're saying that if one of your kids was hurt, you would just leave them to suffer so that the rest of the group wasn't exposed to what *may or may not* be happening outside?"

"I'm saying if one of my kids were injured, I'd do everything in my power the protect them from whatever the hell is out—" Footfalls emerge from the tunnel, announcing Aidan's entrance. My instincts scream to wave him down, warning him to avoid this conversation. Chest heaving as he gulps breaths of air, he raises a hand toward each man, as if brokering a deal. I freeze in place, unable to tear my eyes away. *Please don't fly directly into the hornet's nest.*

Chapter 9

"Arguing…isn't…going…to…help…anyone," he huffs between exhalations. I should really teach him how to build up a runner's endurance. It could be a useful skill these days, especially if we're ever faced with another tornado, or whatever else the sky decides to drop on us. Besides, other than scrubbing dishes and picking up Snickers' poop, I don't bring much else to the group.

The men cease their verbal fire, allowing Aidan a moment to catch his breath. His presence diffuses the disagreement, at least temporarily. After a few minutes that stretch into awkwardness, Aidan resumes his interruption.

"Look," he pleads, "Jeff's not a kid anymore. He's got the right to make his own decision. If he couldn't talk, that would be one thing, but he is fully capable of telling us what he wants. All we have to do is ask."

Aidan runs a hand through his messy brown mop of hair, shaking his head. "If it was me, I'd want to have a say. You two can argue until a new stalagmite forms, but I don't think anyone else should decide for him. There are reasons to stay and reasons to go, and he knows what they are. We all have to do what's best for him right now and the only way to know that is to ask him." Shamed silence descends, blanketing the cavern in a calm quiet. The tension dissolves like a wispy cloud.

Apparently tired of being Riley's hostage, Snickers seizes the moment to announce his displeasure. His frustrated "Yip!" startles us both. The rat terrier squirms in her arms, attempting to disembark. I meet Riley's wide eyes, sharing a flicker of panic at the thought of being discovered eavesdropping. Without a word, we tiptoe back to our room as quickly as we can. The movement appeases Snickers. He settles until we reach our room, where Riley promptly releases him from her hold.

"What do we do now?" I ask. I hate not knowing what's being decided. This impacts all of us. Once that door's open, Riley and I have a choice. We can go check on our Aunt Robin or we can stay here. But for how long? It's not like Aidan's family will magically know when the ash clears outside. The ham radio hasn't been very useful lately and if ash seeps in through that open door, does that mean we aren't safe down here, anyway?

This whole summer has consisted of Riley and I scrambling from one temporary place to another. Home would never be the same without our parents, but when the ash finally settles, where do we land? Aunt Robin is our closest relative, both in proximity and familiarity. Our dad's sister, Aunt Grace, lives upstate, but I'm not sure where exactly. Other than staying at her trailer for our beach vacations, we haven't had much contact with her. This doesn't seem like the time to attempt a family reunion.

Although I've already forgotten the question, Riley's answer pulls me from my wandering thoughts. "We wait a little while, until *they* figure out what they're doing," she says, "And then we interrogate Aidan."

Right. I narrow my eyes and nod slowly. Sometimes that sister of mine is a genius.

After about an hour of stretching out on the bed, distractedly flipping through the few books Riley packed, Aidan pays us a visit. We both sit up. He lowers himself onto the foot of the bed and releases a sigh.

"So, you probably heard what's going on," he says.

Riley hitches a shoulder up and answers. "We heard some commotion, but we weren't sure what would come of it." She's more honest than me. Pretty sure I would have denied hearing anything at all.

"Yeah, it's the same argument as always. Jeff's parents want to leave, and my dad wants us all to stay." He drops his head back and rubs his temples. "Obviously, we were all hoping Jeff would be doing better by now and my dad is so paranoid about the ash and about people finding out that we're down here. I don't know if he's worried that others will just show up if they think this is a safe place and we have supplies."

"I understand," Riley interjects. "They both have their reasons." This is one of those times when a sense of exclusion tiptoes out of the corners of my brain where paranoia resides. Where do we fit into this? Riley and I are on our own; we're not a part of either family down here.

"Right," Aidan continues. "So we wanted to see what you two thought." *I didn't expect that.* "If we open the door, would you two stay or would you leave too?" His shoulders sag as if he's bracing for an answer he doesn't want to hear. He faces me, those blue eyes locking on mine, searching for a reaction.

"We haven't really figured it out yet," Riley says. "But I can't stop overthinking it. I mean, no matter when we leave, Quinn and I have to go somewhere. The only option we really have is our aunt's house. She's our closest relative."

"We planned to stay here until the ash cleared—or cleared enough that it was safe to be outside," I add. "But we're not in a big rush." *Did I really just say that? Not in a big rush to feel the hot steaming water of an actual shower? Or to have access to a toilet that flushes its contents far away? If those things even exist anymore.*

"What's everyone else doing?" Riley asks.

"Well, Jeff and his parents are leaving. He wants to see a doctor and we're all figuring there's some sort of medical care at those safety communes. They're hoping they can get Jeff some help and maybe even reach Matt somehow."

I wonder if they even know where Matt is. The last time we saw him, he told us that he'd been assigned to provide support out west, closer to Yellowstone. The others' cell phones don't work down here, beneath the layers of rock separating us from the surface, so there's no way anyone knows if he's okay.

Aidan crosses his arms, shrugging his shoulders. "I get it, nothing's gonna change for Jeff while we're down here. And it's been a few weeks. At least that's given the ash some time to settle, so when we open the door, we'll just seal it back up after everyone who wants to leave is out. We'll just need to figure out a way that someone could alert us if they wanted to come back."

"And it's all temporary," Riley adds. "I mean, no one was going to stay down here forever."

"Maybe we'll find out the ash is gone," I say with inflated enthusiasm. "And we can all leave together."

After everything we've been through, that sounds *way* too easy. And these days, *luck* doesn't look favorably upon us.

Disbelief clouds Aidan's features, but just as quickly, his thoughts shift. "It's possible. I just wish it wasn't this way. My dad's pretty riled up about the change in plans."

Riley leans forward and rests a palm on his arm. "Somehow, this will all work out. And maybe Quinn's got the right idea about the air clearing up. I mean, it doesn't happen often, but now and then she's right about something."

A smile cracks Aidan's stoic face.

I appreciate her effort to lighten the mood but swat her shoulder, nonetheless.

Chapter 10

Riley circles back to Aidan's original question: what we're going to do.

"Is it okay if Quinn and I take some time to talk about this?" she asks, eyeing me. All I can offer is a blank stare in return. We know so little about what's left of our world, including who survived nature's wrath. *Is half the population gone? More than half?*

Maybe I expected that Aidan and his dad would know when the outside threats had passed, and it was safe to return to the surface. We'd all happily load up our belongings and bid farewell to our dark, but thankfully temporary, home. Riley and I would go to our Aunt Robin's house. And hopefully, we would stay in close contact with Aidan and Jeff.

Never mind the miniscule detail that society as we know it may be crumbling above our heads. We don't know if stores still stand, or if they've been looted, leaving nothing but barren structures with shattered entrances and collapsed shelves. Does money still matter? We didn't use any money on our trip to Virginia. We may have *borrowed* transportation and food along the way, but we didn't need actual cash until we headed back north.

But that was a different time. The East Coast was still rebuilding from an earthquake when a tornado swept through Delaware, right through the trailer park where Riley and I were staying. Now that devastation has erupted out west, we aren't sure how many people are migrating east, either by their own choice or by government intervention.

Aidan's voice draws my wandering thoughts back to the present.

"Sure, my dad asked that Jeff take at least another day to consider all the repercussions of opening that door. But if you decide to go, it should be at the same time as them," he says, scrunching his face. We both nod, not sure what else to say.

"Tomorrow my dad's gonna mask up and take one of the boats outside to try and gauge the air. Jeff's dad will probably go too. While they do that, I'll be scanning the radio for anything that can help us." He scratches Snickers' ears and rubs his belly before wishing us a good night.

Riley and I follow the motions of readying for sleep. There are really only two options—stay or go. Unwilling to form a definite decision, we agree to base it on what Scott finds. If the ash has cleared, there's no reason for us to stay. And we've got an aunt anxiously awaiting our return.

I attempt to banish worry from my thoughts, but sleep hovers just out of my grasp. *One day.* That's all we've got to figure this out. I don't truly believe that anything will stop Jeff's family from leaving here, and maybe that's exactly what they should do, so the very least we can do is to prepare them for whatever awaits when they breach the surface.

Of course, Riley's out cold within minutes of resting her head on the pillow. As I shift and twist, desperate for a position that will lull my body to sleep, her breathing grows deeper, mocking my inability to do the same.

Eventually, boredom overtakes me, and reality releases its hold on my mind.

Much too soon, anticipation yanks me from sleep, even amidst the chilled air and incessant darkness. It's a milder version of Christmas morning excitement, although the only possible gift awaiting me today is information. And none of it good.

My body's timetable senses that it's earlier than Riley and I usually rise, but time is irrelevant down here. There are set mealtimes, but other than that, each day is a blur of the last: tackle chores, bathe, and make sure Snickers is accounted for and has food and water.

I rush through an abbreviated morning routine and dash to the main room. Tapping my toes and scrutinizing my fingernails, I tamp down the rising impatience. I'd guess about twenty minutes pass before Aidan joins me. We grab a quick breakfast and climb the steps to the radio room.

Expectation morphs into boredom with each passing minute. The only transmissions we pick up are disembodied voices rambling about technology—repeaters, circuits, transceivers, and an abundance of other words that tempt my eyelids to flutter closed.

By the time my rumbling stomach confirms it's ready for lunch, Aidan switches the radio off and rises, frustration nearly boiling over his features.

"This is useless." He shakes his head, pursing his lips. "We're wasting our time."

"But what else can we do?" I rest a hand on his shoulder, imparting a soothing calmness. "Let's take a break and get something to eat. Maybe we'll have better luck this afternoon. It was afternoon when we heard Taves yesterday, so maybe it'll be around the same time today."

Unconvinced, he nods and blows out a defeated sigh.

"Alright. We start over as soon as we're done eating," he agrees.

While the mention of freeze-dried meals conjures images of astronaut ice cream, the reality is not nearly as delightful. My three-cheese lasagna in a pouch resembles lumpy balls of undercooked dough bobbing in a river of thick gravy. I slosh a spoon through the muck, as if that will whip it into an appetizing state. It doesn't.

Thankfully, my sack of slop tastes slightly better than it looks. I avert my eyes and swallow each scoop as Aidan updates his mom and sisters on our unproductive morning. They show little interest, likely preoccupied with the layer of tension that blankets most interactions lately.

Jeff's mom grabs food and retreats to eat with him. Before leaving, she mentions they packed some belongings last night. They decided to leave most things behind, though, planning to return or make trips back and forth, depending on how much medical care Jeff needs. Their truck is parked in a lot near the entrance at the top of the steps, so as long as the ash didn't cause any damage, they have transportation. At the very least, one of them will return to let us know the diagnosis and treatment.

Scott and Jeff's dad had disappeared down the tunnel leading to the lake and boats this morning. When no one saw or heard anything for several hours, Kaylee and Jessa went to check on them and found two frustrated men elbow-deep in fuel and grease, so the girls reported back.

On their first try, none of the boats would start. All they can figure is that the fuel tanks suffered from disuse. The caverns closed to visitors right after the earthquake hit and hadn't reopened since. The site wasn't prepared for an infinite operational shutdown.

Their plan was to drain and replace the fuel and then test the engines, using whatever apparatus they could find in the maintenance closet on that level. It's not a good sign that they haven't returned for lunch yet.

Aidan's mom announces that we're taking a full inventory of what food is left this afternoon, which prompts a round of sighs. A bit too eagerly, Aidan reminds her that, after our unsuccessful morning, he needs to return to monitoring the radio. He insists my ears are needed as an additional layer of accuracy in hearing and reporting whatever messages we pick up. She reluctantly agrees.

We're excused as soon as the last plate is collected for washing. Riley scowls and sticks her tongue out at me as I follow Aidan up the steps. I shrug, but I'm thrilled to escape what's sure to be hours of boring, mind-numbing tasks.

Chapter 11

Within five minutes of reaching our destination, I reconsider the potential entertainment value of counting cans of beans with Riley. I enter the room, prepared to spend every ounce of energy on a message I *know* we'll pick up. That thought quickly shatters, along with my confidence.

"It won't turn on at all!" Aidan's fingers fly over the dials, pushing and twisting frantically. He even whacks the side of the radio in case that'll wake it up. "What am I doing wrong?" He steps back, inhales a deep breath, and slides his narrowed eyes across the device.

I bounce on my toes, allowing some nervous energy to escape. *I don't know how to work that thing, but I need to help. Somehow.*

"Let's start over. Why don't you tell me what you normally do, and I'll give it a try? Maybe it's just tired of you." He ignores my attempted joke but seems to relax slightly. Maybe he's skipping a step that we'll catch if we just slow down.

"Fine." He points and motions, guiding me through switches to depress and buttons to turn. I follow every instruction precisely, but my efforts yield the same useless results.

He paces the room, like a caged jungle cat, mentally inventorying nonexistent options.

"Is anyone in the group good with electronics? Like troubleshooting electrical stuff?" I ask tentatively. I don't want to inflame his frustration, but if all we've got left is physically assaulting the nonfunctioning radio, then I'm not too proud to admit we need help.

He stares into the distance but responds. "The only ones who might be able to figure it out are trying to get the boats to work. We can't ask them to walk away from that because we can't solve our own problem." He hesitates for a breath but continues. "We really screwed up. If we just heard that message yesterday—"

"But we didn't." The edge in my tone is sharper than intended. I've wasted enough time asking myself "what if we did this differently" and "where would we be if that never happened." Those kinds of thoughts are dead weight I refuse to bear. Attempting to soften any lingering impatience, I try again.

"What if we offer to help them with the boats? We may have reached a dead end with the radio, but maybe they can use an extra set of hands or two."

He shrugs, unconvinced but agreeable. "Okay."

We trudge down the steps, neither of us eager to admit defeat. Tracking down his mom, Aidan updates her on our new plan. She's focused on overseeing the inventorying efforts but agrees we should be helping somewhere. Within minutes, we're on our way to the inside lake, Snickers on our heels. I'm sure he just wants to see his fish frenemies, but I don't foresee his vocals being a hit if everyone's already stressed.

Aidan's and Jeff's dads are surprised to see us, but quickly accept our offer to help. We're charged with aiming flashlights, fetching wrenches, and rummaging through the ramshackle closet for whatever random gadget they need.

Snickers prances along the dock, stalking and pouncing above each fish that sways through the water. Dropping his front legs flush with the wood, he raises his hind legs, readying to launch an attack. He refrains from loud yaps, opting for low growls instead.

About half an hour later, the tinkering pays off. We claim victory over the first boat, revving its engine in a celebratory rumble. Between that and our own buoyant exclamations, Snickers scurries back into the tunnel. He may be a worthy opponent for the trout, but he's not willing to risk facing the noises bouncing around him, closing in.

Capitalizing on the breakthrough, we repeat the process on the other three boats, testing each to ensure the maintenance worked. As Jeff's dad slaps Scott's back, the two share a hearty laugh like the old buddies they are. Aidan nudges my shoulder, grinning. We still have to figure out what's wrong with the radio, but at least this boosted his mood.

By the time we're done, dirt streaks both men's faces. Exhaustion etches lines around their eyes. They've been working on this since the early morning hours, under time's constant pressure. I've only been helping for a few hours and my body's begging to drop right here and curl up on the ground.

Aidan must notice, too. Concern laces his words as he motions toward me. "Quinn and I can clean up down here if you two need a break. You haven't eaten all day." The last thing I want to do is haul all the junk we pulled out back to the storage area, but he's right. They deserve a break more than I do.

Glancing at his watch, Scott nods. "There's still some daylight left. I say we grab a bite of food, wash up, and then take one of these beauties for a cruise to see what's happening outside of these walls."

Jeff's dad agrees, slapping his hands together. "We'll take you up on that offer." As they turn toward the tunnel, he calls over his shoulder, "And thanks for your help today."

Chapter 12

Aidan and I retrieve the tools and empty gas can, stashing them in the open pockets of space within the maintenance closet. We take a final peek in each boat for any stray screwdrivers or funnels that eluded us during our sweep of the area and then scan the dock one more time. I wouldn't call our work orderly, but at least it's done.

As my tired eyes skim the water, I notice something. Or rather, a lack of something.

"Hey, where did all the fish go?" I ask. "Snickers left a while ago. They should be enjoying their time without him running up and down the dock."

Aidan twists his lips in a dismissive "pfft" and hunches a shoulder. "Maybe it spooked them when we started the boat engines. Who cares?"

"I don't really care; it's just the first time we've been here without those beady little eyes peering at us from below."

"I'll bet Snickers scared them away. You know, he's always asserting his dominance around here. And it's a good thing for him they don't understand English. I mean, a name like Snickers doesn't exactly instill fear." He chuckles, extending a hand toward me. I smile shyly and intertwine my fingers with his. Ready to rejoin the others, we start for the tunnel. Just as we're about to pass through, he tugs me back. I turn toward him slowly, my heart dancing and my lips quivering in anticipation of a kiss.

Instead, he angles his head to the side like a dog. "Do you hear something?" he asks, face scrunched up in confusion. Not expecting that response, I mirror his expression.

"I don't hear anything. What do you mean?" I've gotten used to the distant dripping sounds and of course every cough, sneeze, and step that's amplified by echo.

"It's like a swooshing sound. It sounds far away, but…"

"Nope, I don't hear anything, but I'm tired and I feel dirty. Let's go."

"Oh, well, if you're feeling dirty—"

I smack his arm. "You know what I mean!"

We part ways in the main room. Both sets of parents sit at a made-up meal table, but only the men eat, catching up on the lunch they missed. Aidan and I wave as we pass the group, then continue to our rooms.

I'd love a bath right about now, but I've got to check the schedule to make sure no one else is using it. As I turn the corner and step into our room, Riley sits up in bed, folding a book closed. Snickers startles at her feet, cracking a wary eye open, unwilling to fully wake from his nap.

"Thanks a lot!" she snaps. "I had to rearrange every box, pouch, can, and bag of food, and then calculate how long it will last with all of us down here versus if three fewer people are eating it."

"That doesn't sound like a big deal. I bet you didn't even need my help. Look, my afternoon wasn't all that exciting either," I say, guilt washing through me. Discomfort twists in my stomach as her glare intensifies.

"But having help would have gotten it done much faster and could have made it a little less boring. I can just imagine what your afternoon was like," she teases. "Oh Aidan, can you light another lantern? I can't stare into your baby blues in the dark." She reaches for me, puckering her lips and making obnoxious smooching sounds.

I lightly smack her away, chuckling. "Hey, we were working too! First the radio wouldn't turn on, so we tried to fix it. Then, when we couldn't figure out what was wrong with it, we helped get the boats started. Now Aidan's dad can take one outside and see if any of the ash cleared."

"Really?" Her eyebrows jump as she crosses her arms. "It sounds like you gathered no new information, and we still know nothing about what's happening outside or what else may be coming. So your entire day was basically spent *not* gathering intel that could help us." She tries to maintain an air of annoyance, but her cheeks twitch to stifle laughter.

I shake my head and admit the truth. "You're right. We got nothing." Any guilt I carry from our lack of success crumbles, dissolving in the shadow of her silliness.

Without another word, we both burst into laughter, allowing

every grain of worry and regret to float away on the echoes of our absurdity.

Chapter 13

I gather clean clothes. No matter how long I might have to wait for a turn to wash up, it'll be worth it. As I fold them into a compact, neat pile, Snickers defies his earlier decision and rises on the bed. Suddenly alert, he watches the ceiling, as if it's changed from the same smooth surface that's hovered overhead since we got here.

"What's up with him?" Riley asks, nodding toward the terrier.

"He's been a little off today." I squeeze onto the bed beside him and trail my fingers along his back comfortingly. "He freaked out when they started a boat engine. Took off running. I guess he came back here."

"Well, he's probably never heard a boat start before. Of course, that scared him." She sidles to his other side and wiggles his ears.

Completely ignoring us, he releases an abrupt bark. Tufts of brown fur rise along his spine as his eyes search the ceiling. He's never acted like this before. Until now, he seemed to love being here. Tension twists in my gut. This can't be about the boat engine anymore. *What does he sense that we can't?*

"It's alright, boy," Riley whispers nervously. "It's okay."

Without acknowledging either of us, he leaps to the floor and rockets down the tunnel that leads to the main room.

Riley and I stare at each other for a moment, unable to offer explanations or theories for the sudden behavior change in our dog.

A thundering bellow rumbles through the cavern, sending a shockwave through my chest and shivers up my spine. Riley gasps.

"Let's find the others! Now!" Riley screeches.

I nod and jump to my feet. My instincts scream to run. I dash toward the tunnel without looking back. Her footfalls thud as loud as mine. Her choked breathing mirrors my own: clumsy gulps of air stifled by panic.

Aidan's family had the same idea—they stand frozen, waiting in the main room. Riley and I aren't the only ones gasping for breath. We all wear matching expressions of confusion and concern.

Our wide eyes turn to Aidan's dad. He's the authority down here. But right now his scanning gaze exudes dread. Jessa shrieks, "What was that?" He shakes his head, slightly tilted upward, ears tuned in anticipation of another strike or sudden outburst from our cavernous residence.

Pounding footsteps announce Jeff's parents' arrival. Meeting their alarmed eyes, Scott shouts, "We've got to check the door!"

While the adults work out details in varying frantic tones, I motion for Aidan. A creaking sound echoes off the walls. He cautiously steps toward us, twisting his head to track the ceiling as if it's about to come crashing down.

"What's happening?" Riley screeches before I can. Aidan's eyes slide to his dad, who's darting around the main room, gathering seemingly random items. Jeff's dad rushes up the steps to the entranceway.

Jeff's mom retreats down the tunnel, probably to check on him since he can't join us. Aidan's sisters trail behind their mom as she strides in our direction. Words spill from her mouth before she reaches us.

"We might have to leave. Quickly. Just in case, we're going to help get Jeff get ready to go while the guys check if the seal is still secure." Her eyes flicker between us as she blows some stray wisps of hair off her face. "I think we've got enough help down here. Why don't you three head up in case they run into any trouble?"

Aidan hitches a shoulder. "Sure." The rumbling sound escalates and recedes almost rhythmically.

"Thanks—and be careful. All of you." When Aidan nods his affirmation, she wraps an arm around each of her daughters and leads them down the tunnel toward Jeff's room.

Aidan attempts to side-step around us, but Riley and I bump into each other and block his path. Confusion dulls his reaction. *I've never seen him like this, as if he's drifting in a flood of jumbled thoughts, unable to focus on anyone.*

I clutch his arm, anchoring him to this conversation. "Aidan, what do you know?" Riley trembles in anticipation, her lower lip quivering. Her hands shuffle and tumble, displaying their worried dance.

Eyes still distant, he mutters, "I…I'm not sure." This is the guy who gives a dissertation when someone asks a simple question about a rock. I didn't know he was capable of providing such a brief, noncommittal answer. Gripping his shoulders, I shake him gently in an attempt to bring him back to the present.

"Aidan, what? What is it?" Our eyes lock. While mine hold frustration and fear, his express confusion and calculation. He looks between Riley and I, finally comprehending our escalating state of alarm. He pushes a hand through his dark mess of hair and focuses on us.

"I'm sorry. I'm just running through all the possibilities in my head…of what could be happening out there. You know, the radio's been pretty useless. I'm trying to figure out what's making that noise."

"And wh…what are you thinking?" Riley bites her bottom lip, nodding for him to continue yet dreading what he might say.

"So that noise was a rush of *something*," he starts. "It could be air, debris carried by a powerful gust of air, water, or an object like a plane or tank." His voice trails off as he retreats to his thoughts. "But the reverberations, I don't think we'd have them unless it was rock collapsing. It's more like…water lapping or wind tunneling."

With a quick yip, Snickers dashes past us. *In the panic, I almost forgot about him.* His ears are perked like furry antennae, honing-in on something we can't hear.

"He knew," Riley mutters, following his line of vision. "He

could sense something was happening."

We collectively scurry closer to the steps, where Snickers seems fixated. He's run up and down that stairway a hundred times since we've been down here. What about them has suddenly captured his attention?

Releasing a yelp, he trots forward and bends his head down to sniff the rock. I shake my head, rolling my eyes. Maybe he doesn't know what's happening. I thought his keen senses were alerting us of impending danger, but he's probably just looking for a spot to mark.

Riley strides to the terrier and swipes him up into her arms, then leans forward, running her fingers along the rock. Turning toward us, she raises her palm. Her fingers glisten in the dim light. "Guys, what's this?"

Chapter 14

Snickers wasn't sniffing, he was drinking. Well, attempting to drink from the narrow flow of water trickling down the steps.

"We've seen water dripping from plenty of rocks down here, so what?" I ask. Aidan pushes past me, shining a flashlight up and down the stairway.

"This is different though," Aidan's tone is serious. "There aren't any formations at the entrance that would cause a sudden, constant drip. Wait here, I'll be right back. I'll just check with my dad to see where this is coming from."

He shines the flashlight upward and carefully navigates the incline. The echo of pounding footsteps reaches our ears a moment before shouting bursts from the upper chamber. "Aidan!" At the sound of his name, he pushes his legs to move faster.

"I'm coming…on my way," he says between labored breaths. Although he hasn't traveled very far, I imagine the emotional strain of uncertainty weighs him down as he pushes his body to conquer the slick steps. They serve as a reminder of all that Jeff lost when he tumbled down them.

Before he takes even two steps, a command echoes down. "Get to the boats! Get your mom and the girls. Take a boat out of here! The rest of us will catch up with you!"

"What's happening?" Aidan questions. His legs jitter, ready to continue propelling him upward, but the urgent assignment halts him in place.

"It's a flood, and this seal isn't gonna hold!" his dad shouts. "Get to the boats! We have to leave!"

Aidan, Riley, and I freeze. We must have misheard him. As if to counter our disbelief, the flow stutters for just a moment before flaring to a constant stream. Stirred by either the fresh flow of water or the shouting, Snickers surrenders to a yapping fit. He attempts to scurry around Aidan to investigate higher ground.

Luckily, adrenaline overtakes Aidan's reflexes, and he grabs the terrier, preventing an escape. Closing the gap between us, he hands me the dog and tells us to go to the boat dock and wait for him there. Urgency swells in the charged air.

"Should we grab any of our things first?" I ask. Riley eyes me nervously. When she shifts focus to the steps, her mouth drops open and she points. Gravity pulls a cascade of water over the rocks. Shallow puddles form in grooves along the stone and dirt floor. Rivulets snake from the base of the steps, forming a community of vein-like arteries seeking lower ground.

"No! There's no time. It's not worth it. Water's fast. Faster than us," he calls over the escalating commotion. "A few inches of fast-moving water can carry a car away! Just imagine what that would do to a person."

His brief lecture comforts me, even though the reality of his explanation does not. This is the Aidan I need right now: decisive and focused. My survival instincts are running ragged from everything that I've had to face already this summer: an earthquake; the car crash that took our parents; losing Riley; a tornado; freeing dogs from a psychopath's property; facing the barrel of Jim's gun; and leaving our aunt behind while we retreated to dwell underground for an indefinite amount of time. *How much more can we take?*

Motion from a tunnel snatches our attention. Aidan's sisters rush toward us, closely followed by their mother.

"It's getting worse, isn't it?" his mom cries. Terror etches worry lines along her forehead. Before Aidan can answer, her ears and eyes are drawn to the rushing water.

"There's some kind of flood. When they went to open the door. I don't know," he stammers. "But Dad said we should all get to the boats."

She nods in understanding but her haunted expression conveys incoherence.

"Girls, go with your brother. I'm going to help Jeff's mom get him to the boats," she says, turning slowly as if mustering bravery.

"No, I'll go help with Jeff. You all go to the boats, and we'll catch up with you," Aidan counters.

His mom turns, stepping toward him, and places her palm

on his shoulder. "I don't know how to drive those things, let alone start them. You do. It's better if you get down there first. Take your sisters, Riley, and Quinn and drive one boat out to the lake. I'll take a boat with your dad and Jeff's family. The lake isn't that big, we'll find each other out there."

Defeated, Aidan nods. Rubbing his temple, he swallows any potential hesitation and asserts control. "Alright, grab flashlights and follow me. Stay close and watch for flowing water. Even just a few inches of it can drag you in the wrong direction."

"Take care of each other—all of you!" Although the fear is tangible, her tone is commanding, like I envision my own mother would react in this situation. She pauses for a moment, stilling her gaze upon each of us. It reflects genuine concern, not a superficial afterthought.

She casts a sad smile and nods toward Aidan just before we part ways. While she dashes toward one tunnel, Kaylee trails behind Aidan down another. Riley and I follow. Movement pulls my eyes to the right. A figure sprints to catch up with her mother.

"Jessa!" I scream. "You're supposed to come with us!" My voice bounces off the walls, halting Aidan in his tracks. The others skid to a stop, sliding on rogue pebbles dotting the path.

Jessa glances back but ignores the plea. She slinks into the shadows, disappearing into the darkness. I wave an open palm forward, motioning for Aidan to continue. "Don't worry. I'll get her! Just keep going!"

A flash of relief passes over his features. He faces forward again, launching back into mission mode. Riley hesitates to follow him, her eyes questioning if she should stay with me. I shake my head feverishly. "I remember how to get to the boats.

I swear I'll be there before you guys leave. Take Snickers. I'll be faster without him. Make sure Kaylee doesn't try to run off too!"

Cradling the dog to her chest, understanding seems to renew Riley's resolve. She nods sharply before trailing behind Aidan and his younger sister.

Chapter 15

"Jeeessssssssaaa!" My former track and cross-country training kicks in and I catch up quickly. "Jessa, what are you doing? You're supposed to come with us." Somehow, I muster an authoritative tone, even though the girl is fifteen, not much younger than me.

Her body trembles as she turns to face me. Tears streak her cheeks. "I…I want to be with my mom." Those are the only words she can muster before her lower lip quivers, threatening to erupt into hysterics.

I reach out and touch her arm, attempting to offer comfort, though I fear even the slightest touch will compromise her stability. It's delicate, at best.

"She said it would be better if you came with us though. We'll all be together on the boats. Why don't you just come with me, and we'll catch up to Aidan and Kaylee and wait for your mom at the dock?"

As she contemplates my words, grunting and shuffling sounds resonate behind her. We both angle our necks toward the source.

"Stop struggling!" I've never heard Jeff's mom so commanding. She and Aidan's mom sway clumsily in their attempt to carry a twenty-year-old man whose legs no longer work. I sense it wouldn't be so difficult if he wasn't fighting them.

"We're not leaving without Dad!" Jeff shouts, his voice clear even amid the clamor.

Jessa and I rush to help, but it's nearly impossible for four sets of arms to leverage pivotal points of support on one person. The confines of the tunnel limit every movement.

"We're okay," Jeff's mom barks. "We'll get him out to the main room, and we can talk there." Jessa and I retreat slightly, letting them lead the way. The pace is excruciatingly slow as the sound of rushing water reaches my ears. Thin lines of it teem across the path, snaking and converging. The flow is getting stronger. Aidan's words whisper in my mind. *Even just a few inches of flowing water can drag you away.*

When we reach the main room, the others drop into chairs after lowering Jeff into one. All three of them breathe heavily, recovering from the effort. Anxiety swells within my chest. I'm not used to telling adults what to do, but they don't have time to sit and catch their breath.

"We should really go," I say with as much authority as I can muster. Before anyone can respond, booming voices blast from the top of the steps.

"Get to the boats!" Scott shouts.

Jeff's dad appears close behind him, roaring, "Now! We've

gotta go!"

Within seconds I realize history is about to repeat itself. The men struggle to maintain balance along the slippery steps, but the rushing water proves too powerful.

In flashes of elbows, knees, and everything in between, they crash into each rigid stone of the incline, reaching the bottom in seconds.

The gathering torrents closing in on us fade into my periphery as Aidan's mom jumps to her feet. Jeff's mom rises slowly, a silent panic sweeping over her features. The chamber thrums with shock and urgency. Both women scramble to reach their husbands, offering help and assessing injuries.

"I'm okay," Scott huffs, pushing to his feet. "We can't stay here. If that water doesn't slow, this whole cave will be flooded in no time."

"He's right," Jeff's dad agrees, cradling his right arm but rising, nonetheless.

As the adults hash out an escape plan, my eyes meet Jeff's. He jerks his head back slightly, in a "come here" gesture. With the others distracted, I quickly slide into a chair next to him. He leans toward me, narrowing his eyes. "I guess this is what they were talking about, you know, in that message you tried telling me about."

"This flood, or whatever it is, yeah, it must be." He's finally getting what he wants—to leave the cave, but in the midst of chaos. Any flicker of happiness he might have had at the prospect of leaving has been snuffed out by nature's latest tantrum.

"This isn't how it's supposed to be." He rubs his chin as his eyes drift to a random shadow along the wall. "Aidan and I should be packing for fall semester. My biggest problem should be which parties to hit. But these damn legs won't work and the world's gone to hell!" His jaw clenches with a rage that smolders just below the surface, revealing a demeanor that mirrors a volcanic eruption. He shakes his head in frustration and disapproval.

A weight settles in the pit of my stomach. I understand his anger—how it feels to be powerless and hopeless. I wish I could take it away from him, from all of us.

"Hey, we've got to get out of here, and that's what we're doing. Maybe things are better aboveground than we think." Leaning toward him, I grasp his forearm and project determination. "We're going to get you help. And maybe we'll even find a party or two, eventually."

I pray my promises aren't empty. I'll do whatever it takes to right a wrong that is bigger than all of us combined. It's a lofty goal, especially given that we haven't even gotten ourselves out of this cave yet.

Chapter 16

"Quinn!" My heart seizes in alarm at the frantic call. Aidan's dad rushes over to me, suspending my conversation with Jeff. "Go to the dock. Make sure Aidan left. If he didn't yet, get on that boat and make him leave. Got it?"

I nod feverishly, fear gripping every cell in my body. *Alone. I've got to go find them by myself.*

"If he listened, and he's gone, wait there for us," he instructs, gripping my shoulders and leaning down to meet me at eye-level. "Don't come back up here. Stay put and we'll find you. Just stay close to the dock, okay?"

My head bounces in affirmation. Satisfied I understand, he releases my shoulders and turns back toward the others. I repeat the instructions in my head: *If I see Aidan and Riley at the dock, get on their boat. If they're gone, just wait at the dock for everyone else.* I can do this.

Tension surges as Jeff's dad argues that the best way out is higher ground—the entrance at the top of the steps. Scott counters that the water's rushing in too fast and it's too slippery to traverse while carrying Jeff. If they lose their footing and fall backwards, they won't make it out of the cave at all.

This must have dominated their discussion while I was talking to Jeff. The room is like a gasoline drum, one spark away from exploding. The rising water doesn't care how long they allow tempers to flare in discord, it doesn't require their time or attention. Nothing we do will interfere with its intent to destroy whatever remains in its path.

I twist toward Jeff and wrap him in a forceful hug. "I'll see you soon!" He squeezes back but quickly releases me. "Go!"

I nod, reinforced by his confidence. He's right. We *will* see each other soon, but right now my only mission is to catch up with Aidan and Riley's boat. They might still be waiting at the dock for more of us to show up.

Clutching one of the smaller lanterns, I slog through the ankle-deep water, splashing down the tunnel, praying I remember the way. Aidan's led us to the boats a handful of times. It's probably a solid ten-minute walk if you hustle, but we've always taken our time, since we seemed to have plenty of it.

I draw in a deep, calming breath to counteract my overactive mind. Muted conversations echo behind me, vying for attention. I force my feet to keep going. I don't want to be separated from Riley and Aidan, even if it's just because they're a few feet away from me on another boat.

Relying on the map in my memory, my mind screams to push through the current faster. As I descend, the water flows freer and faster. I realize that it's leading the way. If I just follow the current, it will guide me to the lowest point in the chamber. Its overzealous pace rushes to merge with the existing body of water. My heartbeat thuds in my ears in response to the images playing in my mind: a rising wall of water chasing and dragging us all under its veil. Rag dolls tossed aside, our bodies battered and hollow.

Squeezing my eyes shut, I will the thoughts away. The rushing current, gravity its eager accomplice, seizes that moment to yank me off balance. My arms shoot out and I lose my grip on the lantern. It smashes against the wall as I land hard on my butt, soaking my clothes in the cool, muddy water. It drags me farther down the path, and closer to my destination. But unlike what you'd find at an amusement park, this ride is lined with jutting rocks, sword-like stalagmites, and absolutely nothing to slow or stop my descent.

My arms flail, uselessly reaching for a non-existent branch to grip. The lantern's gone and I'm dragged farther into darkness. A scream bubbles in my throat, but it's quickly squelched by the murky splashes spraying across my face and soaking my hair. A chill seeps into my bones. I welcome the tingling numbness the cold brings. It lessens the pain of each gash and scratch carved into my backside.

The path widens, rock walls retreating as I rush past them. I've nearly made it to the dock, but I have no ability to stop. My heart thunders as adrenaline sizzles through my veins. This ride is ending soon. And my only hope is for a smooth landing.

Chapter 17

I rocket out the slick chute, hurdle across the boat dock and plunge into the icy water. Finally, my body hovers in suspended immobility. It's a welcome change from the uncontrolled velocity that brought me here. That is, until a frigid jolt engulfs my body. Immersed in the churning lake, my insides feel hollow, and my limbs seem to bear lead weights.

The chilled air must serve as a natural air conditioner, seeping all the way to the lake. Never mind that it's full-fledged summer aboveground. Down here, seasons are meaningless.

My mind slows as the cold envelops my body. *The boats. I'm here for a boat. Riley. Aidan. Where are they?*

They were here, and not too long ago. Three electric lanterns cast dim beams of light toward the dock. My vision blurs, but they must hang from something. They dangle in the air, slightly swinging.

I swirl in the water, achingly slow, taking inventory. Three boats remain docked. That means one has left. Without me. Panicked, I dog paddle toward the direction of an opening that Aidan pointed out on one of our exploratory adventures. It's where the cave funnels into an outside lake. It may not get us far, but at least it's out of the caverns, away from the rushing water. And right about now I'd welcome any barrier between me and the icy cold. Instead, I'm caught in its paralyzing wake.

My heavy limbs protest progress. They refuse to propel me forward at more than a jellyfish's pace. Maybe that's appropriate, since my arms would much rather dangle listlessly and allow the water to dictate their movement.

I never actually saw the opening, but I trust Aidan completely. I'm certain I'll reach the lake if I just keep going in this direction. The question is how far away it is and how much longer my mind and body will cooperate.

My jaw twitches and my teeth chatter. A repetitive instinctual fight for warmth. Common sense tugs my eyes back toward the dock. I can't be more than a few yards away. *Why am I even trying to swim to the opening?* Aidan's dad told me to wait here if a boat was gone. My muddied thoughts swirl, creating a wake of residual confusion.

Frustrated, I squint my eyes closed and beg my brain to wake. As I tread water and tune into my senses, something glides past my leg, a smooth body skimming through the water. A scream rips from my throat. *The trout. I forgot they're in here too.* Another one bumps into my thigh. Maybe it's the same one. Or maybe a hundred surround me.

I jerk my head back and forth, searching for fins and scales or any indication of just how outnumbered I am. It does no good. The limited clarity the lake once offered is shrouded in brown billows of stirred up dirt and algae. My mind capitalizes on the opportunity to conjure images of Jaws torpedoing through the water with the sole intent of swallowing me whole. Never mind this is a freshwater lake. The cold is rendering me irrational.

I can't stay here, just treading water. I should swim for one of the other boats. It would be a welcome barrier between me and everything that lurks unseen below the surface. Not to mention how nice it would be to escape the frigid waves churning around me.

When another unseen body bumps into mine, a shriek echoes in the chamber. It takes a moment for my numb brain cells to realize the sound came from me. A dull throbbing pulses behind my eyes. It's all I can focus on until a welcome distraction arrives.

Shouting echoes through the cavern. Aidan's dad ushers the others to a boat. As they maneuver onto the benches, he notices me bobbing in the water. Cupping his hands around his mouth, his lips part, but no words reach my ears. I've been too cold for too long. My limbs tingle with pinpricks of pain.

Helplessly, I watch as he sidesteps around everyone and motions to me. Hands flying, he communicates a plan to his wife, daughter, and Jeff's parents before boarding another boat. The boats rock back and forth, swaying in motion with the strengthening current that pours out of the cavern. Jeff's dad powers the motor on his boat and peers over his shoulder, awaiting confirmation that the rest of his crew is ready.

Aidan's mom raises her free arm, giving a shaky thumbs-up. Her other arm wraps around Jeff. He sits in the center of the boat; the others flanked around him for protection. Their attention shifts my way, but their gazes hover over my head. *Do they not see me?*

Jeff's dad pitches a thumb in the air before turning back to the controls and navigating the boat away. *No! Don't go. Don't leave me here.* The words blare through my mind, but my jaw is too busy chattering to form any other sound.

Chapter 18

Just as I'm ready to relinquish myself to the frigid depths, I'm jerked out of the water. My head lolls back as my body slides over a stiff surface. My heavy eyelids flutter open and closed. Familiar blue eyes, glistening with panic, search my face.

Aidan's dad leans over me. His lips form words that my muddied mind is slow to comprehend. "Quinn! You're going to be okay! We're gonna get you out of here and warm you up." When I don't respond, he takes a step back, seemingly evaluating my ability to stay upright on my own.

My eyes drift to the bench supporting my weight. I tremble from head to toe, arms wrapped around myself as I hunch forward. It's like my body slid into an upright sitting position based on muscle memory, because I don't remember even noticing a seat.

He grasps my shoulders, evaluating my state. "I'm going to drive this boat out of here so we can meet the others, but I need you to hold on. Can you do that?" Slowly, I nod. I want out of here. I want Riley. And Aidan.

"Okay. If you feel you're getting woozy, slide down to the floor. At least that way you won't fall overboard and back into that water." I blink, hoping that is enough of an acknowledgement. There's no way I'm sliding to the floor, but I won't admit it. I've got to be upright to help find the other boats.

His head twists back and forth, eyes skimming up and down the bench-like seats. He blows out a frustrated breath. "We don't have any blankets. Try to stay huddled. We don't want you to lose any more body heat." He holds my gaze for a few seconds before giving me a sharp nod and rushing to the front of the boat.

My ears are still thawing when the engine ignites, and a low rumble vibrates through the floor of our rectangular red craft. Relief dares to flicker through me. Throwing a glance over his shoulder, Scott motions for me to hold on. I comply, lowering my arms and wrapping my fingers around the edged barrier between me and the frigid water below.

The current grows stronger as we navigate away from the most recent life we knew. Confident that I'm not going anywhere, Scott focuses on easing the boat through the churning waves. They're nothing like the ocean's wrath during a storm surge, but they slap the sides of our meager transport, intent on tossing us off course.

My chilled extremities grow feverishly numb. Every scratch, bump, and bruise screams in searing agony thanks to my unplanned tumble-turned-mud-slide to the water. I think I liked it better when my mind and body were both numb.

Punishing thoughts form as my brain defrosts and my cheeks flare with shame. *I'm such an idiot.* I had one job to do—make sure Aidan took a boat. And if he didn't, I was just supposed to wait for the others and get on their boat. Instead, I gave them all one more worry, one more barrier to their own safe escape.

My throat sputters in a ragged whisper, an attempt to call to Scott, to explain what happened, but I let the words die on my lips. He doesn't need excuses or explanations. It doesn't matter. All that matters now is finding our loved ones and getting as far away from this place as we can.

Feeling slowly returns to my limbs, restoring a sense of clarity to my mind. I slightly relax into the rigid seat. The surrounding walls of rock loom closer as we venture farther away from the boat docks. Water cascades down them, spurting through crevices and gaps. The dozens of mini-waterfalls would be stunning if not for the power they hold and destruction they promise. My mind flashes to Aidan's countless explanations of how water can cut through rock, creating formations over time. And now it's overtaking our temporary shelter and swallowing everything we left behind.

Tears pool in my eyes, hovering in suspended anguish. *Where are they?* I *need* Aidan and Riley. I can't face yet another life-changing event without them. They've become my constants in this unstable world.

The walls narrow to a tunnel, perfectly sized so that the boat can glide through without touching the surrounding rock. A lantern rests on the bench next to Scott, casting a glowing three-foot radius. The flowing current jostles our boat forward, propelling us toward an opening as dark as a moonless night.

This must be where Aidan and Riley's boat passed through. "Yes!" my mind screams. I don't care about dry shoes or warm clothes. I just want my sister and…I'm not sure exactly what Aidan is to me. I guess he's my friend, although that sounds like one trivial step above an acquaintance.

The time I spend with him is never enough. Our connection has strengthened with every laugh, tear, and adrenaline rush since we met. *At least it did for me.* Beneath the soreness every inch of my body bears, my stomach flutters as I wonder if he feels the same.

Whatever happens next, I don't want to lose him. He's got his family and hopefully we have our aunt, and maybe we can even locate some other relatives, but no matter what, I'm not willing to part ways. Not that anything has been up to me until this point. That probably won't change anytime soon.

As we near the opening, Scott turns toward me. "You already look a little better," he smiles, relief softening his features. "They should be right outside here waiting for us." I nod and allow a return smile to tug some feeling back into my cheeks.

The moment dissolves in an instant as a deep howl echoes around us. Chased by thudding raindrops, it dampens our escape to the lake outside, both figuratively and literally. As we breach the opening, a steady stream of water pelts us from above.

Chapter 19

I scan the outside world for the first time in what feels like years. Although the air is heavy with humidity, I gulp its freshness. I can barely see beyond the lantern's heroic efforts to light the way, but I sense no hint of ash anymore. It's like the chalky haze that plagued the atmosphere after Yellowstone erupted was never real.

For just a moment I wonder if it's been this way for some time and we had no clue, or if this monstrous downpour is the cause. Has it cleansed the atmosphere? If so, at what cost? We were just chased out of our underground shelter by a flood of fury intent on dragging us under its relentless surge.

"Quinn, hold on!" Scott reminds me. "This is a pretty rough storm."

Yeah, one these boats were never meant to weather. The vast expanse of nothingness nearly renders our lantern useless, barely breaching the torrential cascade. My mind tries to fill in what we should be seeing, but the dark sky severely hampers visibility. I struggle to grasp our location. The restless lake tosses our boat as the motor battles to propel us forward. My mouth drops in awe as I realize how high above ground level we truly are.

This isn't exactly a lake anymore. It's more like a rough ocean. Visions of a tsunami flash through my mind. *Where did all this water come from?* It's like we entered the cave and emerged weeks later to a completely different world. What was once a parking lot, where we last saw our Aunt Robin, is now an endless expanse of water. Turning in a slow circle, my brain stutters as it comprehends our surroundings.

In the distance, buildings peek out from the fluid darkness. Their exposed roofs rise only a few feet above the water's shifting surface. More striking than glimpses of what I can see, is what's missing.

I can almost envision the paved asphalt, sparse trees, and patches of green grass imprisoned beneath the rolling rush of dark water. The world we sealed ourselves away from is submerged. Questions no one can answer flash through my mind. *Is our aunt okay? What happened to our house? What do we do now?*

Racing winds swirl across the submerged landscape, fueling waves, wind, and rain that our boat must conquer. Suddenly, the tourist vessel that can comfortably seat about twenty bodies feels small.

Surprise etches Scott's features, but he pushes the motor to carry us faster. A yellow spotlight flashes, beckoning us toward it. The other boat. I audibly sigh. *Finally. Something's going right.*

When we draw near, Scott cuts the engine, and we drift

toward the mirror image of our vessel. Even over the hammering raindrops, barking erupts. I'd recognize that excited yap anywhere. Aidan practically lurches over the side, reaching for us. "You made it!" He grabs hold, tethering the boats together with his grip. His dad rushes to help.

As they strategize, Riley rushes toward me with relief and concern. Snickers struggles in her arms, twisting his slick body in an attempt to free himself, defying her commands to settle.

Her eyes trail over me, taking in my disheveled appearance. Like her, clusters of hair cling to my ears and neck, while my soaked clothes suction themselves to my body. While the rainwater soaked her from above, she doesn't know that the lake tried to yank me to its bottom.

"Quinn, what took so long? We were talking about going back inside to look for you."

Before I can respond, movement catches my eye. Only then do I notice Aidan's sister, Kaylee. Her eyes bounce between the guys' conversation and ours. Her lower lip twitches, as if words linger just behind it. She shifts on her feet. I can't tell if she's scared, cold, or angling to catch her dad's attention. Maybe all three.

Shifting Snickers into the crook of her arm, Riley tugs mine with her free hand. She lowers her chin, that brown gaze boring into mine. "Hey, what happened?"

I squeeze my eyes shut and blow out a sigh. "It was a mess. Nothing went like it was supposed to. I ended up in the lake and nearly drowned from the cold."

"Quinn! I'm so sorry we weren't there," she starts, but Snickers' frenzied barking blocks out her voice. Squinting into the night, I follow his line of vision. Movement, beyond the storm's punishing downfall, swirls just below the water's surface. Slick bodies twist around each other, further infuriating the terrier. They dart around the water in a cluster, as if teasing him.

Are these fish from the cave's lake? Or did all this water wash them inland from far away? I turn back to Riley as he squirms his way out of her grip.

"Snickers, no!" She shifts her attention a moment too late. The rat terrier launches away from my sister as we both scramble to catch him. His nails clack on the bench seat as his little legs struggle to gain speed. Before anyone can reach him, Snickers propels himself over the side.

"Noooooooooo!" Kaylee snaps out of her trance. She trails on Riley's heels and together they slide across the boat's slippery floor. I dash to the front of my boat, keeping pace with them. Leaning over the edge, I stretch as far as possible, calling for Snickers and scanning the water's roiling surface for a bobbing brown head. Riley and Kaylee do the same.

Peering into the dark waters below, any sound or splash he makes is easily hampered by the pouring rain and howling wind. Shifting weight rocks the boat. *Please don't let us capsize. I can't go back in that water.*

"What happened?" Aidan's dad shouts, projecting his voice over nature's current display of fury.

"It's Snickers—he jumped overboard! We're trying to find him!" Verbalizing it gives this nightmare truth. My eyes drift over his shoulder as I force the words out. They must have found rope because Aidan straddles both boats, securing them together with a series of makeshift knots.

A shriek yanks my attention back to the water. "There! He's there!" Riley screams, pointing in the distance. But I don't see any sign of that furry little head. Darkness swallows the space just beyond their boat. Riley motions again, but the pouring rain blankets any visibility from where I stand.

Brushing past me, Scott lunges for the bow. Reaching beneath a seat, he quickly retrieves what looks like a space-age handgun. I realize it's a handheld spotlight. *Of course, a cave tour boat would have at least one powerful flashlight.*

He grasps the thick orange handle and squeezes the trigger, releasing a thick bolt of dense light. Skimming it across the tossing waves, he aims where Riley thrusts a trembling pointer finger. After a few sweeps, his hand stills. "I see him! The current's pulling him away."

A second beam of light zeroes in on Snickers. Aidan holds it steady, having found a matching spotlight on their boat. Even from a distance, I recognize the fear in Snickers' shifting eyes. His mouth forms a yelp as water splashes around him, churning as nature's force fights to stifle his life-preserving motions.

Amid a raging storm and flooding waters that threaten to claim us all, my gaze drifts to Riley. Her eyes lock with mine. My mind processes what she's about to do faster than my vocal cords can form words of protest.

Climbing onto the bench-like seat closest to her, Riley hurdles over the side and plunges into the dark water below.

Chapter 20

In that instant, the last wisps of childhood slip through my fingers. I can't lose my sister or Snickers. I've lost enough already. Kaylee screams as Aidan scrambles to locate Riley. Scott eyes me warily, as if I might jump ship too.

If I could bring them both back, I would. My battered body would follow them anywhere. But I know from the time I spent in that water, all it does is slow your mind and your body. You're lucky if you can just save yourself, let alone someone else too. Maybe it's not as cold as it was inside the cave, but it can't be much warmer.

"Quinn, take the light!" Scott shouts. Without thought, my body complies. As soon as the spotlight is under my control, he brushes past me. Running his hands along the inner wall of our boat, he quickly retrieves a pole stored behind the seating bench.

"Aidan, take the rescue pole!" Scott passes it to his son before hopping into the other boat. Kaylee grasps the spotlight with both hands, freeing Aidan to meet his dad. She nods at me, and we both aim the surges of light in tandem, training the beams on Riley as she paddles toward where we last saw Snickers.

"Come back!" Aidan shouts, his dad echoing the sentiment. They launch the rescue pole into the water. It lands at least a yardstick away from her. She ignores it, pushing through the churning swells, drifting farther away as she splashes toward Snickers. He seems to realize that her arms are much safer than the adventure his swimming excursion delivered. His muscles launch into overdrive as he paddles in Riley's direction.

When he's within arm's reach, Riley surges, fingers outstretched in anticipation. The next moment freezes time and space. Although it lasts mere seconds, my brain interprets it as stretching on forever.

A wave surges. The little brown head we're all focused on swirls in the tumbling flow, pulled farther out of Riley's reach. Within the blink of an eye, he's carried away, out of sight. *There's no way any of us can reach him.*

Despair clouds my vision and chokes the words rising in my throat. *Noooooooooooooooo!*

"Riley, swim back here right now!" Scott shouts, his voice carrying the commanding tone of a parent that you don't dare disobey. Defeated and likely out of energy, she obliges.

Kaylee sobs openly, running shaky palms over her face. "He's gone…he's gone…and where's everyone else?" Scott rushes to her side and wraps an arm around her. "Did anyone see the other boat come out of the cave?" he asks, panic rising with each syllable.

I shake my head dumbly. *How could I have forgotten about them?* I was so relieved to see Riley and Aidan. But as soon as we reached them, Snickers distracted us all. It's not too late. He can't be that far away yet. As soon as Riley's back on board, we'll turn both boats toward where we last saw him and shine those spotlights across every inch of the surface until we find him.

Aidan confirms that the third boat didn't pass on his watch as he and Scott toss the rescue pole back in the water. Riley splashes within reach of the extended steel bar, but as she stretches to grab hold, her eyes widen in terror. She bellows a panicked scream just before she's yanked below the surface.

Fear seizes my heart as it batters my ribcage. Riley's hands thrash, shooting blasts of water right back into the waves they sprang from. Her head emerges and she gasps for air. "Mmmm…!" She struggles to form words between gulps of oxygen. "Sssss!" The battering rain easily diffuses any sound she makes, but her panic is palpable.

I scream to no one in particular, pointing at my sister. "She knows how to swim! Something's really wrong! She needs help!"

"We're getting her out of there!" Scott commands. "Kaylee, Quinn, move back." My instincts beg me to jump in the water, but his words are stern and he's much stronger than me. If he's planning to save Riley, I need to stay out of his way. I shuffle back a few steps so he can focus on only one person in distress, not two.

As the water drags Riley under once again, Scott yanks the rescue pole back to our boat. He sweeps it through the water right below us before sharing a knowing look with Aidan. *What? What's the plan?*

A single nod triggers Aidan's next move. He drops into the

water cautiously, seemingly feeling his way to avoid obstacles until he reaches Riley. She's too focused on treading water and scrounging for air to notice his approach.

"Riley!" he shouts. In that moment, my mind flashes through a dozen movie scenes where the person being rescued nearly drowns their rescuer in a panicked frenzy to survive. The two people I need most in my life at this moment are in danger.

As if wishing for something will make it come true, I make a mental vow that they will both be okay.

Chapter 21

I watch, my stomach churning with dread, hope, and disbelief. When she notices Aidan's approach, Riley thrashes with a renewed energy. I was hoping the sight of him would calm her, knowing help had arrived. Instead, it seems to reignite her agitation. Aidan continues to shout—the only way to ensure she'll hear over the raging storm and restless water.

Seconds later, he dips below the surface, then pops up for air a few times before returning to battle whatever's trying to steal Riley from us. My sister continues to struggle. Tears prick my eyes as I silently offer a barter of everything I've ever owned if they can just make it back to the boat safely. Bile rises in my throat, in tandem with the realization I've got nothing to barter. I've lost everything I've ever owned. Between what we had to leave behind in the cave, to what's probably drifting in a watery grave in our childhood home, to anything I left behind at Aunt Grace's trailer. All I've got, and all I want right now, are the people I care about.

A few excruciating minutes later, Aidan emerges from the roiling surf with triumphant energy. Relief and exhaustion flash over Riley's face. Together they half-paddle, half-flop their way toward us.

I rush to the front of the boat, sliding on the wet deck, nearly tumbling overboard. Scott whips his head around, his eyes flashing. I grasp the rescue bar and yell, "I can help!" He nods, biting back any thoughts of banishing me to the slightly safer back of the boat. When Kaylee realizes what I'm doing, she quickly joins us, wrapping her hands around the pole tightly, turning her clenched knuckles white.

The three of us work in unison, hampering eagerness with caution as we reach, clutch, and tug our loved ones to safety. It feels as though their lives could slip through our fingers at any moment, and none of us is willing to let that happen. As they cling to the pole, we draw each of them closer and hoist their watered-down frames aboard.

We deposit Riley and Aidan on the vessel's bench-like seats. Chests heaving, they both greedily inhale air. The rest of us mirror their actions, but to a lesser extent. Somehow the emotional toll of witnessing their struggle was worse than the physical exertion of the rescue effort.

By this time, we're all drenched, some of us from the pounding rain and others from the unforgiving flood. Although shivers course through my body, Riley and Aidan fare worse. They both visibly shake. Besides fending off whatever refused to release Riley, they had to push their muscles to fight the frigid water.

Scott drops to his knees, resting one hand on Riley's shoulder and the other on Aidan's. His eyes rake over each of them, faltering when they land on Riley's ankle. Gashes mar her pants, exposing tattered skin and seeping blood.

With a quick once-over of Aidan, confirming no injuries, he leans closer to Riley.

"What happened?" He motions toward her ankle as he gently lifts the hem. Angry slashes crisscross her pale skin. Her hands tremble as she answers, staring down as maroon crests the slices in her skin.

"My foot got stuck...like something grabbed me. The harder I pulled, the tighter it clamped around my ankle. I couldn't...I couldn't get away." Her lower lip trembles and I rush to her side, sliding an arm around her shoulders.

Shifting in his seat, Aidan offers his opinion. "I couldn't see anything in the water, but when I dove under and reached for her ankle, it felt like a thick wire was wrapped around it. Maybe phone lines? Power lines would have electrocuted us."

Scott nods slowly in contemplation. "All this rushing water easily could have downed some poles. If the lines didn't snap, they could be caught in the current, snagging anything that crosses their path. Either way, we've got to patch this up as best we can."

Regret etches his features as Aidan continues. "All I could do was pry the lines apart. It took a few tries they were so tight. I knew it had to hurt, but I didn't know what else to do."

"It's really not that bad," Riley says. Facing Aidan, she flashes a shaky smile. "And thank you. The worst part was being dragged under and not able to get away. I couldn't have done it myself, and I'd much rather be up here with a few cuts than struggling for breath under there." She points to the murky rush of water, shivering at the reminder of its implied threat to swallow her whole.

"We're going to wrap that ankle and then find our other boat." Scott's eyes sweep over each of us, perhaps assessing whose journey to hell and back over the past few hours has been the least demanding. He chooses his daughter. Other than him, she's the only one who was able to avoid taking a swim today.

"Kaylee, check under the seats for anything I could use as a bandage. A cloth would be ideal, something long enough to tie around her ankle." She complies immediately, clumsily navigating the slippery surface, dropping to her knees every few feet to search beneath the seats.

Taking advantage of the momentary lapse in action, I rise, take just a few steps around my sister, and slide onto the seat beside Aidan. His eyes track my movement as Scott awaits a response from Kaylee, either affirming or denying anything that could be used as a makeshift bandage.

Leaning close to his ear, I whisper the sentiments in my heart. "I'm glad you're okay." I squeeze his arm. "Thanks for bringing Riley back."

He shakes his head, raking a hand through his dripping hair. "Don't worry about me. I'm just glad your sister's okay. And you, too. From what my dad said, your little excursion wasn't exactly a dip in the pool either."

"No, it wasn't." I gulp, trying to wash away the lump in my throat, and conjure enough bravery to let him know what he means to me. *What have I got to lose?* "All I could think about when I was out there was you…and Riley…and how much I need you both." I pause for a moment, allowing my words to sink in, and awaiting a reaction. He watches me intently, his eyes drifting from my eyes to my lips and back again.

"No matter what happens next, I don't want to split up. I don't know where we go from here, but I don't want to just say goodbye and never see you again."

He slowly raises his arm, gently cupping my cheek in his palm. Somehow, his icy touch conveys a warmth that eases the chill. "Then we agree to it right now, Quinn. That won't happen. We'll figure out a way to stay together. We'll figure this out together." Amid the misery, we find a reason to smile. I grasp his free hand in mine and entwine our fingers. Though it passes quickly, the brief exchange of hope and promise forge a connection deeper than friendship.

The brief act of solemnity awakens an inner drive that refuses to accept defeat. My heart aches knowing that Snickers is somewhere out there, as well as the rest of Aidan's family. And Jeff's. We can't ignore that. There's got to be a way to get them all back.

Sloshing footsteps snap me out of the moment.

"I can't find anything!" Kaylee shrieks, frustration overtaking her already-fragile composure.

Scott rises to calm his daughter. "It's okay, you tried." Our eyes shift to one another in silent contemplation of our best course of action before he turns back to face Riley. "You know, I bet a sock would be perfect. If it was long enough, it would wrap around your ankle, and we could tie it gently."

If it's all we've got, it's better than nothing. As I open my mouth to volunteer my sock, a beam of light pierces the dark, landing on us. Instinctually, we all shrink away from the blinding beacon, throwing up our arms to block its glare.

"It's them!" Aidan shouts. "They found us!"

Chapter 22

Relief shudders through me. *They're okay and they found us.* Now we can focus on the only other one of us who's missing. And with another boat in our entourage, we can cover more ground with more eyes, searching for that little bobbing head. Sprinklings of hope flutter within me even as the storm above rages on.

The vessel nears, its beam blinding and motor humming. The closer it gets, the less it resembles our own boat. A booming voice reverberates through a megaphone. A limp hand, shriveled from being trapped beneath the icy water for too long, wraps around my own, startling me. Riley stands beside me.

"This is the 126th National Guard Rescue Squadron. Please remain calm. We are here to assist you and lead you to safety."

The National Guard? Where did they come from? My hand clenches Riley's tighter. I'm betting shock and fear radiate from both of us.

At least two sets of eyes watch us from the enclosed area with all the controls. They peer at us through thick rectangular windows, shadowed bodies shifting as they adjust switches, dials, and whatever else they've got in there. As the boat drifts closer, two uniformed soldiers greet us from the deck. Cloaked in dark slickers, they cautiously approach the side of our boat.

"We request permission to come aboard," one says, his eyes sweeping over each of us as well as the empty bench seats. In an instant, they've assessed how many of us there are and that we likely stole, or "borrowed," the boats we command. The emblazoned Couturier Caverns logo gives us away, even if the flat, oblong observation transport would never pass for a privately-owned vessel.

Scott steps forward, gently guiding Kaylee toward Aidan for comfort. "Yes, permission granted," he answers. While one soldier raises a rope and deftly begins mooring our tiny fleet to them, the other climbs over the railing and into our space. Rain pelts his rounded helmet, reminding me of a construction hard hat with an annoying spotlight, relentlessly focused on blinding every retina on board.

Scott shakes his head, as if clearing away the momentary shock. "We have some injuries. Do you have a First Aid kit or anyone who can help us?" He nods toward Riley as the rest of us stare, open-mouthed.

"Yes, sir. We can help." He stops and raises a hand, twisting his wrist, motioning toward the other soldier. I can't make sense of the movement, but the other guy seems to understand. He strides inside the boat's wheelhouse. While he's gone, the first soldier continues.

"Sir, you should know that it's not safe out here. We're patrolling, looking for survivors. It's good we found you when we did." His dark eyes evaluate us and our collective condition. "Once we're secured," he pauses, throwing a nod over his shoulder to his comrade, "you can all board our craft and we'll deliver you to a safety commune."

Safety commune. Matt's warnings about those places flash through my mind, lodging a sinking feeling in my stomach.

"Thank you for the offer," Scott says. "But this isn't all of us." He gestures to me, Riley, Aidan, and Kaylee. "There's another boat...and..." He verbally stumbles, unsure how to explain Snickers' disappearance, and hopefully his upcoming rescue. "We need to find the rest of our group."

"Sir, we're in the midst of a natural disaster," the soldier's tone grows stern, edging toward impatience. "Our crews are performing search and rescue missions in the immediate area. Like we found you, another team is just as likely to find them and bring them to a safety commune."

The other soldier perks, adding to the conversation as he clutches what looks more like a mini suitcase than a First Aid kit. "You're more likely to locate the missing members of your party if you come with us. And based on what we've seen, your vessel is in no condition to maneuver through this storm. We're offering you the safest option at the moment."

"Can you check," Scott asks, "before we leave the area? Can you make sure the rest of our group was found?"

"Sir, we can sweep the area for them on our way to a drop-off point for your group, but we don't have the capability to access the current intake list for the surrounding communes.

And besides, it's changing by the minute. Our sole mission right now is retrieving survivors and bringing them to safety. Our Intake Team can determine if the people you're looking for have been located."

"They were in *a boat* just like *this* that *should* have been directly behind us," Scott says. "If they were found, it more than likely would have been by you."

"I'm sorry, sir," the officer holding the First Aid kit says. "We have not encountered any other boats like this today." Aidan pushes through our little cluster, his head pivoting back and forth between our visitors. "You're out here retrieving survivors—from what exactly?"

After a moment of skeptical silence, the answer hits us like an anchor to the gut.

Chapter 23

"Haven't you heard?" The soldiers squint their eyes in disbelief. "A tropical storm is tearing up the coast. Warnings have been flashing on road signs and emergency broadcasts all week. We began evacuations two days ago."

I can almost hear the question buzzing in his mind. *Where have you people been? Living under a rock? Um, yes, as a matter of fact, we have.*

After a momentary pause, he continues.

"We may not be getting the worst of it this far inland, but it's taking its good old time moving on. Models predict it will pass sometime tomorrow, but the storm surge is so strong, it's been rolling farther inland than the models projected. Teams are performing search and rescue missions from Maine to Delaware. Everyone we locate is to be brought to the designated shelter."

He takes a step closer, stressing his next point. "This process is in place so that we can help the greatest number of people in the most efficient way possible. We know you want to find your family, but chances are they've already been picked up and taken to a commune."

He pauses for a moment, focusing on the only adult in our group. "Look, there are others still out there who need our help. We've got to continue with our mission. Lives are depending on it and every minute is critical."

Scott releases a sigh, running a hand through his hair. "I understand. What you're saying makes sense, but can you check her ankle," he nods toward Riley, "before you take us to the shelter?"

"Yes. Let's get you all transferred to our craft, and we'll check her wounds as we head for the closest commune. Each one has limited medical capabilities, but they can definitely do more than we can."

Once we've abandoned our two boats and boarded theirs, I slide into a seat beside Riley. The boat eases through the water slowly, gaining speed as it carries us farther away from our tethered vessels, and the last place we saw Snickers. My heart sinks deeper with every passing minute.

A soldier approaches, clutching a hard plastic orange case with black handles. He kneels before my sister. "Okay if I take a look at this?" He motions toward her ankle. She nods tentatively. Considering we were about to tie a sock around her wounds, I have a feeling that whatever he offers will be more than sufficient.

"Distract me, Quinn," she pleads. *With chaos erupting in every corner of my mind, that request is easy to fulfill.*

"I can't believe Snickers is gone," I whisper, locking eyes with her. Amidst the rain pelting the deck and echoes of the others' conversations, she clings to each word. Dropping her chin, she shakes her head slowly.

"If I had a better grip on him, it never would have happe—" I stop her before she can finish the thought.

"No! It's not your fault! There was nothing anyone could do. Everything happened in a whirlwind. I mean, I can't believe just a few hours ago we were sitting underground, complaining about counting cans." Once again, our lives have taken drastic turns in what feels like the blink of an eye.

"Yeah," she agrees. "I'd give just about anything to be back there now."

"Miss, I'm going to clean this up and wrap it, okay?" The soldier waits for Riley's confirmation. When she nods, he rolls up her pant leg as far as it will stretch before retrieving a few items from the open medical case.

Aidan shuffles to Riley's other side, plops down and leans toward us. "This storm must have been what Taves was talking about. This must have been the announcement we missed."

I hope our aunt heard the message we did not. Maybe she's waiting for us at a shelter right now, along with Aidan's mom and sister, and Jeff's family.

When Riley cringes, I slip my hand into hers. The soldier dabs her cuts with an antiseptic wipe. She flinches, bracing for the rush of pain, crushing my fingers with a strength that likely rivals Wonder Woman's. As he presses a bandage to her ankle, wrapping a long white strip of gauze around it, Scott's conversation with another soldier drifts to my ears.

"Are the communes in contact with each other?" Scott asks. "Because if the others in our group aren't at another site, then we have to go back out and find them."

"Yes, each site uses a master intake system. You will be asked to provide some personal information, but it allows us to ensure that survivors are accounted for. In this case, you can see how it helps us reunite families."

Another soldier chimes in. "If you'd like to provide a description of who's missing from your party, we can alert the other teams in the area. It might help us find them faster. Or help determine if they've already been picked up."

"Yes, I can describe their physical features. You already know the type of boat they're in," Scott starts.

"Why don't you follow me to the wheelhouse. I'll take some details down and dispatch them to any nearby teams."

"Thank you, I appreciate that," Scott answers.

"You'll still want to provide that information to the Intake Team at the commune. They can share it throughout the region and if your party is already on site at a facility, someone will put you in touch with each other," the soldier explains, quelling at least some worry.

But it still leaves one question burning in my mind and smoldering on my lips.

"What about dogs?" I ask, interrupting their conversation. "We lost our dog out here. Is there any chance he could be at a safety commune too?"

The soldier contemplates for a moment, but his shifting gaze confirms my fear. "At this time evacuation and sheltering procedures do not include companion animals."

Riley squeezes my hand, this time fueled by a different sort of pain. One that we share, deeper than words can describe.

"But what if one of these rescue boats saw him out there? If they saw his little head bobbing in the water, would they just ignore it?" I can't help myself. I know I should be thanking these people for helping us, but all of us still have family members out there.

Two of the soldiers eye each other before one closes the distance and stands before me. "Look, we're just people too. If I saw a dog out there that needed saving, I'd scoop him up and worry about what to do with him later. I wouldn't leave him behind."

I nod gratefully, a weak smile—the most I can offer. *Let's hope they're all like this guy.*

Chapter 24

The boat rushes past city buildings, by no means skyscrapers, but recognizable even in the hazy conditions. I sense we're speeding toward higher ground. Either that or I'm growing accustomed to a water level that easily blankets cars, fire hydrants, and parking meters.

I train my focus upward, unwilling to acknowledge any floating debris beyond what's forced into my periphery. Tree branches or garbage I can handle, but I'm not ready to face the remains of any victims of this nightmare.

Dormant streetlights bow toward us at an uncomfortable closeness, as if their giant bulbs are eyes scrutinizing our every move. The top edges of traffic signs slice through the wake as we pass, imprisoned in the watery depths. Every direction bears unthinkable destruction. The kind that makes you wonder how and where you'd even begin to piece it back together.

The churning motor slows as we approach a long, flat-roofed building. Hugging the brick wall as if it's a traffic lane, our boat winds around to the back of the building. Although the sign at the front of the bus loop is nowhere to be found, I recognize the elementary school. It's not the one Riley and I attended, but it resembles our own.

With the engine settled, we drift toward a concrete loading dock. *I bet this is where all the nasty cafeteria food is delivered.* I envision giant tubs of pasty-looking mayonnaise and enormous cans of questionable meat slathered in gelatinous gravy.

A female soldier greets us on the dock. "This way, folks, if you'll follow me, we'll get you processed and settled. We've got generators, so we can offer you many of the comforts of home." She patiently waits as we disembark, offering a hand up to anyone who needs steadying as they transfer from the rocking boat to solid ground.

"Thank you," Scott says. "One in our group is injured. Not sure if you can fast track us, or even just her for now, to any medical personnel you may have?"

"Just one moment, sir," she raises a hand and steps closer to the boat, talking to the team that remains on board. After a few furtive glances toward Riley and her injured ankle, the soldier returns to us.

"The intake process is very brief. It sounds like the injury has been tended to for the time being. As soon as you're all processed, we'll get you settled with a place to relax, and we'll have a nurse check out that ankle." She smiles, but it's not one that invites questions or dissent. With a sharp nod, as if we've conceded, she turns on her heel and leads us through the door.

We follow her through the snaking hallways, slowing our pace to match Riley's. The soldier doesn't seem to notice. Once we catch up to her, she deposits us at the end of a line of people. At a quick glance, there can't be more than a dozen. Like us, they stand in small groups, clothes dripping with remnants of the storm that steered us all to this spot. Residual drips and drops collect, trickling onto the smooth tiles our feet trudge along. Gravel and dirt mix, forming a thin but muddy slop. Hints of the once shiny waxed surface peek out from the dirty sheen our shoes have cast.

"Just wait here," our escort instructs. "Intake stations are set up in the office and someone will help you as soon as possible." Once again, she turns on her heel, this time making a swift exit. I guess if we have any questions, someone in the office will answer them.

Those in line ahead of us speak in hushed voices. Some quietly sob while others rock back and forth in a self-soothing motion. At thirteen, Kaylee's easily the youngest one here, and other than two other groups, the line is comprised of middle-aged and older couples. *Maybe the younger families evacuated sooner.* Considering our own parents, I believe they would have evacuated soon after the warnings started, before the converging water wielded its full power. If there was enough time, they may have tried to reach family members—even those who live out of town but still in the line of fire for this storm—like Aunt Grace—to check on them.

As we wait, my eyes sweep over what would normally be the main entrance. Two sets of glass doors serve as a barrier between us and the outside. Once we pass through the first set of doors, we wind into the office, but if we continued down that short stairway instead, we'd reach the second set of doors.

Only we wouldn't be coming or going through them, that's for sure. A temporary barrier protects the school's inhabitants from nature's latest flash of power. Every inch of glass is boarded up with wood sheets. Slouching bags of sand, in stacks of three, rest along the bottom border where floor meets wall.

It doesn't look like much, but the area is dry, so it must be working. And no one seems to be concerned about it holding up.

Riley brushes up against me, pulling me from my observations. "I can't believe we're in a school. How many people do you think are here already?" she whispers, shifting her weight from one foot to the other. She cringes, her features pinched in pain.

In the adrenaline rush of finding Aidan and Riley, and then arriving here, my own bumps and bruises drifted from the forefront of my mind. I'm sure once we're settled, they'll promptly remind me of their presence. But my sister has had no such reprieve.

"Riley, your ankle! You shouldn't be standing here in this line! Let's find someone to help you." I tug her arm, motioning toward the nurse's office. *What better place to set up medical people?* "We can start there!"

"No!" she hisses, jerking me back toward her. "I don't want to draw attention to us. Let's just keep a low profile and stick with Aidan's family for now."

"Are you sure?" She's obviously in pain and the whole reason we're here is to get help. Her reasoning makes no sense.

Riley startles the thought away when she clasps an icy hand around my own. "What if Aunt Robin is here? I don't want to take away from Aidan's family or Jeff, but after we ask about them, we can ask about our family," she whispers, shifting on her feet impatiently. I squeeze her hand, inviting anticipation to seep through me. "All I want right now is to get into that office so we can find out if anyone we know is already here."

She's right. How many places could there be like this? This one really isn't that far from home. Our aunt could be here! Just as quickly as belief ignites, fate reminds me what the past few months have proven—raised hopes are too often shattered hopes.

I nod. "Yes, we'll stay right here and find out what we can when we reach the office." Riley forces a smile, but her eyes glisten with anguish. I'm not sure if it's physical or emotional, but I'd be willing to bet it's both.

Chapter 25

A line of people winds around a corner before us. Although everyone varies in height, weight, and other physical features, we all mirror the same bewilderment. Unseeing eyes disregard colorful posters that adorn the olive-green walls. Drug free school zones and anti-bullying messages fade into a meaningless background.

Some people cross their arms, a silent protest to the wait or the muffled conversation they're in. Others shift uncomfortably, a nervous energy trying to escape as they anticipate what's to come.

As I focus on our destination, and just how many people are ahead of us, a stifled sob infiltrates our circle. Riley hears it too. We glance at each other, then search the others for signs of audible distress. Aidan and his dad engage in a serious discussion, but it's imperceptible by their hushed voices. They pause now and then, throwing suspicious glances at the soldiers that stride up and down the hallway.

That leaves only one other person. Behind us, Kaylee stands silent. Her haunted eyes confirm that her mind is thoroughly processing everything that's happened in the past few hours. She wraps weak, shaking arms around herself. Her skin erupts with goosebumps and she shivers. Her lips part as her teeth chatter; the faint tapping amplifies in my ears as I absorb her pain. I understand the numbness, the disbelief, the distant acknowledgement that life can never be the same again.

Without hesitation, Riley shifts closer and wraps Kaylee in a hug, as if she can squeeze the sadness and memories away. Unshed tears flood my eyes. I'm caught somewhere between feeling like an awkward observer of a private moment and someone who's seeing her own past flash before her eyes. I imagine this is what my sister and I looked like when we struggled to face the loss of our parents.

But I was lucky enough to have my sister with me. Just as easily, Riley could be missing right now. And if I had to go through that anguish again, I'm pretty sure it would break me.

Before I can stop myself, I utter the words she wants to hear, regardless of a complete lack of confidence or evidence. "It's okay, Kaylee, I bet we'll find your mom and sister soon."

She doesn't acknowledge my words. Instead, she clings tighter to Riley, squeezing her eyes shut and blocking out the sights and sounds that serve as constant reminders that the life we all shared just hours ago is gone.

Once again, our world contracts to a void and expands to change. I already mourn the loss of our little community, of the flawless way we worked together to build a life in a less-than-ideal setting. For all the times I complained about our temporary underground home, I'd give anything to return to one of those moments—scrubbing clothes clean in the icy water, gathering for a slightly-tasty meal, flirting with Aidan when we'd disappear into the shadows. But now they're just distant memories, unimportant, and irrelevant.

In this moment, nothing matters: where the next meal is coming from; if there's anything dry and warm to wrap ourselves in; where we go from here. If Kaylee's anything like me, all her brain wants to do is forget in an obstinate refusal to acknowledge the truth. In time, she'll understand that acknowledgment doesn't require acceptance.

Aidan and his dad notice our little scene and end their conversation. Scott gently approaches Kaylee, thanking Riley for her efforts. As she steps out of the way so Scott can take over comforting his daughter, Aidan slides an arm around my shoulder and brushes his lips against my hair. "She okay?" he whispers.

Afraid a whimper will escape if I try to respond, I clamp my lips closed and shake my head.

"When can we go back to the cave?" Kaylee asks, each syllable dripping with misery. "We have to find Mom and Jessa."

Scott wraps an arm around his daughter. "We all want that, honey. But I can't put you in danger and what's happening out there isn't safe." He swipes a hand across his chin and lowers his voice, speaking calmly like he's trying to coax a scared animal out of a trap. "If you could stay here with your brother, maybe I could go back out there and help look for them. The teams won't know where to look unless—"

"No!" she shrieks. The outburst draws us all in closer,

forming a protective bubble to shield her from unwanted attention. Scott's eyes shift to Aidan as he pulls her closer and offers a soothing "Shhh, it's okay, I'm right here. I'm staying right here."

Chapter 26

Amid the mini-emotional breakdown, we're completely oblivious to the line's movement. A tall, thin soldier taps Scott's shoulder. "Sir, I believe you're next." He points to a laminated sign peeking through the interior window that connects the main office to the entranceway. The wall bears an enormous poster featuring cartoonish children of various ethnicities smiling and waving as if they're at an amusement park instead of school. It's a welcoming image but utterly tone-deaf in the moment.

A counter that's got to be at least six feet long separates us from three soldiers processing new arrivals. They stand on the opposite side from those waiting to enter, alternating between asking questions and entering information into a laptop. The set-up reminds me of a bank, but with less privacy and minor injuries plaguing every few customers.

The counter is divided into three cramped sections, each

labeled with a large black number printed on white paper taped to the flat surface. How many people have passed through these doors? How many people died before they could be rescued and deposited here?

Motioning for us to follow him, the soldier directs us inside the office. "Looks like number 3 is open."

"Thank you," Scott mutters distantly, likely distracted by the gravity of our situation. His eyes glaze over each of us. I'm betting his thoughts are focused on the ones who are not here.

As we step toward the third slot, a short, plump soldier beckons us to her station and explains that she'll need to ask us a few questions before she can assign us a safe place to stay while we all wait out the storm. My mind inventories possible options of where that might be. Apprehension coils in my stomach as Matt's description of the government's safety communes flash through my mind: like warehouses, no privacy, food rationing. And he said they were filling up as fast as they were being set up. Are people crammed in the gymnasium? Are they set up in rows, separated by flimsy sheets, powerless to muffle tears and sniffles?

Before the process can formally begin, Scott thrusts a finger toward Riley. "Someone in our group is injured. Can she get some medical attention while I answer your questions?"

The soldier, Tavares, according to her name badge, smiles sympathetically. "There is a brief wait to see a medical team member anyway, so we'll get you processed first. That way you'll be all set and won't have to wait as long to get her injury checked out."

Scott turns to Riley. "You doing okay?"

She nods appreciatively.

I have a feeling that even if she wasn't doing okay, she wouldn't admit it.

The cramped space grows stuffy as the new arrivals cluster across from the soldier that's been assigned to process them. It's a harsh contrast from the icy waters and merciless downpour we just escaped. Humidity is the unpleasant byproduct of our collective water-logged garments and a ventilation system clearly unable to filter the congested air.

Still, I marvel at the effortless presence of electricity. Lights, even harsh fluorescence, are welcome after the time we spent underground, bathed in darkness and shadows. I'm certain I never gave generators a second thought in my life before, but now I'm grateful for their invention.

Behind the counter, beyond the soldiers' workspaces, sit two large desks that face each other. Their previous occupants were probably the school secretaries. Between them, a photocopier the size of a washing machine dominates the communal area. Two side-by-side offices, their lights on and doors closed, round out the rest of "their" side. It's plenty spacious for the handful of soldiers shuffling between their workspace and the copier, or occasionally to one of the larger desks to grab a form or paperclip.

Our side must have been the office's waiting area. A magazine rack monopolizes the limited space, displaying outdated flyers announcing PTO fundraisers and field trip permission forms. Four metal chairs line the windowed wall that provides an otherwise unobstructed view of the hallway.

I nudge Riley and point to an empty seat, but she shakes her head no. I don't press. My legs wouldn't mind the respite, but a sense of urgency binds me to the counter. Now that we've made it this far, neither of us wants to miss the chance to hear what's happening, as well as if the others are already here.

As Aidan's dad divulges names, ages, and physical details about his family members, my attention drifts to a middle-aged woman being processed next to us. Her wild eyes dart around the room as she tugs a thin blanket around her shoulders. She's too frantic to focus on the information she's being asked to provide.

"My husband, he's still out there! Has anyone found him yet?" She turns her head from side to side, searching the room, eager to find anyone who can answer her question.

"Ma'am, I assure you we have teams scouring the region for survivors. If he's out there, our crew will find him and bring him here. Now you can help him by answering a few questions so we can get you settled." He raises his eyebrows in anticipation of her reply.

She shakes her head, squeezing her eyes shut. I know what's coming next. I recognize the defeat. Shudders and tears chase her words. "What's happening out there?" She thrusts a trembling finger toward the entrance we all slogged through.

His response is unnervingly even. I know some occupations require a calm demeanor in emergency or potentially explosive situations, but it makes me want to jump over the counter, grab his shoulders and scream until he stops everything to find this woman's husband.

"A series of tropical storms," he says casually, as if he's explaining tomorrow's breakfast hours. I scan his features for empathy or acknowledgement of what we've all been through, but he maintains an emotionless mask. The people surrounding us are other survivors. Like us, they probably lost family members, homes, and any sense of security in a matter of moments. Guilt and grief will sear their memories, clouding nostalgia with regret.

"How many people are out there looking? Will they keep looking until they find everyone?" Words tumble out of her mouth as she edges closer to hysteria. She presses the heels of her palms to her temples, eyeing every person and object in the room suspiciously.

My attention shifts to the soldier, who maintains a stoic expression. Can he relate? Has he lost anyone? Or is he numb to the suffering right before his eyes? He answers the questions in my mind quickly when he picks up the conversation right where he left off.

"Ma'am, right now, it's critical that we process as many people as possible. We have procedures in place to ensure everyone's safety." When she stares at him mutely, he continues. "More help is on the way. We're expecting a team from the Federal Emergency Management Agency any day now and the American Red Cross is already on the premises to help survivors prepare to transition to longer-term shelter after the water recedes."

With a sigh, he shifts his focus to the laptop and taps the keyboard. His tone softens slightly, although he still doesn't directly answer her questions. I guess no one can, though. He can't exactly promise that they'll find her husband. "Now, let's get you entered into our system. That way we can get you checked out by our medical personnel and assign you temporary quarters while we help others who are arriving."

The woman relents. She answers his questions, probably clinging to the hope that she can get answers sooner that way.

Tuning out of the depressing scenario unfolding beside us, I turn my attention to our own situation.

Chapter 27

Riley stands beside Scott at the counter, probably providing details about the two of us he wouldn't know. We're not all related, but I'm hoping they keep us together.

After about ten mind-numbing minutes, Tavares announces that we've been entered into the system, and she has assigned us a space that can accommodate all five of us. Based on the information provided, which Riley and Scott must have supplied while I was focused on our surroundings, we'll each be given a dry change of clothes along with bedding materials.

I flinch at the woman's last three words. "Riley," I whisper, squirming my way in between her and Scott. "What do they mean five? What about Jeff? And his family? And the rest of Aidan's family?"

Her posture radiates defeat, although it could be pain from her untreated ankle. "None of them are showing up in the database." She bites her bottom lip and welling tears reflect in her eyes. "If they were picked up, it wouldn't have been too long ago, so they could still be going through the intake process at another site."

"Will they keep checking and let us know if they show up?" I ask, the dread in my gut hinting that I already know the answer. A fat drop hovers on Riley's eyelash, unable to hold its midair suspension for much longer. Please, please, please let them be at another commune.

"Just about everyone who's come in is missing someone," she explains, swiping a lone tear trail from her cheek as if that can make the emotions fueling it disappear as well. "They can't keep tabs on every single person unaccounted for at the moment. She said we can come back tomorrow and wait in line for a turn to check the status of missing family members."

"Did they know anything about Aunt Robin?" I have to ask, but if they did, I'm sure Riley would have told me already.

She shakes her head miserably. "Not yet, but we can ask again tomorrow."

The more she says, the less I want to hear. She's already sounding like a pre-recorded message. Hope deflates further when we're directed out of the office, away from the only source of information that could lead us to our lost loved ones.

Another soldier greets us in the hallway to escort us to the next phase, a medical check-in. This place is reminding me of Langley in that everyone we pass becomes a nameless, faceless blur. Anxiety and sorrow choke the air, overwhelming my senses. My only mental escape is to narrowly focus on taking one step forward at a time, and nothing beyond that.

We're ushered to a classroom next to the nurse's office and encouraged to sit until someone can see us. Scott paces the room while the rest of us plop into chairs neatly tucked under a round table stacked with workbooks.

After a few moments of silence, a camouflage-clad woman arrives, carrying a vinyl tote bag bearing a common medical symbol: the white plus sign in a red circle. She sweeps into the room confidently, placing the bag on the table as her eyes dance across a tablet screen.

"Alright, it looks like there are five in your group and one of you suffered some ankle lacerations recently." She looks up from the screen, awaiting confirmation. "Riley, I believe."

"That's right," Scott says as Riley rises and takes a few cautious steps toward the newcomer.

"That would be me, but my sister Quinn got banged up pretty bad out there," Riley volunteers. "They patched me up on the boat ride here, and it's really not too bad. Maybe you could check her instead." She motions for me to join her, standing before the doctor.

"I can certainly check you both. From the sounds of it, your injury is a bit more serious, so let's have a look at you first. Please have a seat over here." Riley complies, lowering herself into the chair facing the doctor. Deftly unwrapping the dressing, the doctor slips glasses on and leans closer to the injured limb.

As she examines the wound, she asks, "Can you tell me how this happened?" Her eyes track the gash from front to back as she gently twists Riley's leg for a better view. After she's satisfied by the visual inspection, she retrieves the tablet and documents Riley's condensed version of her overboard adventure.

"They did a good job cleaning you up," she affirms, unzipping the tote bag and withdrawing a few foil pouches and a roll of tan bandage. "I'm just going to spread a pain-relieving gel over the wound and cover it with a reusable bandage. I understand you were already treated with an antiseptic, and it looks clean, so I won't put you through that sting again."

She pauses for a moment before holding Riley's gaze, as if silently assessing my sister's ability to comply with her instructions. "I want you to keep it dry and don't unwrap it. Leave that to the medical personnel here, okay?"

When Riley nods, she continues. "Stop by the nurse's office tomorrow afternoon. Someone will check it again just to make sure it's healing cleanly. Don't want an infection creeping up." She flashes a quick smile before patting Riley's knee and pushing back in her own chair to face me.

"Next," she nods to the seat beside Riley, and I quickly slide into it. "So, tell me what hurts and what happened."

"I fell…" I don't want to admit we were living in a cave. It would probably just invite a slew of more questions. Why didn't I think about what I'd say? Of course, she was going to ask that.

I inwardly cringe at this sudden inability to form a cohesive sentence. "So I fell down what was…like a mudslide and…I just got banged around a little. Just a few bumps and bruises."

"May I?" she asks, reaching for my shirt sleeve. I nod.

As if she's done this a hundred times, she rolls my sleeves up one at a time and slides her gaze along my limbs. When she's done with both arms, she bends over and hitches my pant legs up a few inches. Clinging to my skin, bonded by the damp material, that's as far as they'll go with relatively minor strain.

"From what I can see, it's just as you said, minor bumps and bruises. Is there any specific area that hurts? For instance, if a rock or stick struck you when you were falling?"

"Nope, nothing like that." I shake my head, ready for my check-up to end. She reaches into the tote bag and retrieves two small white foil pouches.

"Here's some acetaminophen. It's a general pain reliever. It should help your body forget its tumble." She deposits the pouches into my hand. "Take two pills tonight and two when you wake up. If you still feel sore after lunch tomorrow, tag along with your sister to the nurse's office and we can give you some more, okay?"

"Yes, thank you." She nods, effectively dismissing me. I scurry away before she changes her mind and expects me to bare any more skin.

"Sir, it looks like you got a little banged up out there as well," she turns her attention to Scott. "Would you like me to take a look?"

"No, I'm fine," he dismisses her offer quickly. "Will that be all?"

"Just one more order of business." She reaches into the bag, unzipping another compartment. "We're vaccinating everyone who comes through our doors as a safety precaution, but I can make quick work of it. According to our records, some of you have already been vaccinated, so I'll only need those of you who haven't gotten it yet."

Chapter 28

The mood instantly changes as tension swells, and silence descends. I wonder if they know I was never vaccinated. The sergeant told me to say that I was if anyone ever asked me. But do they have proof? They won't just take my word for it.

Riley and Aidan got the injection at Langley, so other than me, that leaves Kaylee and Scott. My eyes dart to him. Does he know what Sergeant Bowen told us about the vaccine? As his mouth forms words, red-hot fury flares on his neck and cheeks. Any wonder about how much Aidan shared with him is clear in his reaction.

"You're not putting a needle in any of us! I know what that thing is!" He jabs a pointer finger at the syringes with distaste. "My son already got it and I'll be damned if anyone else here gets one of those."

The doctor startles. Maybe we're the first to object. Perhaps by the time others have reached the medical check-in part of the process, they're willing to accept a quick shot in the arm if it's the last thing standing between them and a few blankets. Or, the expectation of being reunited with their loved ones may hamper any dissent. My mind flashes to the woman next to us in the office, pleading for someone to find her husband. It didn't take long for her spirit to cower in full cooperation.

"Sir, please calm down. This is standard procedure to protect every person who seeks refuge here." The doctor's perfected response reminds me of when the gang and I tried to enter Langley Air Force Base. The guards at the gate gave us a similar speech. I didn't think too much of it until Sergeant Bowen admitted that the injection is really a nano-tech tracker, a tool to help the government monitor and manage the population to prepare for a dwindling supply of resources.

Scott rises, determination fueling his trajectory. Maintaining eye contact, he points at the syringes as if they're overflowing with poison. "I know what's in those things." His voice is a low growl, poised to erupt at any moment.

Just minutes ago, this woman had no hesitation in treating us and making sure we knew what to do next. Would she really attempt to inflict harm on us in her next breath? I study her features. Knowing the truth about the injections, I can understand Scott's fierce refusal. But genuine confusion flashes across the servicewoman's face. Maybe she doesn't know.

"Sir, think of this like a flu shot. It's meant to build immunity in each person who enters this building to prevent the spread of illness. There's nothing in it that will harm you. And it's a requirement in order to enter the common areas. The last thing we want right now is illness or an outbreak. We're housing many people in close quarters and we just want to keep everyone healthy." The soldier pauses, awaiting a response.

Thoughts slide together. Do any of these people know what they're injecting into civilians that show up for help? Or is this being kept from them, too? Sergeant Bowen didn't say if others knew about the trackers or if it was just him. Are we all being lied to?

Scott drops his hands to his sides and inhales a calming breath, attempting to diffuse the anger that's nearly reached its breaking point. "Allergies run in our family, and none of us will be injected with any substance until I'm able to speak with someone who can explain exactly what is inside that needle."

His posture readies for a challenge for just a moment before it softens. He exhales a deep breath, and the fight leaves him just as swiftly as the molecules passing through his air passages. "Please, we're already separated from the rest of our family. And some of us have had allergic reactions to medication in the past. The last thing we need is a medical emergency that could have been prevented. I just need to know what's in that needle, but I'm willing to listen."

Sympathy reflects in the soldier's green irises just before they drift to the tablet. Her delicate fingers hover just above the screen, suspended as she weighs each option flickering through her mind. Pursing her lips, she leans toward Scott. "Alright, I understand. You've provided most of the required information and more than half of you did already receive the vaccination at another site. And I'm sure you're all exhausted."

Sympathy was definitely the better road to take. Defiance seemed to be leading us to a dead end.

Her fingers drop, pecking at the smooth surface as she continues. "It looks like Scott and Kaylee are the only ones in your group not yet vaccinated. I'm flagging your records. Tomorrow, when Riley," she nods toward us, "and Quinn, if she needs more pain reliever, visit the nurse's office, I'd like you both to tag along and we'll get this all wrapped up. In the meantime, I'll look into getting an answer as to any potential interactions for known allergies."

Scott agrees, relief settling into his features. "Yes, of course. I appreciate it. Thank you."

"You're welcome." She eyes us questioningly, a flicker of doubt passing through her thoughts. She doesn't believe we'll be more cooperative tomorrow. I know if Scott has his way, we won't.

The doctor zips her tote and rises. "If you could all wait here, someone will be in to escort you to a living space. It will just be a few minutes." She strides out the door and down the hallway, the sound of her footfalls fading with each step.

Chapter 29

We linger in combustible silence, awaiting our next visitor. Memories of the past few hours swim in the surreal. What started with ten humans and one dog is now five humans. We lost more than half of our little community in mere hours. The sting grows numb, likely undermined by exhaustion. So much has happened in a compressed timeframe that my mind protests focusing on any one memory for more than a minute or two.

Another soldier appears in the doorway, rapping tentatively. So many names and faces have sailed past my periphery tonight that I don't even bother to scan his name badge. His welcoming smile and kind eyes immediately set me at ease. It'll be soon now. I just want to surrender to dark nothingness and forget this day ever happened.

He motions toward the door with a brown clipboard. "This way, please. You'll have a classroom to yourselves tonight. It's just a precaution, to quarantine you somewhat, until you're all vaccinated." His tone is even with no hint of judgment. I wonder if all the soldiers were injected, too. If they really believe the purpose is to prevent the spread of illness, then it would make sense that they all get it. Not that I'm willing to ask.

Along the way, he points out restrooms and locker rooms where we can shower. He calls our attention to handwritten signs taped to the walls, directing visitors through the maze of hallways to help them locate the cafeteria, gymnasium, and office.

We don't travel too far from our first two stops. The nurse's office is just a few yards behind us and the office is one sharp turn away from there. They probably kept us close by so they could monitor us. It makes me wonder how Scott will handle tomorrow's expected vaccinations. What if he refuses again? Will they kick us out? I'd rather our group be quarantined away from everyone else anyway. At least it gives us some semblance of privacy.

The rooms we pass are dark, apparently vacant, but we know others arrived before us. Echoes of occupancy drift through the space—like the dull noises you hear through the door in a hotel room: a random thud, shuffling footsteps, muffled conversations.

Our guide slows his pace, pausing outside room 126. He depresses the flat handle and swings the door open. Stepping over the threshold, he swings an arm along the wall, flipping the light switch on.

Turning toward us, he motions inside. "I'll be back with some bedding materials. Why don't you go in and check it out?"

Scott nods and the soldier marches down the hallway. We walk single-file into our latest temporary home. Rectangular ceiling lights bathe every corner of the room in harsh fluorescence. Stacked desks form an orderly row that runs along the windows. They're positioned to encase half a dozen additional desks balanced atop the counter running the length of the room. Low bookshelves, crammed from end to end, reside just beneath the counter.

Shiny metal legs jut toward the ceiling while flat work surfaces kiss as each right-side-up desk rests on its upside-down partner. Besides clearing half of the classroom's floor space, they seem to function as backup reinforcements to the windows. A few bags of sand are tucked within the makeshift structure, but it's unclear what purpose this room serves, other than housing troublemakers like us.

We stand like statues, just beyond the threshold, unsure what to do next. Our only belongings are compressed to our skin, slowly drying. With nothing to unpack or arrange, it's like we're suspended in animation.

Eyeing a stack of chairs tucked in a corner, Scott sidesteps around us and retrieves three of them. Aidan follows his lead, grabbing two more. They position the seats in a small circle and motion for everyone to sit.

The hard plastic surface offers no cushion, but exhaustion tugs at my muscles. Thankfully, the pain reliever has kicked in and traces of soreness fade. My body molds to the chair, eager for any reprieve.

Grief and loss weigh heavily in the silent room. Snickers should be curled up on Riley's lap right now, completely unaware of nature's raging fury outside. Jeff should be cracking inappropriate jokes to Aidan under his breath while the rest of their family members mingle and comfort each other. I know some of them better than others, but each one leaves an emptiness in their absence.

A few minutes later, a sharp rap on the door jars what little relaxation had briefly settled through me. Scott rises, facing the man who led us here as well as a taller soldier who's joined him.

"We've got some cots and mats for you," our escort says. He jabs a thumb toward the hallway. "They're right outside the door. It'll just take us a few minutes to get them set up."

"Great, thank you very much," Scott answers. "Do you need any help?"

"No, sir. All in a day's work. We'll have you outfitted for some rest in a moment."

They work quickly and efficiently, although their supplies seem to have fallen short. They align four cots, which swallow most of the remaining open space, before retrieving two folded bundles of gym mats. Perhaps they were once an inviting, bright blue, but now their dull hue reveals years of punishment dealt by sneakers, knees, and palms.

"We ran out of extra cots," a soldier explains. "Maybe, for the time being, one of you could sleep on the mats. They make a decent cushion. We're expecting more supplies to arrive any day now."

The other soldier chimes in. "In the meantime, here are some bedding and clothing packs. If you don't need anything else, we'll leave you to get settled." He deposits a small mountain of sealed bags on the cot nearest the door.

"Thank you, we appreciate it," Scott says before they nod and leave. As their footsteps echo down the hallway, he's already shifted into action mode. "I'll take the mat, you kids take the cots. Now let's get our sleep areas set up, wash up, and get some rest."

"I'll take the mat," Aidan offers. "You'll probably wake up with a sore back if you sleep on it. Besides, I've spent most nights in the past months sleeping in a dorm bed, a cabin, or a cave. My body's adjusted to sleeping on anything remotely close to a bed anyway."

"Alright," Scott agrees. "I'll take the cot right by the door. We'll set the mat up in the corner at the back of the room so no one's traipsing all over you when they come and go."

With that settled, Aidan unfolds his temporary bed, sliding it into the corner, and we each grab a bedding pack. Kaylee claims the cot next to her father before announcing that Riley should sleep on her other side. I get it, Riley's been a source of comfort to her since our forced cave evacuation. But it's still a kick in the pride when you're so blatantly omitted as someone's first, or second, choice.

Dropping onto the only cot left, which is the closest to Aidan's makeshift nest, I tear into my clear plastic pack. It contains a folded blanket, sheet, and pillow. They remind me of the ones we had at the cave—more practical than luxurious, but better than nothing.

Chapter 30

Set up takes a few minutes. Other than the clothes we wear, we don't have any other possessions—besides whatever the military provided to us.

"I can't believe they don't know where Mom and Jessa are... and Jeff's family," Kaylee mutters. "We shouldn't be here without them." She plops down on her cot and Riley rushes to her side, wrapping an arm around her hunched shoulders. The younger girl looks as though a slight breeze could topple her even as she sits. Tear stains streak from her puffy eyes and her jaw trembles. Shivers course through her as if Riley's comfort coaxes the pain to manifest itself.

My heart aches as I watch her try to contain the emotions plaguing her mind. I recognize the pain that no person or pill can heal. Riley brushes her free hand over Kaylee's hair, smoothing it down, and whispers a shushing noise. I'm glad she has some inkling of how to handle the girl's abysmal state.

Resting her head on Riley's shoulder, a fresh river of tears rushes from Kaylee's eyes. I turn away, certain that the sight will release the sorrow pooling in my own eyes at any moment. Her emotional outpouring tears at the scab of my own heartache.

Riley and I spent one week mourning the loss of our parents, and most of that time fluctuated between a blur of shock and denial. From there, we battled one crisis after another, with only a few brief intervals.

Focusing on all that's left of our group, I latch onto Aidan and Scott's hushed conversation that grows louder with each word.

"I'm going back to find the others. I need you to stay here and make sure everyone gets some rest. You'll all be safe, and I'll be back as soon as I can." Scott's determination is steadfast, even in his disheveled state. In our chaotic rush to escape the rising water, I hadn't noticed how everyone fared physically.

Gashes mar his shirt and pants. Fresh scratches peek through the gaps, revealing slices the cave's harsh edges must have made in our attempt to vacate. Random strokes of mud paint his cheeks and forehead.

"How do you know they'll let you? What if something happens to you?" At the sound of his voice, my eyes bounce to Aidan. Raw emotion clouds his eyes. He runs a shaky hand through his hair and glances at his sister. If his dad leaves, he's automatically promoted to the oldest adult in our group. And he's barely out of high school.

My chest constricts as I silently process the options and possible outcomes. This could be the last time Aidan sees his father. I quell the recesses of my mind that try to claim the thought as an overreaction. Never had I imagined that the moment my small family climbed into the car for vacation would be the last time we'd all be alive together. I'm certain Riley feels the same way.

Nearly half of their family is missing. And now the remaining members must weigh their chances of finding those lost and if rescue is even possible. The unspoken question is unbearable. Is it worth the risk of losing one more loved one? Scott closes his eyes for a moment, considering his son's words. Shaking his head, he rests a hand on Aidan's shoulder.

"They can try to stop me, but I'll be damned if I don't even try to find your mom and sister, and Jeff..." As his words trail off, Aidan nods in miserable understanding. Is there any chance the others survived? And if they did, can one person find and rescue them?

As if my thoughts transfer to Aidan's brain, his breathing increases and he blurts words out in a frenzied rush. "I should go with you! You can't do it alone!" He glances toward me. "Can you and Riley keep Kaylee safe?"

I nod furiously. Turning those hardened blue eyes back to his dad, Aidan awaits affirmation. It doesn't come.

"Son, I need you to stay here and take care of your sister." He leans closer, his words barely audible "We can't both go. If we both didn't make it back..."

Reality slams into me as I comprehend why I could hear his whispered words. The background noise has faded. The sobbing has stopped. At the first mention of her name, Aidan's sister must have tuned in to the conversation.

Chapter 31

Pushing out of Riley's grasp, Kaylee charges the few steps to her father. Swiping away her running nose and trickling tears, she shrieks. "No! You can't go! No, Dad, please. Don't leave us here without you! Please!"

My heart shudders as Kaylee collapses in her father's arms. He glances at Aidan before squeezing her tighter and whispering in her ear. Aidan rubs his eyes, as if the pain behind them is excruciating. My gaze meets Riley's. Sorrow clings to her eyelashes and the anguished expression I've become accustomed to seeing has once again overtaken her face.

Witnessing this family's heartbreak sparks a flame within me. I don't want any of them to face the losses Riley and I have survived. When Kaylee's cries subside to shuddered breaths, Aidan wraps a hand around his dad's forearm.

"I'll go. You stay here and I'll find them and bring them all back." Whether he believes it or not, his even tone bears resolve. Kaylee tosses her head back and forth, unable to voice her objection. She can't lose anyone else.

Scott runs evaluating eyes over his son. I'm certain he's inventorying every scrape, scratch, and scuff. I don't want Aidan to go, but all I see right now is bravery and strength. Even in his slouched shoulders and slumped posture.

As Scott draws his lips together to respond, I step forward. "I'll go with him. He shouldn't go alone." I match Aidan's determination outwardly. Trepidation flutters along my spine, but I ignore it, choosing to focus on what I know I can do despite what my body believes.

A grateful half-smirk tugs at Aidan's lips before the others rush to react. Calmly, Scott shakes his head and holds my gaze. "I appreciate the offer, but I can't let you do that." At the same time, Riley rushes to my side and entwines her arm with mine.

"Quinn, we barely made it out of there. There's no way you're going back." I look to Aidan, but I know he can't magically whisk a minor away from the acting adult in our group, who happens to agree with the closest semblance of a guardian to me right now.

"I'd be faster on my own anyway," Aidan says, drawing attention back to him. When my narrowed eyes land on his, he cringes and mouths "Sorry." I'm going to assume that he's merely trying to protect me and that he'd welcome my company if it came without opposition.

Scott runs a hand through his hair while his other arm remains firmly wrapped around Kaylee. She watches the conversation leap from one person to another with detached solemnity. There's probably nothing left inside her to express. I remember that sense of numbness after my parents died—a cocktail of shock, anger, and agony.

Instead of smoldering the flame igniting in my core, the objections rising around me fuel it. No matter how unlikely of a rescue squad we are, and even though we needed rescuing ourselves, if there is any chance the rest of Aidan's family can be saved, then we have to take it.

Anger threatens to spill from my mouth, but I choke it back. Adrenaline awakes an urgency, pushing my feet to stomp the ground and my fists to clench. The energy surge conflicts with my sense of caution because these reactions won't do me any good. Tempering my response, I attempt to negotiate, focusing every ounce of concentration I can muster on keeping my tone even.

"The longer we wait, the less chance we have of finding anyone. I'm practically an adult and Aidan needs someone to watch his back out there." Although their scrunched faces appear unconvinced, I capitalize on the momentum and continue. "Give us one hour. Just one hour and if we aren't making any progress, we'll come back." I glance at Aidan. He nods in agreement, flashing me the closest resemblance to a smile that's possible at this moment.

I understand the gratitude that swells within when someone supports your idea, no matter how impractical it may sound. When Riley was kidnapped, Aidan and his friends helped me. They could have walked away and left me behind. When I met them, they were facing their own boatload of problems. But instead of sticking to their plan, they diverged to help a stranger chase after her sister across the country.

Scott releases a deep breath. "Quinn, I'm sorry, but if you were my daughter…in this situation, I would not allow you to go. And I have to treat you as such. I'm not your parent, and I'm not even your relative, but I would want someone to look out for my child if I couldn't."

His reasoning stabs at my heart. If my parents were alive, they most definitely would forbid me from doing something like this.

Riley squeezes my arm. "Why don't we all sit down and think about this. Maybe we can convince some soldiers to send a search party to the cave? They're trained for situations like this. Well, maybe not this exactly, but they're better prepared than any of us."

My brain screams, Nooo! We're wasting time. We need to go right now! But, just like the foot stomping I nearly released just moments ago, I know that response will not yield the results I want.

"I think that's a good idea," Scott says. He turns to Kaylee. "You should get cleaned up, change into the dry clothes they gave us. I'll go talk to whoever's in the office and see what they say, and then we'll get some sleep."

The man wavers between fire and ash. One moment he's a breath away from breaking out of this place and the next he's retreated into the role of responsible parent dutifully forgoing his instincts to protect the only family members he has left.

Chapter 32

We walk to the restrooms in pairs, Kaylee practically glued to Riley's side. Taking advantage of the miniscule amount of privacy we've been afforded, I whisper to Aidan. "I don't know why your dad bothered going back to the office. They aren't going to do anything. You heard them when we got here. Everyone's missing someone and they're already searching. Do you honestly believe they'll listen and go look where he says?"

"No, I don't." His chin and cheeks are harsh angles, tension hardening every feature. "They're going to focus on what would have been heavily populated areas, not a cave that had exactly ten human residents that no one was aware of."

"I just wish there was something we could do." My words hang unanswered, an impossible call to action. He doesn't speak for the rest of our trek, but an intensity swirls in his silence. As we part ways to our designated facilities, I only hope that he'll include me in whatever ideas are churning through that brain right now.

As we all settle into our beds, Scott returns. Scratching his forehead, his eyes drop to the white tile floor, and he confirms what Aidan and I suspected: rescue efforts are in progress, and we can check back again tomorrow to see if our missing loved ones have been brought here or to another commune.

I'm thinking they should just play their standard messages on a recording over the loudspeaker. We know rescue teams are out there retrieving people; otherwise, it's anyone's guess where we'd be right now, but being tucked away in a classroom makes it feel as though time is an endless measure of nothingness. As though progress has stopped. We have no way of knowing what's happening beyond our four walls.

I should just be grateful for the privacy—at least we aren't huddled together in the middle of a cramped, humid gymnasium. It's probably like being trapped on an endless plane ride—trying to tune out a baby's whimpering cry, holding your breath every time someone nearby spews germs into the air by sneezing or coughing, and crumpling yourself into the smallest form possible to squirm past too many bodies packed into the space.

Settling into an almost-comfortable position, I wait for my body to release my mind from consciousness. The others succumb to sleep quickly, clouding the room with calming exhales that grow slower with each passing minute.

I gulp down the knot in my throat as my body processes true heartache. I would give anything for Jeff and Snickers to burst through that door, with the others close behind. Riley, Kaylee, Scott, Aidan, and I would gladly sleep on desks or sitting upright in chairs if it meant the rest of our group was here. Because they belong with us.

In the stillness, the slightest movement catches my eye. The figure closest to the door rises, a fluid shadow among the darkness. Drawing no attention other than my own, Scott slips out the door. I don't protest or alert the others. I knew where he was going as soon as he settled into his cot with his boots still on, and it's not the bathroom. We're safe but his wife, child, and friends may not be. I understand his driving need to find them.

I roll to my other side, but too soon, surging memories threaten to trigger tears. I focus on Aidan's back, wishing I could lose myself in his eyes right now. After about ten minutes, I assume he's asleep and I'm ready to join the rest of the room by closing my eyes and just breathing until I'm swept away from the present. I'm ready to forget the fear, pain, and loss this day has brought—even if it's just temporarily. As I allow my eyelids to drift closed, Aidan twitches slightly, soundlessly. If I wasn't observing him like a stalker, I never would have noticed.

Squinting, I crane my neck to get a slightly better view. He twitches again. My heart aches as I sense his silent battle to contain a brimming agony for all that's lost. Sweeping my gaze across the room, I confirm, albeit with limited visibility, that the others remain unmoving.

Like a cat, I slink across the floor on all fours, attempting to squelch any sound from my movements. This wouldn't look good if anyone else woke up right now.

By the time I reach Aidan, his whole backside shudders. Unsure of how he'll react, I swallow the rising doubts and let instinct lead my words and actions. His pain is palpable and though I can't take it away, the very least I can do is share it with him.

I slowly climb onto his folded gym mat. Momentarily surprised by the shifting surface, he releases a sharp intake of breath. As his head turns toward me, a wet track of tears reflects in the dim moonlight. Avoiding my eyes, he turns away and shakes his head, as if refusing my unspoken offer of comfort. He stills, facing away from me, probably hoping I'll leave him alone.

Instead of retreating, I slide onto the mat. Coiling my body around his, I reach across his shoulders and wrap my arms around his trembling frame. After a moment's hesitation, he turns toward me and buries his face in my hair. We don't speak. I understand loss and there are no words I can say that will make this any easier for him. Physical closeness is all I have to offer. I blanket him in a protective cocoon as all the sorrow he's been suppressing seeps out.

Hot tears soak my hair, likely leaving behind a tangled mess. But it's worth every knot and every limb that goes numb as I hold him in the tightest embrace possible. As waves of sorrow and regret drag him deeper into despair, he clings to me like a life jacket.

When the tears finally stop and his breathing stills, I allow my body to relax into the mat and my mind to drift into oblivion.

Chapter 33

Sunlight pierces my eyelids, growing brighter by the second, signaling that morning has arrived. As my senses return from a deep slumber, someone repeatedly clears their throat. It's better than a screeching alarm clock, but as realization dawns, my discomfort grows.

"Ahem. Aaaahemmmmm."

The slits of my eyes budge open a crack, just enough to confirm that my apprehension is justified.

"I believe your cot is over there, young lady." Aidan's dad towers over us, uncrossing his arms only to point toward my empty sleeping area. Heat flushes my cheeks. Last night, I didn't exactly consider how this would look in the morning.

"I...uh," I scratch my head, willing a believable lie to materialize. Riley and Kaylee watch the spectacle from their cots, eyes wide. Neither has the decency to feign disinterest.

Aidan startles awake, raking a hand through his disheveled tufts of hair. Absorbing the situation, he clumsily jumps to his feet. "Dad, nothing happened. I…had a nightmare or something…and Quinn rushed over to wake me up before I woke all of you."

Doubt flashes in his dad's narrowed eyes. He's not buying it. And it doesn't explain why we were both still asleep. My cheeks flare in a visual manifestation of shame and mortification. I wasn't trying to do anything wrong. I was just trying to comfort Aidan when he was clearly suffering, but I can't say that. I won't call him out for a moment of weakness that he trusted to share with me.

I may appear to be in the wrong, but I'm not the only one here withholding information. My jaw drops as I prepare to expose Scott's absence while the others were asleep last night, but the thought fades before any words form. Only now do I notice the dark circles beneath his eyes and the worry lines creasing his forehead.

If he had any good news to share, I believe that would take precedence over my little infraction. Which likely means that there is no good news.

"So, now what do we do?" Riley interrupts, rising to her feet, brushing away nonexistent lint on her sleeve and tilting her head toward the door. "We should find out what their plans are for us today." Thank you, Riley! Her interjection works to distract Aidan's dad. He glances her way, but his eyes dart toward us once more before focusing on her.

"They said we should report to the cafeteria for breakfast when we woke up," Scott says, running a hand through his hair just like I've seen Aidan do a hundred times. "But I'd like to talk to someone in charge and find out a bit more about this operation. Why don't you all go get something to eat and I'll catch up with you?"

"I'm coming too," Aidan states unflinchingly. Scott's jaw drops, likely to counter with dissent, but Aidan's blue eyes pierce his father's. He exudes a sense of determination that either wasn't present or bubbled just below the surface yesterday.

"Why don't you both see what you can find out? Kaylee, Quinn, and I will grab seats for us in the cafeteria. In case there's a line or something, we can at least get a head start and you can meet us there," Riley suggests.

Scott considers her words for a minute before agreeing. My sister has diffused another moment that could have ended in an argument, or at the very least, awkwardness. When I squeeze her hand in gratitude, she doesn't even flinch, effectively safeguarding my secret acknowledgment.

As we ready to leave, instinct tugs my eyes downward. But the one I seek isn't here. By now he'd be whining to go outside, eager to do his business. With a wistful sigh, the rush of loss floods my being.

The five of us trudge to the locker rooms and ready for the day. Physically, at least. When we're all done, we part ways. Aidan and his dad disappear down the hallway leading to the office while Riley, Kaylee, and I follow the hand-scrawled signs directing us through the maze of passages. We pass classrooms, a library, and a few janitor closets. Several of the rooms appear to be temporary quarters, much like our own.

My eyes volley from window to window beside each door,

attempting to glimpse what's inside. Makeshift areas are separated by curtains, creating small spaces for clusters of cots. It reminds me of a restaurant, where they ask you how many are in your party. Except this isn't a table you sit at for an hour-long meal. It's an uncomfortable excuse for a bed when you don't have one anymore. It's a presumption of safety at the sacrifice of privacy and autonomy.

The view into each classroom is the same. The uniformity of the setup suggests spaces were prepared before people arrived seeking shelter. Unlike our classroom, which lacks any privacy barriers or cots. I'm guessing we were shuttled into the space so that they could better keep track of our vaccination status. Eyeing the other setups, I'm grateful for Scott's refusal.

We pass a few other people, mingling at water fountains and bathroom entrances to swap stories. After one left turn and two right turns, we reach what initially appears to be a dead end, but a rectangular black sign with white block letters announces that we've reached our destination.

Sure enough, the spacious hallway leads to a large, recessed room lined with glass windows. At least a dozen rows of rectangular tables fill the space, perfectly parallel. Six round stools extend from each table's side. The round orange seats look sturdy but stiff.

Though we're among the newest residents, we easily blend in with the room's occupants. A general sense of despair hovers over every muffled conversation. Distress etches wrinkles and frown lines into the faces surrounding us.

Some people seem to form instant connections in solidarity with each other, while others avoid eye contact altogether.

Everyone here is processing some sort of loss, and a collective dampened spirit chokes the air.

Riley nods toward the line funneling out of the food serving area. It's only about five-people-deep and appears to be moving. "Let's get some food and grab a table. It's not crowded, so the guys should be able to catch up to us pretty quickly."

Grabbing trays, we shuffle down the counter, settling on runny eggs, greasy sausage, and barely-browned toast. Just as we claim a table and lower ourselves onto the round seats, Aidan and his dad stride through the open doorway. They spot us immediately and beeline to join us. Before either opens their mouth, I sense the news is bad.

His jaw tense, Aidan's dad mutters, "They still won't tell us anything. Just keep saying the rescue missions continue and they're focused on areas where survivors have been spotted or reported."

"And, of course, they had us leave our boat behind, so it's not like we can even just take it and go," Aidan adds.

"Might as well get some breakfast," Scott says, temporarily defeated.

Wearing matching scowls, they rise and join the growing line of hungry residents. Riley, Kaylee, and I push food around on our plates, swallowing an occasional bite here and there. When the guys return with their meals, we weave pointless small talk around stretches of dejected silence.

Just as we finish up gathering trash and utensils to pile on our empty trays, an announcement blares over the public address system.

"Attention everyone, breakfast is being served in the cafeteria.

It will be available for another hour, so if you haven't eaten yet, we suggest you do so now. Also, the floodwater outside has officially started receding. While that is good news, the surrounding areas are not yet safe for public movement. However, we have been able to open the atrium, centrally located within the building, as a common area. This open-air patio is accessible from the hallway directly outside the office. It is opposite the front entrance doors, which remain barricaded for safety. If you have questions, please stop by the office."

"It's really receding already?" Aidan mutters. "How's that even possible?"

"Hey, with everything nature's thrown at us this summer, I'll take any help she wants to give us," Riley says, shrugging.

"You know what could be happening?" Aidan rakes a hand through his messy tufts of hair. "This area is loaded with limestone and the weight of the flood water could have caused sinkholes. It could be like a never-ending field of land mines out there."

"No more talk about sink holes, okay?" I don't like where this conversation is going. "I've had my fill of those things after the last one."

As I replay the announcement in my mind, I'd much rather have heard something like, "Everything has been restored and everyone's loved ones have been found. You can all go home and return to your previous, normal lives." Except that normal, for Riley and I, is a constantly-shifting continuum. At one point, it was spending the night in military barracks and another time it was teaching our dog where to do his business underground.

My heart sears in instant regret of the mental flashback to

Snickers. If we can't find five missing humans, the chances of reuniting with our scrappy little dog during this mess must be next to nothing. No one's tracking animals that are brought to safety communes. And, as we learned when we were first picked up, they aren't supposed to.

Disposing of our trash and returning our trays, our little group loosely assembles, wandering down the hallway to return to our room. I have a feeling every minute we spend here is going to pass by slower than the last. It's not like a campground, where Riley would probably eagerly drag me to bingo or craft time to assemble a colorful beaded necklace.

This place promises the necessities to survive, without the frivolity of entertainment. Not that I'm expecting a talent show or volleyball game anytime soon, but we've got to pass the time somehow.

Chapter 34

Each minute ticks by in painfully slow progression. Scott paces the room in a continuous loop, lost in whatever thoughts blaze through his mind. Aidan rearranges chairs stacked against the windowsills, contorting his body to gain a clearer view of the outside world.

Riley wanders the room, running her fingers along spines of the books nestled within the shelves resting beneath the windows. Kaylee and I laze on our cots. Mine didn't get much use last night, but it is more comfortable than the gym mats Aidan's got to sleep on.

In her exploration, Riley discovers a pile of worksheets and a cup of sharpened pencils on a round table beside the vacant teacher's desk. "Who wants to brush up on their math skills?" she asks. The closest thing to a response she gets is a groan and a half-hearted snort.

She flips the paper over and holds it up proudly. "Back side's blank! How about a round of hangman or Tic Tac Toe?" When she's greeted with a similar reaction, her focus narrows on me. Throwing my hands in the air, I try to make light of my refusal.

"Hey, I've been entertaining you for seventeen years, it's someone else's turn." She rolls her eyes and centers on the most impressionable member of our group.

"Kayyyyyleeeee. You know you want to," she teases. The younger girl lifts a shoulder up and mumbles, "Okay." I don't sense a true hesitation, though. Her lips quirk in a half smile when she slides a chair out from the table and plops into it.

I watch them settle into a simple rhythm, a temporary distraction from what I fear is a permanent loss. For the moment, I'm grateful that the five of us are together. It's no substitute for our missing family members, but at least we can offer each other some comfort.

Peering around the room as if he's taking inventory of us, Scott abruptly stills. "You all stay here. I'm going to see if the soldiers need any help. There's got to be something I can do around here. And maybe I'll overhear more about their operations."

"That's a great idea." Aidan abandons his post by the windows and turns toward his dad. "I'll come too." When Scott's jaw tightens, Aidan quickly adds, "Think of it as another set of ears, especially if they split us up."

Scott tilts his head in consideration before his eyebrows shoot up and he nods. "You're right, and it's not like they'll put you in danger." His eyes drift from me to Riley and Kaylee. "You three okay staying here?"

All three of us nod with surety. I could help, but now that I've eaten and my body's had a taste of relaxation, my muscles beg to sink further into the swath of taut cloth. The cot is much more comfortable than Aidan's nest of gym mats, which I will avoid tonight. No need for another spectacle tomorrow morning.

I'd bet Scott and Aidan would prefer that Kaylee stay here anyway, and she shouldn't be alone. Still, I'm glad they at least asked it as a question instead of assuming we'd all stay back because we're females.

"Alright, we shouldn't be gone too long." They both throw a casual wave over their shoulder before strolling out the door.

My eyes drift out of focus as Riley and Kaylee giggle, sliding a sheet of paper back and forth between them. I draw in a deep breath, allowing any wandering thoughts to fade to blackness. My mind completely disconnects from consciousness, slipping into a soothing void.

"Quiiiiiin, it's time to wake up," a familiar voice tugs me from oblivion. Riley hovers over me, watching intently as my eyelids flicker open. "Scott and Aidan are back, and we're all ready to go to the cafeteria. The sooner we grab lunch, the sooner we can go to the office and see if there's an update. They said we could check back this afternoon, so maybe we can beat the line if we can get there right after it becomes afternoon."

An announcement over the loudspeaker yanks me from my momentary disorientation. "Attention everyone, lunch is being served in the cafeteria. Please make your way there to select a grab-and-go bag or a tray. You are welcome to eat in the cafeteria or any common area. Please be sure to discard all trash in the proper receptacles and return all trays and utensils to designated bins in the serving area when finished."

I sit up on the cot and swing my legs over the side. They're all watching me, like I'm an experiment, the vessel for a chemical reaction that could fizzle out or ignite at any moment. With a yawn and stretch, I bid farewell to my recent dreamless state and rise on unsteady legs.

Chapter 35

With purpose, we parade down the hallway, a renewed motivation that was nonexistent this morning. The line is just forming, so we take our place in it. Soon enough, we snag trays and push them along the stainless-steel chute running parallel to the counter of offerings.

Launching me back to memories of my school's cafeteria, none of the options look appetizing. Maybe this food was tucked away in the corners of what I imagine are massive freezers, left over from the last school year. If that's the case, how much is there and how long until it runs out?

Gulping down any hesitation, I load my tray and offer a genuine "thank you" to those who plate the food, replenishing servings as they're taken. I settle on macaroni and cheese, green beans, and applesauce. No mini cartons of chocolate milk grace the stainless-steel cooler, so I snag a bottle of water.

We neatly file to a long table, planting ourselves on the attached stool seats. Just like the kids that would normally fill the space, we know exactly what to do. We just lack the animation that typically sparks the air during lunchtime at an elementary school.

Riley, Kaylee, and I fill three seats on one side of the table as Scott and Aidan sit across from us.

"So what did you guys end up doing while you were gone?" Riley asks. That's right, I completely forgot they were going to offer their help, hoping to gather some intel. Aidan and his dad share a grin before answering.

"Well, let's just say it wasn't exactly what we expected," Aidan starts, stabbing a forkful of macaroni.

Scott finishes explaining. "They had us out on the dock, where the boat dropped us off when we got here. A supply of cots was delivered. We helped carry them to the gymnasium."

"So the good news is I should be able to get a cot tonight," Aidan continues. "But the bad news is, that gymnasium is a nightmare."

"What do you mean?" Riley leans toward their side of the table, mirroring my curiosity.

The guys share another glance and Aidan scratches the back of his neck, an obvious stall tactic.

"Packed. People everywhere, sectioned off by shower curtains. You can hear every sound and smell every body odor imaginable." He crinkles his nose. "I'm pretty sure I picked up some barn animal scents in there."

"It's just one more reason not to get that vaccine," Scott says. "I'm sure they won't forget that we're here and that we didn't all get it. If they try to push it on me again today, I'll refuse. They can't force it on us. And they won't split us up."

The conversation settles as we all contemplate what comes next. Riley's got to get her ankle checked again. My aches from being tossed around in the cavern have faded, so I'm not visiting the nurse's office today. Besides, I don't want to draw any attention to myself. I was never vaccinated, but I believe Sergeant Bowen said I was, at least in their database. I'd rather avoid any situation that might uncover that untruth.

"I didn't realize how hungry I was," Riley says. "We're really lucky we don't have to worry about regular meals on top of everything else." We all nod solemnly. If only everyone were here.

Chatter is sparse, not only at our table. The low hum of voices reaches my ears, but the words are distant and sporadic.

Between alternating bites of macaroni clumps and stringy beans, I watch others spill out of the food line with their trays. The space slowly fills, giving us a clearer picture of how many others are here. As I scan the unfamiliar faces, one warrants a doubletake.

"Why does that woman look so familiar?" I nod toward a table diagonal to ours. Riley's eyes search the row until they land on the one person who stands out amongst the others. Perched on her seat, she drizzles a cream-colored dressing over a plate of salad greens before cutting a roll in half and lightly buttering one side. Her posture signals confidence, and a slight distaste for cafeteria-style eating.

Wispy blonde hair sweeps just above her shoulders and her complexion practically glows, physically contrasting nearly every other person here. The rest of us share a washed-out pallor and a depressive air that hovers like a collective cloud.

And this woman notices it all. As she daintily chews, she observes every distant gaze, every mechanical movement, and every lost soul. If she's facing loss like the rest of us, she hides it well below the surface.

"You're right, Quinn," Riley murmurs, leaning toward me on her elbow. "She does look familiar." Our conversation grabs Kaylee's attention. She twists in her seat and follows our line of vision.

"That's Amy Kehm," she says, as if that clears everything up. When we stare at her, she continues. "She's on TV. The show is…Dad, what's that show? I've never seen her in real life, but that's her. I can tell."

Scott and Aidan turn, practically broadcasting our fascination with the local celebrity a dozen feet away. Whether she notices or not, she has the decency to ignore our gawking. We quietly return to our meal.

"You're right. It's Good Day PA. She's the host," Scott says. "I guess we're all the same here though."

"Well, one thing's for sure," I mutter. "I'd say it's anything but a good day in PA."

Chapter 36

We finish our meal and clear the table of trash before taking the familiar path back to our classroom.

"I'll catch up with you all soon. I'm going to check in at the office to see if they have any information," Scott rushes past us before anyone can respond.

"Aidan, your dad's gonna get himself kicked out if he doesn't quit bugging them," I say.

"I'm pretty sure that's the goal," he says, raking a hand through his mess of hair. "At the least, I won't be surprised if they ban him from checking more than once a day."

I squeeze his shoulder. Kaylee and Riley round a corner. Just as the distance between our two small groups seems to grow, our casual steps skid to a stop. Apparently, as soon as our sisters turned, they nearly collided with a cluster of three girls, probably around Riley's age. Now, the five of them face each other, apologizing for the near-crash.

Courtesies are exchanged and we shift around each other, just a few yards from our room. Before I take two steps, a squeal rings through the air.

"Aidan? Is that you?"

Surprise flares as the sugary sweet voice registers. *Who is this?* All three strangers scrutinize his face, then break into huge grins. "It is you!" Until now, I felt like our world consisted of only his family and mine, but this is a cold splash of reality. I've only known him for a few months. He's obviously lived a lot longer than that and known lots of people.

"Hey," he answers, hesitantly. "I guess you're all here for the same reason I am."

"Our families evacuated together a few days ago," one explains, twirling a lock of thick auburn hair. Her pearly white fingernails suggest she just had a manicure. *How is that even possible?* I've washed my hands a dozen times since leaving the cave and bits of stubborn dirt are still caked under my nails. Her green eyes trail over him. "They brought us here."

"Yeah, it sucks! We're all jammed into that gym, can barely breathe without tripping over someone," another girl adds. Several inches shorter than me, she rests both hands on her hips, clearly indignant with the accommodations. She doesn't look like she's suffered too much though. Her long blonde hair shines even in the harsh lighting. She's certainly not lacking shampoo and a brush.

"Hey, maybe we can catch up a little later," Aidan says flatly. "I'm supposed to meet my dad at the office." He points down the hallway, as if that confirms his alibi.

"Sure." The smiles fade into smirks, as if they're accepting an unspoken challenge. Brushing past us, their eyes glaze over me as they utter farewells. The only one who hasn't spoken yet calls out first.

"We'll catch up more later," she says, brushing a wisp of short black hair behind her ear.

"Hope to see you again soon," Auburn-hair adds, waving her manicured fingers in the air.

"Bye," Blondie says, keeping it short and sweet.

Awkwardness descends, trailing us back to the room.

"Well, that was weird," Riley announces. "Who were they? And why didn't you want to talk to them?" She plops down on her cot, the full force of her attention trained on Aidan.

I concentrate on keeping my features impassive, as if unwarranted jealousy isn't coursing through my veins. Innocently awaiting Aidan's response, I promise to thank Riley later for saying exactly what I couldn't.

He blows out a deep breath and lowers himself next to me on my cot. "Oh, I went to school with them. We weren't even really friends, so there isn't anything to catch up on…Maybe they were just excited to see a familiar face, you know, with so many people packed into this building, they probably don't recognize too many faces."

"I guess," Riley mumbles, unconvinced. "They just seemed really disappointed you didn't want to talk."

He shrugs his shoulders. "I'm sure they'll get over it."

She agrees, sensing the moment of interrogation has passed. Shifting her focus to Kaylee, she asks, "I need to get this ankle checked at the nurse's office. It feels fine, but they told me to come back today. Wanna come?"

Kaylee nods and they both look to me. "Quinn?"

"No, I'll wait here." I don't need any more painkillers, and nothing will rid my mind of the worthless thoughts swirling through every dark corner of consciousness. I'd rather stew in silence, and besides, if I went, I'd constantly worry that whoever we talk to is silently questioning if I was truly vaccinated at Langley.

The teenage girl inside me flares to life, reminding me that the only thing worse than running into those girls is the feelings of insecurity that linger in their wake. It's so, so stupid, yet I can't shake it. I feel irrationally possessive of this guy I've known for mere months.

Maybe all the life-changing events we've faced together in such a short time have pushed me over a delicate precipice, clinging to the only safety net I had when I was completely alone. As soon as our sisters leave, Aidan inches closer to me.

"Hey, you seem…different. Everything okay?"

I can't admit the truth, it's too embarrassing. He must see it all over my face though, because as I open my mouth to deny my feelings, he raises a hand to stop me from responding. Leaning closer, he rests a hand on mine.

"Quinn, I barely know those girls and I probably should have introduced you, but I honestly just wanted to get back here and forget about them. I do not need to catch up or hang out with them. They're just people who happened to be the same age, at the same school, at the same time. Nothing more."

Dammit. *After everything I've seen and everything I've lost, why does* this *have to spur a flame in my gut that wants to lash out?* Because beneath the calloused layers of regret and sorrow, I'm just an insecure teenage girl crushing on a college guy. And as much as I'd like to tamp down the useless thoughts, they fester, a bubbling waste of emotion.

When we first arrived here, we were just a random group of five within a sea of nameless faces. Now Riley's become Kaylee's surrogate big sister and Aidan's got a fan club running around.

"Hey? You still with me?" He waves a hand in my face. When my dopey smile confirms that he's got my complete attention, he continues.

"Besides, probably half the girls in school had a crush on me, so we were bound to run across some of them at some point." He flashes me a sly grin and nudges my shoulder. "I may have known them longer, but I know you better. And I'd like to know you even *more* better."

"*Even more better?* Really, college boy?" I tease. He knows exactly how to make me laugh when I need it most. My cheeks flush with fire, but it's better than fighting jealousy's bitter pull.

"So I didn't major in English," he chuckles.

"But you have spoken it for…what…20 years?"

"Look, I didn't major in math either." He might be more frustrating if his eyes weren't so blue, and his smile wasn't so lopsided when he laughs at himself.

"Fair enough." I raise my palms in surrender. "You stick with rocks and caves."

He tilts his head as the smile fades from his cheeks. "What about you? I mean, I always knew I wanted to become a geologist, but what do you want to be?"

"I don't really think that matters much anymore," I answer honestly. "Who knows how long it'll be until we just have a place to live, let alone think about a real future."

"You got me there," he says, sadness reflecting in his serious eyes. "But for now, we'll just have to take what we got."

When he wraps an arm around me, I nestle into his side. He rests his chin on my head and we sit in comfortable silence.

Chapter 37

Riley and Kaylee return a few minutes later. They sprawl out on their cots, mostly ignoring our display of affection. Grins pass between them, but thankfully they don't say anything.

"Finally!" Scott bursts into the room, his eager eyes passing over each of us. "They're releasing the names of people brought to the other shelters!"

My heart skips a beat. This is what we've been waiting for, but if we don't get the answers we want…then what? The others must share my worry because hesitation slows their reactions as well.

Scott claps his hands together, his eyebrows knitting in disbelief. "Well, come on! Let's go find our family!"

His positivity overtakes the doom, and one-by-one, we spring from our cots. Maybe it's okay to believe, to assume some part of our situation has to get better soon. As soon as they clear the threshold, he wraps an arm around Kaylee and playfully pushes Aidan's shoulder.

Riley and I follow. When she's certain the others are distracted, she nudges my arm and whispers, "You okay? You seemed upset, but then you and Aidan were getting kinda cozy in there." Of course, she'd detect any rise or quell of emotions in tight quarters with no privacy.

"Yeah, I am." We've got much bigger concerns than a couple of girls running around here who recognize Aidan. I push them from my thoughts and allow a more important topic to bubble between us.

"What if they know where Aunt Robin is?!" I dare to hope; the temptation too great. Haven't we already been dealt enough bad luck for one lifetime?

"She's got to be somewhere close. She insisted on staying home because that's what they told people to do. So if they said to evacuate a few days ago, she would have listened." Riley's words tumble out of her mouth just as quickly as her feet carry her forward. Any residual pain in her ankle is forgotten or overridden by adrenaline.

We practically skip down the hallway. Excitement churns within me, effectively dismantling my brain's cautions. I want to believe she's okay and we'll find her.

Slight hesitation surfaces as I consider what reuniting with our aunt would mean for us. She's our closest family and it makes sense that she'd automatically become our guardian, but I don't want to leave Aidan. The swirling thoughts must slow my pace because Riley tugs my hand. "Come on!" she urges.

Just as we pick up speed, we're forced to skid to a stop, nearly crashing into Aidan and Kaylee when we reach the end of a snaking line of people. *Of course, another line.* This communal living is getting old fast. And we don't even have the worst of it—we haven't had to claim a pocket of space in the gym.

A cocktail of anticipation and impatience electrifies the air. Whispered fears and words of cautious hope hover. Time passes slower than molasses climbing a hill. Scott and Aidan attempt to remain stoic, features guarded, but both sets of blue eyes reflect excitement.

When our turn finally arrives, Scott approaches the counter eagerly. Aidan and Kaylee cram in beside him. Riley and I remain a few steps back, giving them the most privacy possible in the limited space. Huddled together, we whisper, tossing rhetorical questions back and forth. *Did any of our belongings survive the floodwater? Is our aunt's house still standing?*

Although they speak in hushed tones, the conversation before us targets my ears as if they're fine-tuned to eavesdrop. None of the names are showing up in the database. The soldier helping Aidan's family suggests that they were picked up by a rescue team sometime today and haven't been identified yet, or they're holed up somewhere, waiting for the water to recede, or that they were picked up by a rescue team and were unidentified.

Aidan and Kaylee stare at the soldier, awaiting a better answer. Scott presses a fist to his mouth, folding his other arm across his body. I'm certain he's about to confirm my suspicion. If someone entered a safety commune and refused to provide any identifying information, then they might be in that category. But I don't believe Aidan's or Jeff's family would do that, considering it's the fastest way we could all find each other again.

So that would mean they were unable to identify themselves. My hands tremble as Riley inhales a sharp breath. Realization must be dawning on her too.

"How do you…how do you…determine who those unidentified people are?" Scott asks, his voice cracking with emotion. Once again, a somber haze engulfs our group. Swift punishment for daring to believe good news was possible.

"At this point, they're being kept at a holding facility, sir. As the storm dissipates, we're able to shuttle small groups back and forth to help identify those we find. The transport is very limited though. We allow one representative from each family," the soldier offers. "It's the only way we can ensure that each group missing someone has a chance to confirm their loved ones' identities and get some closure."

"Yes," Scott says quietly. "I understand. I'd like to get on that list." As he listens to the soldier's instructions, I wrap my palm around Aidan's forearm.

"I'm so sorry," I whisper. "I'm so, so sorry." The comforting gesture yields the opposite effect of what I intended. Aidan's eyes narrow on me with disbelief.

"It's not them!" he hisses. "There's no proof!" Shaking his head in protest, tears pool in his eyes, but they don't drop. His tone turns fierce. "They're not even giving us any description of anyone they found. For all we know, they could be holding people who washed up from a state away. They have no idea."

Riley steps closer. "You're right. The only thing we know is that they aren't registered in the system, but they could still be out there, waiting for the next rescue boat to show up. There's still hope, Aidan. There's no reason to give up." She flashes me a sad smile. I'm grateful for her interjection. We all experience pain and grief in different ways, and I don't know how to comfort Aidan right now.

These past months have been riddled with questions that have no right answers. Time is supposed to heal pain but our suffering charts an unsteady pattern, with only occasional moments of recovery.

Pulling Kaylee toward him, Aidan wraps an arm around her shoulder. "I'm going to take her back to relax," he says, slowly leading her through the doorway. Scott nods in appreciation. When his conversation ends, he steps away from the counter and motions for Riley and I to take our turn.

"You girls want me to stay?" he asks, rubbing his temples.

"No, we're fine. We'll see you back at the room," Riley says.

Chapter 38

As he passes through the door, just a few steps behind Aidan and Kaylee, I notice the sudden change in atmosphere. In the short time we've been parked in here, those around us must have received similar news. The anticipatory air swirling outside the office now brims with hopelessness. It's as if a giant celebratory balloon was popped, dispersing an ominous cloud of despair.

Riley and I advance to the counter. As my heart pounds, she spells our aunt's first and last name. The soldier helping us taps each letter into the keyboard, his eyes sliding across the screen as the command registers.

When her hands start their nervous dance, twisting around each other, I reach over and clasp a palm around them. She stifles a nervous giggle and drops them to her sides. Reaching over, I take her hand in mine and squeeze.

"Good news. We've located your aunt."

Tears spring to my eyes. Riley snatches her hand from mine and covers her gaping mouth with trembling fingers. "Where? Where is she?"

The soldier flashes a genuine smile. He probably doesn't get to deliver much good news these days. "She entered one of our other safety communes two days ago. It's just a few miles from here."

Two days ago? That doesn't make sense. Hope is an illusion that's tricked me too many times. "But we asked about her yesterday and they said there was no record. How can that be?" I'd rather know nothing than trust what could be a mistake.

"We've had some glitches in our system. The power's been a little spotty, even with generators running. Our database was updating on site, but it wasn't synching with other locations to refresh the data," the soldier calmly explains. "By the time we realized, it was later in the evening, and we didn't want to disturb anyone who had already settled for the night."

My mind continues on that trail of reason. If they told everyone who arrived yesterday, or even before that, to check in again today, they wouldn't have to announce it at all because that would just ignite a stampede to the office as soon as people heard the news. And I can't imagine anyone needs a reminder to visit the one place that's offering information, even if it is minimal.

Clutching my hand once more, Riley squeezes. A smile blazes from cheek to cheek as she faces me. "It's really her!"

We nearly burst with elation, the intense rush muddying our ability to answer the soldier's questions.

"I can send a message to the Intake Team at her location and then we'll coordinate with them to reunite you. We'll need to work out if she'll be reassigned to this location or if you will join her there."

Riley and I meet each other's eyes, but neither of us speaks. *Our aunt's been settled at that place a little longer, and she's an adult. I guess it's up to her. But if we go there, what happens to Aidan's family?*

"She's your closest living relative, correct?" the soldier asks. We both nod. "And according to the information she provided, she is over 18 years old." Again, we mutely nod. He turns his focus to the keyboard and begins typing.

"Let's start by sending an alert to let her know that you're here and wish to make contact."

Riley finds her voice first. "That sounds great, thank you."

"Stop back after the evening meal and we can check for a response. Travel between communes is delayed due to high demand and flood conditions, but once we know who's going where, we can place you, or her, on the transport list."

"Thank you," Riley repeats.

As we float down the hallway, my thoughts swirl. Relief is nearly overtaken by guilt, which slithers through me, accompanying the reminder that Aidan's family feels no such relief right now. Restraining our enthusiasm, Riley and I quietly shuffle into Room 126.

Aidan and Kaylee sit on a cot, slumped against each other. Scott paces before them, rubbing his temples. His tone is low and serious, inviting no argument.

"They put my name on the transport list. When an open spot comes up and it's my turn, they'll take me to where they're storing…the bodies. And I'll need to…identify anyone I can."

Kaylee protests, but he cuts her off. "I know you both want to come, but they won't allow it and it's best if I do this alone, anyway."

Aidan runs a shaky hand through his mussed hair as Kaylee pleads with their father. "But we deserve the chance to say goodbye…if it's really them." She nudges closer to him, seeking a comfort that can't cure the threat of loss they're all facing.

"Both of you, if it is them, it's best that you remember the good times and keep those images in your head. What you might see would haunt you for the rest of your lives. And I don't want that for you."

Riley's sneaker takes that moment to announce our presence. Three heads turn toward us. Scott looks relieved by the interruption.

"Girls, any news on your aunt?" he asks cautiously, probably expecting that we got the same news as them.

Riley rocks forward on her toes awkwardly. "They actually said our aunt is at a nearby commune. They're sending her a message to let her know that we're here. Then we'll need to figure out if she'll join us here or if we'll be taken to her."

Aidan releases a deep breath, his shoulders sagging. "Well, at least there's some good news. I'm glad they found her."

"So she'll be your guardian now?" Scott asks tentatively. "I mean, not that we've minded having you as part of our family."

Riley chews her lower lip. "Well, she's our closest relative. We have an Aunt Grace too, the one who owns the trailer at the beach, but Quinn and I don't have her address or really any contact information."

He nods silently. He must be thinking the same thing I am. These could be our last days together. Who knows where our aunt will want to go if our houses no longer stand? Desolation floods my mind. This is exactly what we hoped for, but she's not going to base rebuilding our lives on what Aidan's family does. She's never even met them, and they probably have no idea what comes next either.

Why did the world have to fall apart? We've lost nearly everything and now we're going to lose them too. Is it too much to want a boyfriend who's just a call or a text away? Is it too much to expect a prom and graduation? Because none of those things seem even remotely possible now or anytime soon.

Chapter 39

When the announcement is made for dinner, we solemnly file out of the room. Riley buries her happiness while I linger on fate's random plans to build and dismantle relationships. Besides, it doesn't feel right celebrating our luck when Aidan's family carries the weight of uncertainty in their every step.

We shuffle through the line, selecting the most palatable options we can find. Not that it matters much, none of us seems to have an appetite. The meal is mostly quiet, other than the sound of utensils clanging against plates as we push food around in between occasional bites of tasteless sustenance.

Appraising the group's growing lethargy, Scott launches into conversation. Just loud enough for our ears, he asks if anyone has been asked about our vaccination status. We all meet him with the same response—no. He confirms that no one's approached him about it today as we had expected.

He leans toward the center of the table, voice barely above a whisper, "They seem to have forgotten about us. I was planning to ask more questions, to find out what exactly is in the shots, but now I think it's best that we all keep quiet about it."

I wholeheartedly agree. I still don't know who believes I got the shot and who knows I didn't. And I don't want to call any attention to that little detail.

"Sure," Aidan agrees. "I think we've done a pretty good job of keeping to ourselves anyway. Maybe there's enough going on that we're not a priority." Riley, Kaylee, and I nod. None of us wants a spotlight turned on our little group.

After dinner, we trudge back to our classroom. I trail a few feet behind the group, my steps slowed by the inevitable depressive state that awaits. We could all use a distraction. *Are we just supposed to sit in that room and stare at each other?* This place has even less to do than the cave. At least there we could explore. Here it feels like we're on constant lockdown.

Engrossed in a jumble of useless thoughts, I flinch when Aidan brushes up against my shoulder. He ignores my unwelcome reaction, training his focus straight ahead. Keeping pace, he leans into my side, tilting his mouth toward my ear. "I need to talk to you alone. Make up an excuse when we get back to the room. Say you need to go somewhere and meet me at that atrium they opened up today."

Heart strumming in time with each step, my mind flashes with potential excuses to get away. *Where would I want to go? Alone.*

Riley opens the conversation as soon as we enter the familiar space. "I noticed the library's open and there isn't really anything else to do. Anyone want to go see if they have any good books?"

"I'll go," Kaylee volunteers. I suspect she'd go just about anywhere Riley suggests at this point.

Scott squeezes her shoulder. "That's a great idea, maybe it'll take your mind off things."

Aidan shoots me a pointed look, silently urging me to announce my fake plans. Never mind I've had about three seconds to contemplate the perfect fabrication.

"I'm gonna go to the gymnasium and see if I can get one of those new cots," he says, pressing a palm to his back and motioning toward the small stack of mats in his corner of the room. "Those things are lumpier than they look. And since I helped cart in a new load, I'm thinking I should get one."

"Good idea, son. And I may take another trip to the office. I'm sure they're tired of me, but maybe they can tell me how many people are on the transport list ahead of me." Scott gulps and blows out a shaky breath. He's caught between indefinitely waiting for news and demanding a truth that none of us want to hear.

Beads of sweat form along my hairline. I'm acutely aware of being the only one without a plan.

"So I think I'll go to the library too, might as well see what they have." My attempt at nonchalance sounds forced, but no one argues.

"Alright then," Scott directs. "We'll all meet back here when we're done."

Aidan shakes his head, frustration etching his squared jaw, before turning on his heel toward the gym. I force my brain into overdrive as I follow Kaylee and Riley. I am not spending hours flipping through dusty children's books while Aidan's waiting to talk to me alone.

"I wonder if they'll let us check books out," Riley says. "It might be nice to see what that atrium is like."

"*No!*" my brain screams as I paint a neutral reaction across my face. Sure, I could talk to Aidan then, but if we appear too secretive, we'll raise suspicion. And I have a feeling our sisters are highly skilled in the nosiness department.

Kaylee hitches a shoulder up and adds, "I could read anywhere. I just hope they're not all little kid books."

The wooden entrance door is propped open, inviting us to explore the expansive rectangular room lined with bookshelves. They cover every outer wall and form additional rows in the space between. A single soldier stands behind the librarian's desk, his attention jumping between a laptop and a shuffle of papers. He doesn't look up to greet us.

A handwritten sign propped on the desk beside the soldier answers our only question.

Commune residents are welcome to browse the shelves and enjoy the library's offerings; however, no items may leave this room.

Please return items to the exact location where you found them so that we can minimize any disruption to the school's processes and property.

Ah, so he's not acting as a librarian. He's just getting some work done while he's on civilian babysitting duty. Fine with me.

The only mission I have is to escape.

Riley cups a palm around her mouth in a secretive gesture and whispers, "Well, so much for checking out books. Looks like we should find something to read and pick a table."

Kaylee nods and wanders into the stacks. I shadow Riley as she explores the nearby shelves. Once I'm satisfied there's enough distance between us and Kaylee, I tug Riley's sleeve awkwardly.

"Hey, I need to do something." Her narrowed eyes and scrunched nose confirm she suspects I'm up to something. The pressure to invent an excuse is mounting. If Scott notices that Aidan's in the atrium when he's done in the office, we'll have no chance to talk privately.

"Do you need to use the bathroom, Quinn? It's right outside if that's the case."

"No! Look, I've got to stretch my legs." *Yes, that's it!* Shrugging my shoulders innocently, I add, "I haven't been able to run since…I can't remember the last time. I just really need something to take my mind off things and books won't work for me." *At least part of that statement is true.*

After a moment's consideration, realization dissolves any disbelief. She knows I ran track and cross-country in high school, and the skill's certainly come in handy over the past few months—trying to outrun a storm and creepy guy, or two.

Even though formal education is no longer a part of our lives—at least for the time being—just being in this environment reminds me of the days when my biggest concern was locating something remotely edible for lunch or reaching my locker and the next class before the bell rang.

"Do you think they'll let you do that? I mean, the gym's

packed with people and the old no-running-in-the-halls rule probably still applies." *Ugh, she's right. I've really got to get better at planning lies before I voice them.*

"All I can do is ask, right? And if they say no, I'll just meet you back in the room."

"Alright, just don't get lost, okay?" She smiles and turns back to the shelves.

"I think I can manage that. See you in a bit," I whisper and pivot, forcing my feet to maintain a steady pace, even though they're ready to sprint. I won't have much time for a rendezvous. I've got to get there fast, before Aidan gives up on me.

Chapter 40

I shuffle through the hallway, simultaneously trying to blend in with the few others straggling through the corridors, while sidestepping around them at their infuriatingly slow pace. My sneakers squeak out a few high-pitched scuffs, drawing attention to my clumsy gait. I avoid eye contact with anyone I pass, falling back on the useless toddler-playing-hide-and-seek adage of "they can't see me if I can't see them."

The contrast between my physical surroundings and current emotional state is striking. I remember marching down hallways just like this as a kid. The waxed floor scent and brightly-decorated bulletin boards fostered a sense of comfort and familiarity. But now this place is just one more temporary shelter necessitated by a string of disasters.

Slinking around the nurse's office and avoiding any angle visible from the main office, I finally push through the set of double doors leading to the atrium. Fresh air cradles my cheeks. I stand still, inhaling what feels like the deepest breath I've taken in months.

Perfect rows of rectangular windows that rival my height form a glass ceiling. The enclosure reminds me of a giant greenhouse. This area serves as a connecting point from the front of the building to another wing.

Potted plants and trees dot the corners, relishing the golden sunlight streaming through the protective layers shielding them from the storm's fury. Uneven pavers, lodged in place by patterns of brick, carve a winding path that leads from the entrance to the exit, leading into another hallway.

Gaping, my eyes run along the walls. Windows, perched open at 30-degree angles, rise between structural beams, releasing a subtle humid breeze. Three cast iron benches rest among the landscape, their current occupants are refugees like me. Of course, I shouldn't have expected to be the only one here, which reminds me of why I visited the atrium.

Snapped out of the momentary stupor, I pace the path, searching for that tall, muscular frame topped with a nest of messy brown hair. And the bluest eyes I've ever seen. I shake the thought away. *This isn't helping.*

He must have given up waiting for me. After practically broadcasting the urgency for this secret meeting, my mind was too slow to process an alibi. Energy seeps from every pore, disappointment anchoring my feet to the ground. The room's natural beauty fades to vague periphery as my shoulders sag in defeat.

"Are you okay?" a middle-aged woman asks. Her short,

curly hair is nearly as dark as her skin. Concern lurks in her deep brown irises.

I shake my head. "I'm fine, thank you. I was just waiting for someone, but I don't think he's going to show."

She presses a polished nail to her scarlet lips. "You know, there was a young man here. Maybe ten minutes ago. Pacing all over the place, mumbling under his breath."

"That was probably him!" My pulse rockets in urgency. "Did you see where he went?"

She points toward the door opposite of the one I entered. "He stomped out that way, complaining about having to take care of things himself. Seemed pretty worked up. Maybe you should just let him blow off some steam. He didn't seem like he'd be good company."

That tells me all I need to know. *How many other moody guys could have just passed through here? There's hardly anyone in this room.*

"Thank you!" I call as I dash past her and out the door.

Chapter 41

Zipping down the hallway, I dodge passersby. Poking my head in our classroom, I confirm my suspicions—no one's returned yet. There's only one thing Aidan would want to take care of himself: finding his mom, sister, and Jeff's family. And, since the building's front doors are barricaded, not to mention on constant display for the soldiers overseeing intake operations, there's only one way in and out of this place.

I bolt to the library, feet pounding tile in a steady clomp. This time, the soldier on duty levels his gaze on me as I cross the threshold. Eyebrows raised, he watches every movement. Not exactly my most graceful entrance. I flash a nervous smile to convey that I'm not a threat to disturbing the peace.

Riley and Kaylee sit together at a small round table, a small pile of books scattered between them. They've collected enough reading material to last a week, but they're each focused on one book at the moment, lost in its pages.

Sailing past my sister, I run a finger along her shoulder to capture her attention. It works. Her head snaps to the side, seeking the source. When I motion for her to follow me toward the room's farthest corner, she nods and leans forward, whispering to Kaylee.

A moment later, she joins me behind a bookshelf, hidden from view of the library's few other occupants.

"Quinn, what is it? Did something happen?" Her jaw clenches as her hands join, preparing to tangle in their nervous dance.

Tamping down rising panic and unraveling emotion, my throat struggles to form the words. "He's…gone. Riley…he…left!"

"What? Who left? Aidan?" Her palms greet her forehead with too much force. She squeezes her eyes shut, either in frustration or overwhelming worry.

Panic rises with each heartbeat. I nod my head feverishly, buying a little more time to inhale and return my breathing to normal.

"Are you sure? Are you positive?"

Even though he didn't tell me, and I didn't see him go, I sense his absence. It's like an overpowering urgency prevented him from waiting for me in that atrium.

"I just know. He was supposed to meet me, but he disappeared. Look, I have to go find him. I can talk him into coming back. But I have to leave right now, and I wanted to tell you."

"He can't go back out there himself! The last thing his family needs is something else to worry about…or one more loss." She chews her bottom lip and wrings her hands. "Let's go to the office and report it. Maybe they can catch him before he gets too far."

She turns quickly, but instinctively my arm strikes like a snake and my hand latches onto her elbow. Her widened eyes shift from the hand grasping her arm and slide to my face, a hint of anger bubbling just below her confused expression. Before she can yank herself away, I plead. "No, Riley, don't. He's serious, and he *needs* to do this. We can't tell on him. It's such a…a betrayal!"

"Quinn, we can't just let him go. We know what he's about to do. Can you live with yourself if you find out he gets hurt—or worse—out there and we did nothing to stop it?" Unshed tears reflect in her eyes. *I know she cares about him, but she can't understand his driving motivation.*

I speak softly, although I don't believe it renders my words any less meaningful. "When you were missing, I had no one. No one to help me find you. If it wasn't for Aidan and Jeff, their group never would have helped me. Riley, they barely knew us, but they dropped everything to help me find you. They helped me cross states, driving stolen cars, and we weren't even sure where you were. And do you know what would have happened to me if they didn't help?"

She gulps, her eyes dropping to the floor. She shakes her head slowly as her posture visibly weakens from the reminder of my anguish.

"I would have done the same thing," I say, drawing her attention back to my face. "Because even if I had to walk two hundred miles by myself to find you, I would have. It would have been *a lot* harder, but I would have done it. Alone."

Heavy silence clouds the air. My legs jitter, as if suddenly awaking every nerve ending in my body. A plan clicks into place faster than I can make sense of it. "I'm going after him. I have to. And he needs me."

Riley's mouth hangs open in a silent "No." I grasp her shoulders and lean in, pressing my forehead against hers.

"Please understand. I have to help him, the way he helped me. I want to talk him out of it, to talk him into staying, but if I can't...I won't just let him do this alone. And the longer we argue about it right now, the farther away he'll get. I know exactly where he's headed but if I don't go now, I don't know if I'll be able to catch up to him. It's more dangerous if he's alone. I swear, I'll try to bring him right back. I have to do this, Riley."

I'm talking in circles, swirling thoughts manifesting in verbal confusion. I need to find him. Now. And I'll do whatever it takes to get him back—if it's convincing him of what he shouldn't do—or, more likely, joining him on a mission that he can't deny. Because I know he'd do it for me. He already has.

Silent tears track down her cheeks. Her eyes hold true misery. I know I'm putting her in a terrible position, but she's right about one thing—we can't let anything happen to Aidan. At least if I'm with him, he'll have another set of eyes to watch over him.

She wipes her nose, sniffling. "Quinn, what if you get hurt? What if you don't come back?" Her voice cracks with each question. I wrap my arms around her and squeeze, searing the warmth and comfort of the connection into memory.

"I know I'm asking a lot, too much. But he can't do this alone, just like I couldn't find you alone."

"Why don't we talk to Scott? Maybe both of us can go, at

least we could stay together then." Riley's lower lip quivers. *It won't work, and we both know it.*

"We can't both go. There's no time, and Scott would freak out if he knew what was happening. And your ankle, it's still healing. What if you couldn't keep up with me, or Aidan? Besides, Kaylee needs you. I don't know if you've noticed, but she's gotten pretty attached to you. I don't think she could handle knowing everyone's gone but her dad."

She nods, the tears freely flowing. Wiping her nose, she inhales a deep breath. "Go, before I think too much and change my mind. I won't tell Kaylee why you came here."

I squeeze one more time before releasing her trembling frame. "Thank you, for believing in me. I promise, we'll be back soon. Please, just stall for us—tell his dad whatever it takes to keep it under wraps for as long as possible."

Turning away, I sprint out of the library, carrying the weight of my sister's gaze with each step.

Chapter 42

The confidence that fueled my conversation with Riley quickly fades as I pass through each corridor leading to my destination. The walls seem to stretch on forever, while simultaneously closing in, chasing my heels. *What if I can't find Aidan? What if he already left?* A cell phone would be handy right about now. As long as it worked, and we both had one.

I draw on memory, retracing those sopping steps from when we first arrived here. The only way in and out of this place is through what's now a temporary boat dock. It's probably crawling with rescue teams coming and going. Falling back on the knowledge I've gained from watching countless movies, I square my shoulders and force purpose into my stride. Maybe, just maybe, if I walk around with reasonable intention, as if I belong here, I can squash any doubts about my presence.

A jolt in my heart rate confirms my own doubts in the flawed, passing thought. With each deliberate footfall, I creep along the interior edges of the building, clearly labeled as restricted areas. Thankfully, those who are allowed in this section of the building don't tiptoe.

Muffled conversation drifts to my ears a moment before boots rhythmically descend on the tile. However, many there are, they're coming this way. I freeze, scouring my surroundings for a hiding place. Backtracking, I gently twist the handle on the first door I see, labeled Media Room. The knob turns only a fraction before its abrupt halt. Locked.

The footsteps grow louder, closer. Adrenaline rockets through my bloodstream. Backing up a few steps, I latch on to the only other door on this side of the hall. Grasping the handle, I twist and tug with all my strength, as if that's all it takes to open a locked door.

Immediately regretting my carelessness, I spring forward and grab the smooth surface, preventing the door from banging into the wall behind it. With only a quick glance at the confined space blanketed in shadow, I slip inside and slowly pull the door closed.

I don't need a sign to confirm where I am. The harsh sting of bleach sears my nostrils. As my eyes adjust to the dimness, shapes transform into outlines of cleaning supplies—mops, buckets, spray bottles, and a plunger. Shifting as far away as possible from the object that regularly dives into toilets, I wait in suspended silence.

Voices crescendo as the group passes by just inches away, only a simple wooden barrier between us. When the sound fades, I count to sixty. The minute seems to stretch forever as tears pool in my eyes, their only defense against the biting aroma of ammonia blending with a cocktail of other cleaning solutions.

Cracking the door open, I listen for any indication of stragglers or new groups passing through. When silence greets my ears, I push the door open an inch and cautiously peer up and down the corridor. Nothing. Slipping out of the closet, I scurry back to the loading dock.

It's empty. Two rescue boats gently sway in the water. The decks are vacant, and no faces appear behind the windowed cabins. Drawing in a calming breath, I notice how much lower the boats sit compared to when we arrived. It was dark and miserable that night, but I specifically remember stepping off the deck and easily reaching the school's concrete platform. Now I'd have to drop at least a foot to climb into the same vessel.

Laughter swells within the building, and my ears buzz in anticipation. Sure enough, footsteps and chatter follow, growing closer. More soldiers! I can't go back inside, or I'll run smack into them. My eyes scan the dock feverishly, searching for cover. *This was so not a good idea.*

"Hey!" I startle at the angry whisper-shout. Instinctively, I lower my head and lift my shoulders, as if I can just crumple within myself and hide.

"Hey! Come here!" The same grumbling voice commands. The only difference is that it's slightly more annoyed.

Aidan pops out from behind a dingy shelf loaded with work gloves, rusty canisters, and thick belt-like strips with buckles dangling from their curling ends. He waves a hand in the air impatiently, coaxing me to join him.

I hurdle around a ragtag group of metal dollies. They vary

in size, carelessly clustered around the shelf. They actually help camouflage Aidan's body. In passing, the small area perfectly blends into the mundane space. The major risk of being noticed is if someone started poking around on the shelves.

As I shuffle against the brick wall and squeeze in next to Aidan, he latches on to my elbow and raises a finger to his mouth in a "Shhh" command. I huddle against him and squeeze my eyes shut, willing us to become invisible.

My heart stutters, but not in fear. Warmth radiates from Aidan's body, shooting electricity through mine. I should focus on staying completely still, but my mind's consumed by a closeness I didn't realize I craved until it happened.

Less than a minute later, the laughter I heard drifts to the dock. Four soldiers stride toward the closest rescue boat. They each drop to the deck with ease and assume their positions: two inside the cabin and two outside. The engine rumbles to a quick start and they're gone.

Chapter 43

When the hum of their engine fades, I throw a leg out from our hiding spot, ready to emerge from the cramped quarters. A hand clamps around my elbow, freezing me in place.

"Quinn, what are you *doing* here?" Aidan's voice forms an angry whisper once again. When I retract my leg and face him, his hold on my elbow relaxes only slightly. I can't avoid the anger flaring in his eyes.

"Helping you!" My own frustration seeps out. "I came to find you in the atrium, but you were gone. I can't believe you didn't wait for me a little longer."

He releases my elbow and runs a shaky hand through his messy hair. His eyes drop to the ground. We're both vaulting emotional hurdles right now. Hopefully we can ground each other. Somehow.

"It's been a whole day and it feels like no one's doing anything to bring in more survivors. And if they won't, then I will." His tone softens and he raises his eyes to meet mine. "I just…I didn't know what to do…and I can't take it anymore." The anger melts away, replaced by fear and vulnerability. It's a combination I remember all too well.

"Aren't you afraid of getting caught?" I whisper. Sneaking around in a restricted area is blatantly breaking one of the few rules here. My trembling nerves serve as a constant reminder that we're one sneeze away from facing a likely interrogation and punishment.

Since we arrived, they've given us beds and food, not to mention working showers, sinks, and toilets. I can't imagine they'd give us a free pass just because we're emotionally compromised. My thoughts jettison away when Aidan's anger surges like a cresting wave. I'm not used to seeing him this way, and I don't like it.

"So what if we get caught? Are they gonna lock us up in prison? Because that's what it feels like anyway." He's right. What more could they do? They won't throw us out. I mean, they won't even let us leave, I think. And we're already stuck in a classroom, cafeteria, or a common area while we're here. Just waiting and waiting.

I cave, trying a fresh approach. One he often took with me when I could not piece together a reasonable plan when searching for my sister.

"We're going to do whatever it takes to find your family. You're not doing this alone."

The fading sun's remaining rays reflect a thin sheen forming over his crystal blue eyes. He closes them for a moment before wrapping me in a tight embrace. Safety and warmth envelop me.

He drops his head to my shoulder, tangling his fingers in my hair. *That's what he needed to hear.*

"Thank you."

"So what's the plan? I'm guessing this is what you wanted to talk about in the atrium?" We keep our voices low and crouch behind the shelf, just in case anyone else shows up.

"Weeeell," he starts, "I thought maybe I could borrow one of those." He nods his head toward the last rescue boat docked. "But I looked inside and I'm pretty sure that thing has more controls than a fighter jet. There's no way I could even get it started."

He leans closer. "But I overheard a few of them talking out here. They said that one soldier left on a recon mission a few hours ago, around this and the other nearby communes, checking to see how far the water has receded. They said he should have been back already, so that tells me it could be any minute."

"How would that help us? Because I don't think we should swim in this stuff even if it's not deep." *Where's he going with this? The only way out of here is by boat. Unless we wait until the water's gone completely.*

"No, we can't swim in this stuff. There's probably sewage in there, or worse. But whatever boat that guy is using, they were laughing about it. I think they called it the River Rat. It sounded like it was a floating box." He waits for understanding to dawn on me. It doesn't.

"If whatever this recon guy is using is really that small, then I can probably drive it. You know, I was a tour guide at Couturier Caverns for a few summers. I know a bit about boats." *Right, that makes sense. I never questioned why he knew how to drive the tourist boat when we had to evacuate the cave.*

"Alright, so we wait."

"So we wait," he parrots.

Chapter 44

Cramps sprout in my shins and thighs as my body protests the unnatural position. Time drags along with no regard for our comfort or my sister's likely skyrocketing worry. And who knows what Scott would do if he learned the truth about our whereabouts. I'm guessing the first thing would be to report us missing. He's already a regular fixture in the office, so he wouldn't hesitate to seek their help. Soon enough, he'll probably start greeting the intake soldiers by name.

The sun barely blinks from the horizon, plunging toward its nightly descent. Darkness falls faster than I expected. If we have to wait much longer, we won't be able to see any further than what's directly in front of us. Plus, the longer we wait, the more likely one of the rescue boats out there patrolling will return.

Just as I open my mouth to suggest we give up and return to the classroom, movement in the distance catches my eye. A flat, low craft speeds toward us, its churning rumble growing clearer by the minute.

We freeze, like statues, in the cramped space. A single soldier steers the small vessel along the concrete dock, parking it directly behind the only remaining rescue boat. He rises, balancing in the teetering boat before hauling himself onto the dock effortlessly. Pausing, he stretches, extending cramped muscles and twisting kinks out of his neck and back. He audibly sighs in relief at the movement, clearly savoring the ability to stand on solid ground. Within a minute, he strides past us and inside the building.

Aidan squeezes my hand, sending my heart into a frenzy. *It's time.* We have no idea when someone else might show up, but this may be our only chance to check the last place we saw the others. There's no time for hesitation. I wrench myself out from behind the shelf and dash to the boat. A hushed scuffle behind me confirms Aidan's closely following.

I jump to the flat surface, landing on all fours. Quickly scooting backward, I leave enough space for my captain. He slides into the boat with a litheness I don't possess. We both cringe when he starts the engine. Although the crew around here is probably used to the sound, it feels like we've rung the dinner bell for a horde of zombies.

Aidan steers us away from the dock as fast as possible without pushing the motor beyond its limits. The last thing we need is for an erroneous screech or rattle to draw anyone's attention, or the boat to protest our need for a fast escape.

Once we've safely retreated from view, blocked by buildings and structures that rise into what was once a city skyline, Aidan slows to gather his bearings. The fading daylight is blanketed in dusk. *This will not be easy.* His eyes focus in the distance, bouncing from one direction to the next, retracing memories of the streets now entombed beneath murky water.

In the stillness, a distant buzzing churns in the air.

"You hear that?" Aidan asks.

"Yeah, but what is it?" My biggest question is if it's natural or man-made, although I'm not sure I have a preference. I don't want to get caught out here, especially since we've technically stolen a boat from the U.S military. That's got to be way worse than say, shoplifting some eyeshadow. But, given Mother Nature's latest outbursts, I don't really want to see what else she might have up her sleeve.

"I don't know." His eyes search the night sky, but it's useless. Out here, we can't tell what noise bounces off buildings or if the sound is even in front or behind us. "We'll just keep going. Where we're headed is the only thing we know right now."

"I'll keep watching and yell if I see anything." Turning my gaze skyward, I study the inky clouds as they blend into pockets of oblivion. For a moment, I wonder if anyone is watching over us, from somewhere beyond anything we can see.

"There's a small floodlight on the floor," he says. "But we should only use it if absolutely necessary. I don't exactly want to trigger the Bat-Signal tonight."

As wishful thoughts of my parents flicker through my mind, a burst of light emerges on the horizon. "Aidan!" I surge forward, practically crashing into him. Grasping his shoulder, I point. "I think it's headed this way." We track the beam to its source. A flashing green light illuminates the dim outline of an aircraft.

"Small plane…no, probably a helicopter," he says, his eyes

fixed on it. "It reminds me of when we tried to leave that bowling alley on the way to Langley. Remember, there was a helicopter flying around, shining a spotlight along the ground? Maybe they were searching for people who needed help and this one is too?"

His words make sense, but either way, we don't want to be found.

"That's great if they are, but we should go," I mutter as icy chills sweep up my spine. "We aren't looking for anyone's help right now." I was already on edge, but knowing we could also be watched from above ups the ante.

"There's a sign." He points before cranking the motor back on and beelines directly for it. "Maybe we can hide behind it and try to blend in until the spotlight passes."

I nod eagerly. Hiding sounds great right about now. And at least we've reached the outskirts of the city. Distantly spaced billboards, smaller and lower to the ground than those along the highway, rise from the water. They promise the tastiest food, the best shopping, and unique tourist experiences. All I care about is if their displays are wide enough to camouflage us.

Aidan zips us behind the closest sign and cuts the motor. We drift, each of us grasping the edges of the stationary fixture to keep from floating out into the open. The gentle thwapping crescendos in its rhythmic ascent. My heart churns in tempo, waiting. Neither of us peeks around the edge to assess its location or whether a sweeping spotlight lurches toward us.

Not soon enough, the churning fades to a dull pulse. My shoulders relax and I draw in a deep breath. We bid one last pensive glance at each other and release the sign. *The helicopter's gone, which means it's time for us to go.* Before we turn around, ready to assume our posts on the tiny boat, a deep voice slices through the night, shattering our perceived invisibility.

"I'd like to talk to you two," the stranger demands.

Chapter 45

Every muscle in my body betrays me. My mind screams, "Run!" but my feet are suddenly cemented to the floor. Besides that, there's nowhere to go. I'm not about to jump ship and randomly break into a breaststroke, kicking my way through the dull brown water and whatever lies beneath it.

Shoulders hunched, deflated by guilt, we turn as one to face our penance.

Rather than the armed militia I was expecting, a lone boater drifts beside us. His face is cloaked in shadow, further hidden by the black hood draped over his head.

We didn't even hear him approach. My arms jiggle with nervous energy. Do we raise our arms in surrender? Does he have a gun or other weapon? Is this person robbing us? We have nothing except the boat we stole. At least we outnumber him. His boat's not much different from the one we have, so it wouldn't make sense for him to take ours. We were so fixated on hiding from what was above us we didn't bother to check if anything was approaching from any other direction until it was practically tethered to our side.

"About what?" Aidan asks. He stands straighter, broadening his shoulders, painting a fearless image. But trepidation lurks beneath his tone and appearance. I just hope our visitor doesn't identify it.

The man tugs his hood back, letting it sag to his shoulders. With a flick of his wrist, a soft click precedes a small burst of light. He clenches the illuminated tube inches below his chin, as if we're gathered around a campfire and he's about to frighten us with a chilling tale.

The shadows tugging the creases on his face retract as my eyes adjust and focus. Jaw dropping, I nudge Aidan's shoulder. *Is he seeing who I'm seeing?* Those blue eyes narrow and his face scrunches. *Yep, I'm officially not crazy. Or else we're both having the same hallucination.*

"Sergeant Bowen? Wha…what are you…doing here?" Shock coats my words; my voice nearly cracks.

"I wanted to talk to you." He takes a cautious step toward the wall barriers separating his boat from ours. In response, Aidan slides between us, as if he's a protective shield. I can't tell if the sergeant even notices. Whenever they aren't fixed on us, his eyes dart from side to side, as if he's awaiting an ambush. It doesn't exactly foster confidence. Although just a moment before he approached, we were preoccupied with the helicopter in the distance.

My alert factor skyrockets. *Is he one more threat to add to the growing list?* We held up our end of the deal—delivering a satellite phone to his wife—so what could he possibly want with us now?

"How…how did you even find us?" I don't have a tracker and I lost my cell phone way before I even met the sergeant. He's never given me reason to question his actions. Until now. This doesn't feel right.

He raises his hands in surrender. "I know this is strange."

"Yeah, you could say that," Aidan concedes, crossing his arms, standing even taller.

"I can explain." Sliding a bag from his back to his side, the sergeant reaches into it and retrieves a black rectangular block that I instantly recognize. A tracking device. A small smile plays across his face as he notices the spark of recognition in my eyes.

"You tracked us, but how? I don't even have one in me." My head turns to Aidan as he narrows his eyes in distrust.

"I wanted to talk to you one more time. So I plugged in your sister's tracking number. I noticed it remained in proximity to yours," he pauses and nods toward Aidan. "The readings were very faint. They barely registered. Honestly, they probably wouldn't even have been noticeable if I wasn't looking for them."

He inhales a deep breath and continues. "Then suddenly, when I was checking again, the readings were strong. Riley and Aidan were easy to track, but then they diverged. I figured you were with one of them. I took a guess, hoped it was him, and I was right."

I cross my arms as Aidan cocks his head in confusion. I voice what's likely flashing through both of our minds. "So if you found Aidan, and I wasn't with him, you'd have tracked down Riley?"

"I was honestly hoping to find you all together," he says. "But I also don't have a lot of time, so I had to make my move."

Make his move? It's not like he had us lined up in the crosshairs with his finger on a trigger. *Right?* The more he says, the more questions I have. *Is this really the same military officer I met in Virginia?* He clears his throat.

"So you came all the way up here to ask us something?" I clarify, narrowing my eyes. Nothing he's saying makes sense. "You barely know us. What could be so important?"

"You are half correct, but I'd like to explain further." *Now that sounds more like the Bowen I remember.* "Rossana, Millie, and I are staying in a nearby location. Why don't you come and talk with us. I promise, this will make more sense."

My heart clenches with those words. When we got the satellite phone to his wife, Rossana, we knew they made plans to reunite. But after that, our world spiraled into fast forward, and between finding our aunt and then barricading ourselves underground for weeks, I kind of forgot about the people who helped us get there.

"I'm really glad you're all back together." In the midst of distrust and the underwhelming odds of us actually succeeding in our current mission, a sappy smile washes over my face. All they wanted was to be together. And somehow, in this mess of a situation, it happened.

Chapter 46

Either unimpressed or completely oblivious to the romantic notion, Aidan remains a wall of reason.

"We need a minute to talk about this," he says. "Privately. Maybe you could just…drift back a few feet or something? Now we've got helicopters or something flying around to watch out for too."

"Ah, that would be the good old Department of Operational Assets, or DOA, searching for more arms to inject," Bowen says bitterly. "Yes, I'll take a brief ride around the perimeter. Make sure we're alone. When I come back, I expect you'll have an answer."

The sergeant starts his motor and fades into the dusky evening. Convinced he's out of range to hear our conversation, Aidan turns toward me. Under the pretense of privacy, in hushed voices, we debate our options.

"How long has this guy been tracking us? He said when he first started, the signals were really weak, so that's probably when we were underground." He rakes a hand through his hair. "I know he helped you and Riley, but I don't like that he's been watching, just waiting to approach us."

"I don't have a good feeling about this either. He was totally different at Langley. He wasn't sneaking around, and what he asked of me then was to make a side trip, after getting us a car and supplies. It's not like we had any other options. We couldn't say no. But this seems…off."

Aidan crosses his arms, irritation rising. "We barely know this guy and he came all the way up here, in the middle of a tropical storm, to find us? He must want something, but we have our own problems. We took a risk stealing this boat and we're no closer to finding anyone than when we were still sitting on that dock."

"Yeah, we're already out of time, everything's taking too long. And who knows if your dad is freaking out right now." Guilt funnels into a growing unease. "If Riley was out here, without a way to let me know that she was okay, I'd be a wreck. Maybe we should go back, tell them that the sergeant found us and that he wants to talk to us, and see what they think."

"Okay, we can do that. After we look around some more." His posture's stiff, as if he's awaiting a challenge.

I withhold the sigh itching to release. *I thought we just agreed that we should get back to the school.* I tilt my head in question, but don't argue. He needs to know that he did everything possible. And the least I can do is believe in him. I nod and he grabs the floodlight, flashing it twice in the direction where the sergeant's boat disappeared.

A moment later, the rumble of an engine echoes in the distance and the sergeant draws near. When he cuts the motor, Aidan offers our proposal.

"Why don't you tell us where you're staying, and we'll talk to our family about coming to meet with you?"

The sergeant crosses his arms and juts a leg out to the side, planting himself in a firm stance within the minuscule space. "That won't work. In order to protect my family, I cannot divulge their location. I will take you there, but just you two. Right now. Then you can return to your family and discuss my proposal."

My eyes snap to Aidan. Indecision reflects in his irises, matching my own. We've made exactly no progress on the one thing we intended to do since stealing this stupid boat. The longer we're out here, the more likely we are to get caught, and if we don't even get a chance to look for Aidan's family, this whole trip was wasted.

"I've got to check in with Rossana." An urgency overtakes the sergeant's tone as he eyes his watch. "If you just come with me now, I can explain more."

An idea shoots through my mind faster than a bolt of lightning striking the ground. *It's the best chance, maybe the only one, we've truly got.* I wrap my fingers around Aidan's bicep, attempting to convey, "Hold on. I got this." Tossing my chin back and raising my eyebrows, I have one question for the sergeant.

"Does that tracking device still have our friends' ID numbers in it?"

"It does," the sergeant answers warily.

Aidan's lips quirk into a smile. "I like the way you think," he whispers for my ears only. Spending a little time now could buy us information that will save us a lot of time searching. Confidence washes over him as he addresses the sergeant.

"We'll come talk to you," he starts, rubbing the scruff on his chin, "if you can look up where our friends are."

Bowen blows out a frustrated breath but nods his head. "If that's what it takes, fine. I'm trying to conserve the battery, but those few numbers are already plugged in, so I won't need to search for the name and number combinations."

"You have yourself a deal, Sarge," Aidan smiles broadly. "Lead the way."

Chapter 47

We trail him closely, weaving around telephone poles, store facades, and apartment buildings. He slows when we near a multi-story hotel. Our boats line up about a foot below one row of perfectly spaced windows. An identical level rises above, and I'm guessing there's one more hidden beneath the water.

Shuttling behind the enormous rectangular box of bricks, he leads us to the fourth window from the right. Before we cut the motors, a low barking resonates from inside. *I know who that is.*

Sure enough, two familiar faces push through the curtains' slit. Rossana's eyes widen in momentary surprise before she tosses a rope to her husband. He deftly secures his boat and climbs through the opening before anchoring our boat to the air conditioning unit.

We greet Rossana, expressing relief that she made it to Virginia and found her husband. While we talk, Millie circles around our legs, pressing her nose every few inches from our knees to our ankles, investigating every embedded scent we unknowingly carry. I glide an open palm along the short, smooth fur of her forehead, instantly struck by the memory of how she took to Jeff when we first met her. Maybe her family will help us locate his.

Just as quickly, flashes of Snickers bombard my mind, smothering my heart with grief and regret. Once we've met minimum courtesy requirements, an awkward silence proves it's time to get some answers. They didn't come all this way to find us just to sit around and make small talk. Besides that, I'd welcome a distraction from the misery that's sure to follow if I analyze the latest round of heartbreak we've been dealt, losing our four-legged family member.

As Millie settles, Rossana motions for us to sit. A narrow desk bumps up against one wall, but since it offers seating for one, we shuffle toward one of the double beds and plop down on the firm mattress. She and the sergeant sit across from us, on the other bed.

"Alright, we're here." Aidan forces a casual tone, but a nervous energy buzzes just below the surface. "How about we fire up that device?"

Rubbing his palms together, Sergeant Bowen cocks his head to one side. "Actually, I thought we'd discuss my situation first and then check the device. In case it reveals any information that could change your immediate plans, I'd prefer to make certain that you hear me out in full."

Alright, he's got us there. If that thing tells us Jeff is nearby, we'll be out of here before the little dot on the screen can blink.

Without arguing, we present him with our full attention.

"I'm probably the last person you expected to see again, especially after everything that's happened." *Yep, I can agree with that.*

"I've assigned myself a new mission and let's just say it required travel." He attempts a half-smile, but the gravity of our circumstances quells any amusement. When Aidan and I just stare in silence, he continues.

"I got out. I jumped ship, or I guess you could say I jumped jet since I was at an Air Force base." Amid an upended world, his demeanor is more relaxed than I've ever seen. I'm wishing he would just get right to the point. "Thanks to you, and the satellite phone you delivered, I guided Rossana and Millie close enough to Langley for me to intercept them. With a little inside help, I slipped out unseen and we headed north."

The sergeant explains they avoided going home, as that would be too obvious a location if anyone was sent to pursue and retrieve him. Her family owns a relatively remote hunting cabin where they stayed until warnings of the tropical storm arose.

Anticipating flooding, but not knowing how bad it would be, they scouted out the nearest lake and borrowed a boat that was left behind. They carried it back to the cabin and, once the rain came and eventually stopped, used it to navigate back to civilization. Specifically, to find us.

During their time in hiding, he hatched a plan to end the tracking system for good. He needed help but couldn't approach anyone in the service, not knowing if they would listen to his story or if they'd feel compelled to report his actions and his location.

With few options, he started watching Riley's and Aidan's trackers to pinpoint our location.

"We've got our car, some supplies, and weapons. All at the cabin, ready to go when we are." He nods toward his wife. "She was kind enough to pack some of my hunting rifles from the house before she parted ways with your group."

Rossana smiles in return. "Which I wouldn't have done if you hadn't asked."

"And why would we need to know this?" Aidan asks. Urgency slams into me. *This is taking too long.* I really miss the person who zipped through instructions when Langley was on the verge of a lockdown.

"My plan is to fade into the sunset, just disappear into the night with my family, and never return. But before I can do that, I'm taking down this tracking system. If for some reason I can't, then I'll broadcast it to every American alive. They need to know what they're carrying around inside of them."

"And you want our help?" My voice veers toward a nervous high-pitched squeak.

"Well, particularly yours, Quinn. I think you're well suited for this mission." His eyes land on me.

"Her?" Aidan throws both hands in the air. "What do you mean *her*? She's a minor, she can't just run off, and I'm not going to stand by and watch her go."

"The less people on this mission, the better. We can sneak in and out quicker that way." The sergeant implores Aidan to understand, but he directs his response to me.

Lowering his voice, his eyes bore into mine. "We made a promise that we wouldn't separate, so if you go anywhere, I'll be right by your side."

I squeeze his hand and nod. *Yes. I can do this, or anything, on my own, but I want him with me. Always.*

"Before you decide anything, hear me out. I think we can come to some agreement." The sergeant steers us back to the business at hand. He isn't the same person I met at Langley. His reserved demeanor has taken a sharp turn. The soldier I met weeks ago appeared overworked, tired, and serious. This man is fueled by a desire to right an enormous wrong. Between that and having his family back, I'd like to believe he's unstoppable.

I imagine I've changed too since the world turned upside down. Guilt slithers through me when I think about Riley. She never would have come here with me, and I had to do this, to hear him out. Anxious anticipation tickles the back of my mind.

Sounds like the sergeant wants to make one more deal.

Chapter 48

"Look." Eyes downcast, he rakes a hand over his close-cropped hair. It's grown out a bit since he left Langley. "I was part of the project when it began. By the time I fully realized the extent of what it involved, it was too late. I couldn't stop this before, but I can now."

"Why Quinn, though? Why would you find us?" Aidan vocalizes one of the questions fueling my confusion.

Releasing a deep sigh, Bowen rises. He paces the small area, but suddenly, as if a memory jolts him off track, he turns toward us. "I need a team. A small, cohesive group that I can trust to do exactly what I say when it needs to be done."

Scrunching my face, I ask, "And that's me?"

"Well, you and Rossana. Just hear me out. When I left Langley, I had to be fast and quiet. I didn't have time to gather any information that would have been useful now."

"So what are you saying? What kind of things?" Aidan asks, impatience tugging at the corners of his clipped questions.

"Well, for one, if any of my friends or family were vaccinated. If I knew that and had their tracking numbers, I could find them. I certainly can't access the full system that could tell me now." He pauses, perhaps not wanting to admit the obvious.

"So we were the only tracking numbers you had, probably already plugged into that thing." Aidan gestures toward the device.

"Yes," the sergeant confesses. "You were among the last people I…had contact with…before this latest round of natural disasters." He swipes a palm across his forehead as if it pains him to share the next words. "I can't do this alone, and I can't just walk right in and fix this mess. I've got a tracker too, and I imagine someone's got orders to monitor my whereabouts. I take full responsibility for this mission, but it's not a one-man job."

Rossana places a hand over his, squeezing. "We don't even know where our family is, if they evacuated, or if they even… survived." Her last word hangs in a whisper.

"And we didn't want to put them at risk by trying to contact them." The sergeant's voice steadies, as if the simple gesture of physical support renewed his disposition. He leans forward, conveying the honestly in his next statement. "I would never put you in danger, either. This isn't an active combat situation. I'll be there to draw attention my way, to provide a distraction. The most I'm asking for is that you convey a message to someone on the inside who can shut this whole thing down."

"If you can shut it down, then why didn't you do it sooner?" Aidan's words are more curious than accusatory but doubt creeps into my mind. *What's he not telling us? If this thing was so bad, why did he go along with it in the first place?*

Bowen's hands drop to his thighs. "It was too risky to involve anyone at the base. I was only stationed there temporarily. I wasn't even supposed to be there that long." He shakes his head, snapping his thoughts back to the present.

Bowen glances at Rossana before continuing. "And besides that, when I expressed concerns about the initiative, my family was directly threatened unless I continued to cooperate." He pauses, pressing fingertips to his forehead. "I wish I had done more, and I can't change what's already happened, but I have a plan to stop it."

His reason is noble, and I feel like an ass for asking, but I have to know. "Why would we do this?"

"I have reason to believe, from a trusted source, that there's more going on here than just watching people move around. These devices have the ability to receive a signal that could… harm each host."

My eyes dart to Aidan. *No! Harm him? And Riley? And who knows how many others out there?* I choke on ragged breaths, coughing to clear the dread and disbelief.

Aidan's posture folds like he's been punched in the gut. We walked in here to get a location on our friends, but we're going to walk out carrying an unconscionable burden. *Now what?* Before we can contemplate our next course of action, the sergeant continues.

Pinching his nose and squeezing his eyes shut, his confession pours out in a low, deliberate tone. "I will never forgive myself if I don't do this. You've proven yourselves trustworthy. Maybe ask yourselves, what's really left, anyway? The possibility of rebuilding under a government that can pick and choose who lives and who dies? Who gets food and who starves?"

Rossana runs a hand across her husband's back in a soothing motion as she addresses us. "We'll fix this, one way or another. But you've got to do what feels right. And if you can't do this, we understand."

The sergeant nods. "I don't want to separate you from your families, and I don't want to put anyone in outright danger. So go back and talk to them. Tell them that I'm basically offering them the chance to save the world. What's left of it anyway."

"How soon?" Aidan asks. "When does this mission happen?"

"The minute this water recedes."

My mind buzzes with information overload. There's too much to process and time seems to stretch on endlessly. *How long ago did I tell Riley about my plan to find Aidan?* His dad's probably alerted every member of the National Guard of our absence by now.

Observing our glazed focus, the sergeant switches gears. "Why don't we look up your friends," he suggests. "Then we can determine a way to make contact."

He reaches for the device on the floor at his feet and pushes a few buttons, clearly able to manipulate the thing more so than Riley and I ever could. He points at a blinking green dot. "Alright, this one's Jasmine." Then to himself, he mutters, "Sure is bright."

Attempting to gain perspective, Aidan asks, "How specific does that thing get? Can you tell exactly where she is?"

Zooming in for a closer view, the sergeant answers with calm certainty. "She's still in Virginia. Based on the number of trackers around her, I'd bet she's at a safety commune."

Aidan taps my arm. "I wonder how her dad was when they tried to inject him." We share a chuckle, remembering how agitated the man got when just talking about Jasmine being vaccinated. I wouldn't be surprised if he wrestled a syringe right out of a soldier's hand.

"Daniel is still in Virginia as well." I forgot all about Jim's brother. "He's also within a cluster of trackers, so he's likely staying at a shelter." Memories of the Masters brothers swirl, from my ingrained distrust of Jim to my relative tolerance of Dan. That is, until they abducted Riley. From that moment, there was no chance of salvaging any sort of relationship with either of them.

"Now this is interesting," he squints at the screen as he adjusts settings. "I've located both James and Jeff. They aren't together, but their dots…both of their dots are red." Genuine confusion tugs at his features. "I haven't seen that before," he mutters.

Chapter 49

My heart seizes as if death's brutal grasp clamps around it like a vice. Aidan drops to his knees, his shoulders hunched in crushing pain.

Silence saturates the room, other than the soft rap of Millie's paws padding the floor as she approaches Aidan, nuzzling her head beneath his palm. She must sense the sudden shift in his demeanor that radiates a deep-seated need for comfort.

Clenching my eyes shut, I hear the guarded concern when Rossana voices her observation. "You know what the red dots mean…"

Fat drops roll down my cheeks. I brush them away and sniffle before answering her. "We know what happened to Jim." I run a shaky palm over my face, attempting to compose myself. "He had a gun…and he found us, me and Riley. He was going to shoot me but…Jeff shot him first. He died." I shake my head back and forth slowly, wishing I could wipe the memory from my mind. "If Jeff didn't do what he did, Jim would have killed me. Probably all of us except Riley."

"So a red dot must mean that whoever has that tracker is… gone." Aidan rakes a hand through his hair, his eyes shifting around the room like he's searching for a flaw in our reasoning. "Because we can confirm that is definitely Jim's status."

Drawing a hand over her mouth, Rossana shudders. Her eyes flood with sorrow just before her voice rises to an unnaturally high pitch. "Maybe it malfunctioned. Maybe Jeff's just stopped working."

I latch on to her words with fragile uncertainty. It's entirely possible, though. Nothing works 100 percent of the time. And of all people, he's got my vote for unknowingly finding a way to damage or disable his tracker.

"I hope you're right, and anything's possible," the sergeant adds, scratching his chin thoughtfully.

He pauses for a moment as an intensity ignites his next words. "This is exactly why we need to carry out this mission and shut down the whole tracking system. None of this ever should have happened. If people were warned, they could have had time to prepare for everything that's hit us these past few months. And they should never have been injected with trackers."

Goosebumps race down my spine while my stomach churns with anxiety. His anger scares me, even though we're on the same side. Sensing my discomfort, Rossana leans forward and rests her hands over mine. I didn't realize I was trembling until the light pressure she applies stills me.

"We can't know for sure," she says softly. "Maybe he's okay

and just hiding out until the water's gone."

She's got a point, but she doesn't know that Jeff's legs no longer work. If he is there, he's probably stranded. We don't even know if he's alone. No one else with him had trackers. The emotional overload threatens to paralyze me in this spot. I'm sure the same thoughts flash through Aidan's mind. His pain mirrors my own.

"Where? Where is he?" Aidan's voice is rough. He shoots to his feet, burning anger driving him to action.

The sergeant looks to his wife, then back at us. "I can pinpoint him on the map, but do you really think it's a good idea to go? The military's out there performing rescues because it isn't safe."

"So far they haven't been able to tell us anything and I'm tired of waiting. If that damn tracker is wrong, if there's any chance…I've got to know for sure."

Aidan's anger has the opposite effect on me as the sergeant's. A kindling ignites, stirring me to action.

"He's right." I rise on unsteady legs. Although every instinct begs me to curl up in a ball and block reality from any conscious thoughts, that won't do any good.

The sergeant nods, turning the device toward us for a better view. He points to the dot associated with Jeff's ID number. While the scattering of green dots mimic fireflies flashing vibrant signs of life, the red dot barely flickers, its crimson shadow practically fading into the recesses of the black screen.

Swirling a pointer finger over the screen, he draws an invisible line from our approximate location to our destination. The device seems to be more about random number combinations than actual useful directions.

"Hold on," he mumbles, pressing a few buttons in quick succession. "Okay, now this shows us land formations. It's not the clearest imagery, but it gives us a little more perspective."

As they squint at the screen, studying it more closely, my nose wrinkles in frustration. If anything, the map makes even less sense now. It resembles a sonogram, where a ray of light opens up like it's about to swallow a baby's silhouette.

"That's Couturier Caverns!" Aidan practically jumps out of his skin, temporarily forgetting why we're even pinpointing the location.

"That's where I saw your dots, faint beneath all the layers of rock?" the sergeant questions. "You can find it from here?"

"Yes, that's where we stayed the past couple of weeks." Sucking in a shaky breath, Aidan turns to me. "Maybe they're still in the cave…maybe they never made it out…and Jeff's dot is weak because all that rock is blocking the signal." His eyes widen and a nervous smile washes over his face.

Chapter 50

I return the smile, but fear floods my veins, not hope. Bowen said when he was tracking us, the dots faded and disappeared when we were underground. He never said anything about them turning red, and he just mentioned that he never saw red dots on the screen before. So Aidan's theory wouldn't be possible if the sergeant was specifically watching our dots but they never turned red.

Pushing my worries away for the moment, I summon a strength I don't feel and step closer to Aidan. No matter what happens, no matter what we find, the most I can do is support him.

"We need to borrow the device to find him...them," Aidan states.

"I can't do that." The sergeant's words are stern but apologetic. "There's no guarantee you'd return with it, and I need it to contact the only person who can get me into Detrick. Whether you join me on this mission or not, it's happening."

Slapping his palms on his knees and holding the position as if he's about to retch, Aidan inhales a deep breath.

"Look, I'll point you in the direction as best I can, but that's all I can do. You go, find them and then talk to whoever's waiting for you back at the commune. We'll meet up again tomorrow at 1800 hours. If by some miracle the water's low enough to drive through, we'll leave at that time. Either way, I'll need your decision then. This can't wait."

Rossana steps forward, tugging her husband's arm. "He doesn't mean to be so harsh." Although she speaks to us, her eyes narrow on the sergeant. "Since we don't exactly have working cell phones or any other way to get in touch, meeting in person is the only way we can do this."

"But where are we supposed to meet, and how are we going to get there? We snuck out today and stole this boat. I doubt we can pull the same thing off two days in a row."

"Not to mention what we'll find when we get back," Aidan mutters. "They might be out looking for us right now." Worry flashes in his eyes and his jaw tenses. *I don't look forward to explaining our actions to his dad. At least Riley sort of knows what's going on.*

"You walk out." The sergeant's tone is flat, as if we're voicing a ridiculous concern. Neither of us responds, prompting him to elaborate.

"You aren't prisoners there. You have every right to leave, but you need to let them know so they can account for you. The purpose of this process was inherently to help people. It just got diluted along the way, or rather twisted into something perverse."

When I cross my arms and tilt my head to the side, unconvinced, he offers an example.

"Do you remember when your sister was at Langley with the man who abducted her?"

I nod. Of course, I do, I'll never forget the moment we saw each other again after being separated against our will.

"When I was talking to the two of you, what did Mr. Masters do?" The sergeant raises his eyebrows the way a teacher would when trying to coax what they believe is an obvious answer out of you.

Hearing someone refer to Jim with such formality turns my stomach. He doesn't even deserve the nickname Slim Jim after everything he did. I think Evildoing Imbecile would be more appropriate.

"He left. He just…left." I guess it's true. Technically, we're free to go, but the front entrance of the school is barricaded, and the only way out is through a restricted area.

"Okay, even if we can just leave, there's still the floodwater. How are we supposed to get anywhere? We had a boat, but they made us leave it behind." Aidan raises his hands in frustration. "The one we have now isn't exactly ours and I doubt we'll be able to get our hands on it again."

"The water's definitely receding, but I believe it'll be at least one more day before it's low enough to safely drive." The sergeant pauses, rubbing the scruff along his chin. "You'll be under close watch when you return, both by the soldiers and your family members. Take tomorrow to be on your best behavior. And keep this quiet. Tell your family members, but make sure they understand that no one else can find out about it."

"Then what? We either convince them or we don't, but how do we let you know?" There's no way Riley will agree to this. And Aidan's dad? I can already envision a thick vein pulsing on his forehead as we try to explain. I subtly shake my head at Aidan. He must know this battle can't be won. Riley barely accepted me coming here, in what was supposed to be a fast retrieve-and-return mission.

"He'll never go for it," Aidan concedes. "I know my dad. He won't believe it and he won't agree that we should go."

"Alright," the sergeant says, crossing his arms. "Could you arrange a meeting? I can explain exactly what's going on here and what needs to happen. Maybe he'll believe me."

Doubt it. The words flash through my mind, but I don't voice them.

"We'll try." Aidan glances at me but defeat already lingers in the air. Conversely, the sergeant seems to relish the challenge.

"You get him to meet with me and I'll convince him that this needs to happen." He clasps his hands together, eyeing us intently. "1800 hours tomorrow. I'll follow your ID on the tracking device to make sure you're there, but I can pick you up wherever they're docking boats at your commune."

My eyes meet Aidan's. He has to agree to this since he's got a tracker. No one can see me on those devices. With a flicker of a nod, I know he's in. I turn my forehead down slightly in response, a confirmation of understanding and agreement.

"Alright," he breathes out on a sigh. "We'll be ready."

"One question," I murmur. The sergeant nods once, encouraging me to continue.

"What time is 1800 hours?"

Chapter 51

Aidan listens intently, committing the sergeant's directions to memory. I try to follow the information exchange, but the screen might as well be a map of outer space for all I'm gleaning from it. Promising to talk again tomorrow evening, we bid our temporary companions farewell and slip out the window.

My eyes scan every direction, searching for flares of light or bursts of movement. The moon's reflection disguises the water's dull appearance. If my heart wasn't clenched with anxiety and apprehensive shivers didn't race down my spine, this could be an amazing experience. In another time, another place, it would be just me and Aidan, drifting along the gentle water, guided by the moonlight.

But reality is always a blink away, shattering daydreams and crushing hope.

The landmarks rush past us as the boat speeds ahead. I recognize the theater Riley dragged our family to at least half a dozen times. Its enormous three-story cream-colored façade stands tall, stronger than the storm that washed away lives and swamped streets. The marquee sign prominently announces a musical production that will probably never be.

Once we reach the outskirts, billboards rise up, stoic markers of where rolling hills replace asphalt. Before long, fields and brush replace steel and brick. Tension courses from my core to my extremities as we near our former shelter. Memories of our last moments here flash in my mind.

Although the parking lot may not fare as well, Couturier Caverns weathered the storm and continues to dominate the landscape. The solid rock looks just as strong as it did when we first arrived, proving it prevails over water in the short term. Over many thousands of years, not so much.

My heart beats frantically as we breach the cavern's opening. This is where a tour boat would normally spill into the outside lake. Now, everything is a lake. Still, I recognize the enormous gap in the rocks.

"I see something ahead." Excitement churns in his tone while dread blooms in the pit of my stomach. Anytime optimism attempts to flare, that dull red dot flashes through my mind, immediately squashing it.

Aidan's eyes frantically search the calm water, its surface no longer a roaring menace like the last time we were here. Glancing over, the boat's light reflects an intensity in even his slightest movement.

"Their boat! I see it!" His eagerness only solidifies my unease.

This was a mistake. I swallow the lump in my throat and squeeze my eyes shut, effectively trapping the tears that threaten to spill. The boat churns, propelling us ahead slowly toward the familiar red flat-bottomed tour boat. As we draw near, it gently sways in the slight waves of our wake.

He cuts the engine. I sweep a handheld flashlight along the interior as we drift close enough to scan the seats. No one. Nothing. No evidence that the boat recently carried any passengers. Aidan scrunches his face up in confused disappointment before thrusting a pointer finger in the air, physically punctuating his assumption. "Why would they just be sitting here in a boat? I bet they went back inside the cave!"

He cups his hands around his mouth and calls their names, pausing between one each in case there's a reply. The only voice we hear is his, echoing through the chamber. My stomach twists as goosebumps crawl along my arms. A chill I hadn't noticed before dashes up my spine.

"Aidan, maybe we should just go back. To the school. They're probably worried about us and we've been gone a long time. And your dad's probably gonna go ballistic when he sees us." I can't meet his eyes. It feels like the words I'm not saying are only augmented by their absence. *I don't believe we'll find Jeff and the others. I don't believe any good will come from this, so let's go before things get worse.*

"We just got here, and I'm not going back until I find them." His voice is low, his sentiment unyielding. I recognize that drive. It's the same unstoppable determination that led me to Riley after she went missing what feels like a lifetime ago. Gulping down dissention, I turn back toward the water and sweep the flashlight's beam across the surface, resuming my task. Understanding the unspoken consent, he lunges to the front of the boat and takes the helm.

In contrast to the urgency he must feel, Aidan pushes the boat forward cautiously. Maintaining an invisible radius of about three feet around our vessel, he maneuvers through the openings, careful to evade the harsh protruding edges where rock slices through water.

Random pieces of debris, inanimate victims of the storm, drift past us—mangled branches, plastic bottles, and a bright pink soccer ball with alternating black pentagons. His eyes never stop scanning, seeking an alternative that grows more impossible to imagine by the minute.

His arm juts out, pointer finger twitching. "I see something floating. Over there." Following his line of sight, I sweep the flashlight's beam along the rocky edge where land meets water. He's right. Sneakered feet, toes submerged beneath the surface, dangle from dark blue denim. A white shirt stretches across a back bobbing in the lazy current.

Chapter 52

As we draw closer, my eyes sting and my throat clenches. Each breath is a struggle, contrary to the abundant oxygen filling every crevice of the enormous cavern.

"Quinn, close your eyes." His words are a low growl. A merciful warning rather than a domineering threat. I squeeze them shut but wonder what's worse—my imagination or reality. My mind paints a morbid picture of bloated, pale bodies rotting in the contaminated water. As if it refuses to provide a peaceful resting place, instead displaying the empty shells of our loved ones after claiming their souls.

Without question, I wait, turning my back against the scene I cannot watch unfold. Sloshing water tempts my eyes to peek, but weakness invades my trembling frame. I cower, sinking into the boat's stiff surface like chocolate melting on a hot day.

"It's Jeff," he croaks. "He's…he's gone." His voice cracks, along with the tiny piece of my heart that wished against all odds that none of this was happening.

A soft splash precedes a low grunt. As if he's struggling.

"Do you need h—"

"No." He cuts me off, but guilt smooths the sharp edges of his tone almost immediately. "I'm…I'm moving him onto the rocks so…"

"I understand." We finally found him. Aidan doesn't want to lose him again. My voice trembles but I push the next words out. "If you need me, I'm here."

Once again, he calls for those we lost, voice cracking on each name. In return, we're greeted by infinite emptiness. A sudden draft of brisk air sweeps goosebumps along my arms, a chilling promise that our calls will go unanswered.

A few minutes later, the boat rocks as Aidan climbs back inside. My hands shoot to the walled sides, grasping for stability.

Dripping wet, he wraps me in a soggy hug. His forehead drops to my shoulder, and I allow mine to do the same. We mold to each other, frozen in an embrace, for what feels like hours, though it isn't nearly long enough.

When his breathing slows and his grip loosens, I raise my head.

"We should get back," I whisper.

Renewed pain flashes in his eyes. "Quinn, just because… We still might find someone else…We can't just give up."

"There's something I should tell you." I gulp down any hesitancy and force the words out before I can change my mind. "Remember our first night at the school?"

"Yeah." He scrunches his face as if I'm wasting time mumbling nonsense. My eyes plea with him to stay with me. I have a point to make.

"Well, that night, before I crawled over to your mats, I saw your dad leave." I wait for realization to sink in. It doesn't seem to take hold, so I continue. "He snuck out, Aidan. And I can only imagine he snuck out to search for your missing family members. But did you see him that next morning?"

"Yeah, he was pretty riled up about finding you next to me."

"Yes, but his eyes, they just held a sorrow that I can't explain." The memory haunts me. I'd never ask, but I think in that moment he knew a truth that none of us wants to accept yet.

"Why didn't you say anything?" Aidan's tone is more hurt than accusatory.

"I didn't want to rat him out, and when I saw how…hopeless he looked, I just felt worse about everything."

Aidan squeezes his eyes shut and nods.

"I get it." He heaves out a deep sigh. "I guess you're right. We should get back." Defeat is just one more burden he bears, masking his emotions, likely leaving him numb inside.

"We'll tell the soldiers about this. Maybe one of the rescue crews can come here if I describe the location to them. Maybe they can just take a closer look to be sure." Although it's largely squashed, I admire the sliver of hope he carries.

"Yes, we should definitely ask them," I say, bracing myself for whatever awaits us when we return to the school.

Aidan steers the boat in a loop, turning us around. Retracing our path to the outside world, we sputter past subdued surroundings. The night is dull and lifeless. And considering how anxious I was to return to the school earlier, I wish we had a few more stops to make along the way.

Whatever consequences we face for our actions don't matter. We're too consumed with grief to care. Memories of my friend play through my mind, cruel reminders of the laughs and words we'll never share again.

Jeff easily diffused tense situations, turning frustration or anger into humor. He was like a brother. A fiercely loyal, goofball of a big brother. He would have done anything for any one of us, but that selflessness couldn't save him.

Knowing that we have to tell Scott, Kaylee, and Riley, destroying any remaining hope they may hold, numbs my thoughts and movements. I don't want to talk or think. I just want to fade into a dull nothingness.

We spot our destination before passing the last remnants of the city. The school loading dock is lit like a beacon. I can't remember how bright it was the night we arrived, but a warning flares through me, signaling that the display is for us.

Sure enough, as we drift alongside the wall, we have an audience. Four soldiers greet us. One commands us to show our hands and rise from the boat as another approaches with a thick rope to leash it. The other two stand between us and the entrance door. One speaks into a walkie-talkie as his eyes scan over us, evaluating our appearance. The last one carries herself like a snake, coiled and ready to strike. When we step toward her, she launches into an interrogation.

"Considering four witnesses saw the two of you arrive at this facility in stolen property, is it safe to assume that you were the ones who confiscated the property initially?"

Is this woman a lawyer? Because that's all I'm hearing right now, what sounds like legal gibberish. Never mind the information we possess as a result of our crime. Aidan was right. He did what they couldn't.

"Yes, I did it," Aidan says gruffly. "And I can explain why."

They escort us to the main office, past the intake area and directly to the principal's office. *How fitting.*

"Have a seat," our interrogator instructs. She watches us as if we're about to pocket anything in the room that isn't nailed down. "The facility commander will be joining us momentarily."

Great. She settles into a chair, apparently unwilling to leave us unattended.

About five tense minutes later, an older man with graying hair and hawkish features breezes into the room. Traces of old man aftershave chase his movement as he deftly slides his tall, uniformed frame into the wheeled chair behind the desk. Much to her disappointment, he dismisses the woman who brought us here. At least she doesn't get to watch our trial and sentence.

The man's gray eyes pierce us, pinning us in place. He introduces himself as if we should be impressed by his name and rank alone. We're not. I don't care enough to commit either to memory. We're mentally exhausted and dejected, barely clinging to reality after what we found at the cavern.

Chapter 53

"So, you two stole one of my boats today. Granted it was barely more than a floating saucer, but it's still government property at the moment. Do you care to explain your actions?" The man's sharp features slide into an impassive expression, as if he's awaiting a steady stream of ridiculous excuses to pour out of us.

"Yes, I can explain, sir," Aidan starts. "It was my idea. Part of my family is missing, and no one's been able to provide any information. I thought maybe I could find them if I went to the last place where we were together."

The man paints a slightly sympathetic look across his features, though it barely softens the harsh angles.

"Being that only two of you returned, I'm guessing that didn't work out too well for you?" He raises his eyebrows, as if expecting we'll admit that our plan was a complete failure.

"Actually, we did find…one person we were missing. Well, his body." Aidan's words add another layer of reality. The commander's jaw tenses but his gaze softens. He presses a fist over his mouth before dropping it to speak.

"I'm sorry for your loss. If you'd like to share the location, I'll send a team to retrieve your loved one and—"

Pounding erupts, rattling the door. "Sir! I said you would have to wait!"

"And I said that was not acceptable!" Scott's flustered tone breaches the wooden barrier between us. Aidan grits his teeth beside me. Any empathy points we may have just gained are losing their value with each passing breath.

"What in the—" the commander rises abruptly, faster than I'd expect for a man his age. He rounds the desk and yanks the door open. Sure enough, Scott stands on the other side mid-knock. His eyes flash wide as the sudden movement registers.

The soldier attempting to tame him rushes to apologize. "Sir, I explained that you were in a meeting right now. Apparently that meeting is with his son."

The commander releases a deep breath before swinging the door open wider. "By all means, join us." He sweeps an arm out, welcoming his unexpected guest. Scott straightens his shirt and strides through the opening. Relief flashes through his features when his eyes land on us.

"I'm glad you two are safe. And back." As soon as the commander passes, returning to the seat behind the desk, Scott slides a chair next to Aidan and waits expectantly for the conversation to continue.

"As we were about to discuss," the commander says, "in

order to maintain order and civility, we all have to abide by rules. When someone flaunts the rules, word spreads quickly. And words have the power to incite mutiny. We cannot have that, so we have to squelch it at the source."

We've effectively been cut from the conversation as Scott interjects his position. Relief courses through me as the playing field feels a bit more level now.

"Look, we're all under extreme stress, as I'm sure you can imagine. They're good kids, they really are. I guarantee they never intended to damage the boat. And they did return it. Maybe you could just release them to me, and I'll be responsible for them for the rest of the time we're here."

Resting his elbows on the desk, leaning forward, the commander counters, "If they were under your guardianship before their actions today, then I fail to see how you could prevent a similar event in the future."

Crap. He's got us there. Although Aidan's technically an adult. Without checking the database, his age is probably questionable. That perpetually ruffled hair gives him a boyish appearance and those blue eyes wield innocence beyond what they've seen. Forcing my gaze away from my accomplice, I attempt to neutralize the distraction.

"Then what now? Are you going to kick us out?" Scott rubs his forehead, probably inventorying what other options we may have. But there's nowhere else to go. We don't know if our homes still stand at this point.

The commander steeples his fingers, resting his elbows on the desk. "Technically, I cannot turn away civilians while there's still flooding in place. The only solution I see at the moment is community service."

Alighting his focus on me and Aidan, he says, "Tomorrow at 0600 hours, the two of you will report to the cafeteria to assist with meal preparation and cleanup. Staff there will determine when your assistance is no longer needed. Until that time, you will remain under their service for the day."

I don't even have to ask. I know that 0600 hours means six a.m. We both utter the most dejected, "Yes, sir" possible.

"That sounds fair," Scott says, as if our punishment is a welcome inconvenience. Sure, he'll still be asleep tomorrow morning while we're slogging mush into bowls in an assembly line.

The commander smiles, but darkness lurks behind it. Something that raises the hair along my neck.

"Now, there is one more matter to attend to before you're dismissed." This time, he trains cold gray eyes on Scott. "Besides ensuring that this operation runs smoothly, I am required to report the commune's status to my superiors. And they don't appreciate when my building is not at full compliance with the rules set forth."

He pauses, waiting for one of us to complete his lecture. All three of us remain silent. Holding our breath, still as statues.

"We were able to determine that your group was responsible for the infraction that occurred this afternoon. When I reviewed your records, I was quite surprised to discover that not everyone in your party received the vaccination that is required upon entry."

So that's what he's getting at. Great, Aidan and I completely botched up any chances his family had of slipping under the radar. The sergeant's warnings rush through my mind but I'm powerless to share them here.

Scott rakes a hand through his hair. His eyes drop to the ground before landing on the commander, intensity punctuating his words. "Fine. We'll comply."

The three of us trudge back to the classroom. While part of me can't wait to close my eyes on this day, another part dreads tomorrow. Now, besides working in the cafeteria for as long as they decide to keep us, we also have to squeeze in time to convince Scott to go talk to Sergeant Bowen. I don't think we're in a position to ask anything of anyone right now. Plus, we have the awful news about Jeff to share.

Kaylee and Riley barrel toward us, wide-eyed, when we enter the classroom.

"Where were you?" "We were so worried!" "Why were you gone so long?" Their emotions tumble out in a verbal cascade of concern and disbelief. Aidan raises his palms, warding off additional questions.

"We didn't mean to make anyone worry," he says. "My plan was to be back before anyone even noticed I was gone."

"You're a coward! You ran off without telling us! As if things weren't bad enough." Kaylee's fear and short-lived relief erupt as rage. She hurls accusations at her brother as her cheeks flush crimson. She crosses her arms so tightly they could snap.

"Look, I'm sorry. I just…I felt like I had to do something…I really didn't want to upset anyone, but I had to go look for myself. No one was telling us anything here." His head dips and his eyes graze the floor.

Scott wraps an arm around his daughter and leads her to the closest cot.

"Calm down, honey. What he did wasn't right, but he's back now and we've got to be thankful for that. They're both back, and safe." He nods to me in acknowledgement.

"We went back to the cave." Aidan plops down next to Kaylee and drops his head in his hands. "While we were out there…we did find…someone. Jeff's body was there."

There are no more questions. No more details. Only tears, sobs, and shudders.

Chapter 54

Misery slows each step as we prepare for sleep. Scott sets his watch for five-thirty the next morning, promising to wake us. I'm not bothering with a shower until my manual labor is complete.

When the light flicks off, we settle in for sleep. Other than an occasional sniffle or low cough, silence permeates the room. My cruel mind uses this time to focus on Jeff. Tears brim as I remember the first time we met. He put a smile on my face almost immediately. His humor and easygoing personality set me at ease. It's what I'll miss the most about him.

Silent tears wrack my body. I clasp a hand over my mouth to contain any whimpers that may try to escape. Eventually, the sadness seeps into the edges of my mind and releases me into a numb oblivion.

Morning comes too soon. Scott gently shakes me awake

before proceeding to Aidan's corner to repeat. We tiptoe out of the classroom before trudging down the hallway to the restrooms. A few splashes of cold water snap me from the last tendrils of slumber.

When I'm sufficiently ready for a day of forced labor, I push through the door. Aidan waits patiently in the hallway. As we force our feet toward the cafeteria, he nudges my shoulder.

"Sorry I got you into this." He eyes me cautiously, gauging for any hint of anger or blame.

"It's totally not your fault," I assure him. "And besides, it could be a lot worse. So we had to wake up early and we'll be forced to witness the inner workings of that kitchen. Beats scrubbing toilets, don't you think?"

He smiles and runs a hand through his hair. "Agreed." Just as quickly as it quirked, his smile fades and he focuses on what must be his next worry. "I can't believe how mad Kaylee is. She won't even talk to me."

"Well, she's not wrong. I mean, I can see why she's upset." The hurt in his eyes has no bearing on my next words, because I mean everyone. "But you weren't wrong either. No matter how little chance there was in finding them, you took it. And they're all worth it. Your mom, your sister, Jeff, his parents."

He blinks several times, an attempt to halt any unshed tears. He crosses his arms, as if clamping down the swelling emotions inside. I fill the silence, so he doesn't think he has to.

"I know that feeling, Aidan. I know what it's like when one tiny sliver of hope slips past the part of your brain, screaming an awful truth. So many times, when we were at our aunt's trailer, when I would wake up…I'd recognize the surroundings but…

forget what happened. For just a moment."

I take a deep breath, closing my eyes briefly, summoning the strength to continue. "It's like I had all these good memories of the place—going to the beach, jumping in the waves, playing mini golf—and for just a split second, my brain forgot. Forgot all the bad and pretended that it never happened."

Riley would probably say it's a way that we cope. Despair sprinkled with a dash of delusion. Just enough to keep us going, moving forward, when we really just want to disappear.

We reach the cafeteria and weave around the tables. Though we don't see anyone, we follow the sound of distant voices and pans clanking in the kitchen area. The breakfast crew consists of two men and two women who laugh and joke as if we shouldn't all still be drooling on our pillows right now. I'm not sure if they're usually this pleasant or if the prospect of two new people to boss around energizes them.

Chapter 55

Within minutes, we're wrapped in aprons, gloved, and directed to enormous cans of pineapple chunks to scoop into individual bowls. The soldiers scurry around the massive stainless-steel appliances, unloading trays of shriveled sausage and flimsy pancakes.

As soon as we finish our task, we're whisked to the front lines, replenishing servings as temporary residents select their choices and load them onto a tray. Amid the haze of monotony, a familiar voice tugs at my ears.

"Excuse me, miss. Do you have any breakfast meat other than sausage?" I scowl at Riley, unamused by her attempted humor. Kaylee shuffles beside her, barely acknowledging us. *She'll come around when she's ready.*

"You two doing okay?" Scott rounds out the group.

We both nod and Aidan admits, "They've been pretty easy on us."

"Alright, well make sure you get something to eat too, okay?" With that, Scott continues through the line. I thought he'd still be furious with us, but he seems to have gotten over our infraction relatively quickly. I wonder if Jeff is monopolizing his thoughts. Our discovery certainly doesn't renew any hope that the others are safe somewhere, just passing the time.

Halfway through breakfast hours, we find our groove. During our coordinated routine to replenish overcooked breakfast sundries, I don't even notice the three sets of eyes scrutinizing us.

"Aidan? What are you doing back there?" "Is that really you?" *Great.* His fan club has arrived. I should have figured we'd see them.

"Oh, hey." He glances at me, flashing a perfect smile. "This is Quinn. We're…together. Anyway, we got caught doing something we really shouldn't have done and…let's just say, this is our punishment."

Their jaws drop as my cheeks flush. My insides sear with exhilaration and I can't hold back the smile spreading across my cheeks. They mutter their discomfort before scooting down the line. "Ooooookay." "Whatever." "Guess we'll see you later."

Once they're out of sight, he leans toward me, his mouth hovering beside my ear. "I hope that was okay."

"It was better than okay. It was perfect!" I say just before a giggle escapes.

Our service ends after the last fork and plate are loaded into the massive dishwashing unit, which reminds me of those boxy conveyer belt things at the airport that swallow and spit out your cell phone and keys.

They gave us short breaks to eat, and the work actually wasn't that bad. It provided a welcome distraction from the conversations we need to have today.

Our plan is to divide and conquer, or rather, convince. We've got to dispel each argument so that when we come together as a group, we're all in agreement. Aidan will talk to his dad to explain the sergeant's proposal and I'll talk to Riley. Kaylee's the wild card. We're just hoping she does more listening than objecting so that we can each convince our elder family member that the sergeant's mission has to happen.

To dissuade any sort of group discussion, we separate at the library. Aidan promises to send Riley to join me, while he approaches Scott in the classroom. I choose the table farthest away from the soldier on duty and slide into a seat. Luckily, this place doesn't get crowded.

I wait, first gently tapping my fingers on the wooden table, then graduating to tracing invisible geometric shapes along the smooth surface. Each outline tugs my conscious back to Jeff and the others, who are still missing. A circle, like a never-ending cycle, signifying the spirits that will live on even after our loved ones' bodies fade. A triangle, all hard edges and sharp corners, a resilient facade necessitated to protect crumbling emotions. A square, strengthened by its structure, a formidable support bearing the brunt of weakness and vulnerability.

Just as my eyes drift up, Riley rushes through the entrance door. She lowers herself into the seat across from me and reaches a hand toward me. I extend my own, which she grabs and squeezes.

"Are you okay? We didn't really get to talk much since you got back last night." The joking spirit she displayed earlier in the cafeteria is gone. Now that we're alone, her brown eyes hold worry and grief.

"I'm okay," I admit half-heartedly. "It was actually kind of good to spend today working. It kept my mind off of everything else for a while."

"I can't believe Jeff's gone, just…gone." Staring at the desk, she shakes her head. "We never even got to say goodbye. It's just, so much has happened the past few months, so many bad things. I don't know how much more I can take."

I release her hand and scoot my chair closer to hers. "Riley, I have to tell you about yesterday."

"There's more?" She shifts uncomfortably in the chair. "I'm not sure I'm ready for more."

"No, you have to hear this. Aidan's telling his dad right now too." She chews her bottom lip and wrings her hands, bracing for what comes next.

"Yesterday Aidan and I ran into someone." Her eyes narrow, as if we physically crashed into another boat, so I start over. "Sergeant Bowen found us!"

Her mouth opens and closes like a fish craving water. I continue since she's unable to form words.

"He believes…that the trackers can be…used against us." *Why is this so hard to explain?* "He thinks there's something in them that could…hurt us if the military used it. He says the only way to protect everyone who has a tracker is to disable the system."

She watches me intently, understanding unfolding the more I explain.

"He thinks he can do it, but he needs help. Nothing dangerous, just two people to deliver a message while he creates a distraction."

"Quiiiiiiiiin, what aren't you telling me?"

"He wants me and Aidan to be those people."

She crosses her arms and raises her eyebrows.

"Look, I know what you're thinking, but he's got no one else to help him and if we don't do this, something bad could happen to every person with a tracker. That means you, and Aidan, and probably Aunt Robin by now."

She grits her teeth and presses a hand to her head. "So you want to do this?"

"Yes." I swallow the lump in my throat. "I think so. I mean, something has to be done."

Chapter 56

I fill her in on what the sergeant shared with us. She doesn't like it, as we expected, but she's relieved that all he wants right now is to talk to Scott. When I've answered her questions, the best I can anyway, we stroll back to the classroom.

Pushing a lock of hair behind her ear, Riley quietly asks, "Remember my friend Jen from high school?"

I nod. My sister's always been incredibly introverted. Her circle of friends is small, but strong. Jen's been a fixture within that group since grade school.

"Well, she's here." She keeps her voice just above a whisper, as if it's wrong to feel or express any happiness at a time when so many lives are in turmoil.

"Jen's staying here, too?"

Riley nods.

"With her parents and brother. I don't know why I never thought about seeing anyone we knew here. I mean, of course we would. We grew up in this area."

She's right. I hadn't even considered that friends and neighbors could be here. Other than that news lady, I didn't even really notice people we ate near in the cafeteria, passed in the hallways, stood in line behind, or shared a restroom with. There's also Aidan's little fan club, which I'd rather forget about.

"That's good news." Digging deep for any scrap of happiness I can offer, I tug my lips into a weary smile. "And we can always use more good news."

We step into the classroom cautiously, unsure of what to expect.

Aidan sits on my cot while Scott paces the room. Kaylee's slumped in a chair with her arms crossed. Tension swells in the air.

I join Aidan on my cot while Riley plops down on hers.

"So I guess you're up to speed now, too?" Scott asks.

Riley and I nod.

"Well, I'll meet with this guy, but we're not taking part in what he's trying to do." Resolve laces his words. "He's got some nerve hunting you kids down to ask something like that of you."

Aidan shrugs and presses his nose to my ear, whispering, "He's pretty ticked off about this. We need to go along and make sure he doesn't start a war with the sergeant."

"Right," I agree.

After gulping down a quick dinner, all five of us walk to the office. Aidan and I wait in the hallway, preferring to avoid anyone who might recognize us from our last visit there.

My heart thunders with worry. *What if they won't let any of us leave?* Given the recent infraction Aidan and I committed, Scott decided he would request to sign out Kaylee and Riley. Then, once the intake soldiers knew three people were leaving, we'd just swap out two of those people—Kaylee and Riley—for me and Aidan.

A few minutes later, the three of them slowly push their way through the office doors. With a subtle nod, we follow as they stride down the hallway, back to our classroom. As soon as we step into the privacy Room 126 offers, Kaylee and Riley slip matching lanyards over their necks and hand them to us. The simple forest green badges bear two words in white block letters: TEMP PASS.

"Put this around your neck. This gives us access to the dock, both to leave and return." Scott's words hover just above a whisper. His eyes dart from the door to us and back again. As soon as the straps dangle from our necks, he orders, "Let's go."

We weave through the building, anticipation energizing each step. It was only a day ago that Aidan and I stood on this same dock, preparing for our getaway. Yet it's a completely different scene today. With a designated adult, there's no sneaking around or hiding behind a rickety shelf. Shoulders back, we walk with purpose.

Soldiers breeze past us, lips quirked in question until their eyes glance over our all-access passes. The unspoken permission renders us fixtures, three random bodies for passersby to navigate around.

Whether daylight or darkness, there's not much to see back here. Two rescue boats, as well as the much smaller one we commandeered yesterday, are docked. But the difference between last night and today is how much lower they sit. It's got to be a few feet, which means the ground can't be that much farther below.

Eagerness swirls through me. The sooner all this water is gone, the sooner we can leave here for good. Not that I know where we'll go or what we'll do, but I've had enough communal living.

Soon enough, a churning motor sounds and the sergeant's small boat glides toward the dock. This time he's not cloaked in a hoodie, shielding his face from view. Maybe that would be too suspicious looking. Instead, he holds his chin high, conveying an undeniable confidence, as if he has every reason and right to be here. As though he's not here to recruit a team to dismantle the government's plan to track every American.

We climb into the boat, trading subtle nods with our captain. The possibility of being overheard isn't worth exchanging pleasantries. We all know why we're here. Once we've put several blocks between us and the school, the sergeant calls over his shoulder, "Not too much farther."

Subtle changes materialize in the limited snippets of landscape I recognize from last night's trip. Tips of bushes that were blanketed in water now rise from the muck. Larger objects, like trucks and bus shelters, peek at us from their submerged prisons.

Weaving behind a mini market, we advance toward a dumpster. Slimy gray bubbles float atop the murky water surrounding the massive green box. No one acknowledges the putrid stench emanating from whatever festers inside the rusting metal. I fight every instinct that begs me to pinch my nose closed.

"I think this is as good a place as any." The sergeant sweeps an arm through the air, encouraging us to disembark. *Is he serious?* Maybe this is part of his plan to convince Scott. If he's distracted by the smell and desperate to get out of here, will he agree to anything?

Aidan takes the first tentative step, cautiously planting one foot on the flat lid. When it holds, he positions his other foot, shifts his full weight, and rises.

He turns and offers me a hand, which I accept. There's no way I'm falling into the muck awaiting below. We shuffle to the far end of the flat top so Scott and the sergeant can join us. I don't think these things were meant to hold people, but it seems sturdy.

"Thank you for meeting with me. I assume you know why we're here." Aidan and I quietly fade into the background as Sergeant Bowen faces Scott. Completely alert, they appear ready for a debate.

"Yes, my son explained what you told him yesterday. I listened, and considered the options," Scott starts. "But I'm sorry to say that we'll have to decline your request." I should feel relief. We're off the hook. The only adult in our group said so. But instead, a sudden sense of regret flares within me, as if we're making a mistake. Bowen's words to me back at Langley whisper in my mind.

"The government knew about that earthquake in the Atlantic, but they didn't warn anyone. And now this Yellowstone eruption is being kept under wraps too."

Thoughts of dissent flash through my mind, readying to launch a debate, or at least spark additional discussion. *I've got to speak up.* Of everyone here, I've had the most interaction with the sergeant. I don't believe his intentions are malicious. But before I can rattle off reasons we should consider participating in his plan, the sergeant responds.

"You realize, sir," Bowen replies, barely restraining impatience, "where this is headed? We'll all be at the mercy of those who control whatever resources still exist. The government, through the military, can dictate where people live and what food they'll get. The entire purpose of this setup was to monitor the population and all these natural disasters helped move the process along."

"Look, I know you've got an axe to grind, but we aren't in a position to help." Scott's stance is firm even as he visibly grows tired of the conversation.

"I understand," Bowen acknowledges. "And I wish you luck. But there's one more thing you should know." He pauses, giving Scott the chance to refuse his words. When Scott remains fixed in place, Bowen continues. "I helped work on the tracking device system that's being injected into civilians. And I have reason to believe, from an expert medical source, that the nano-technology swimming in our bodies has the ability to terminate its host."

He turns on his heel, the movement fast, likely fueled by his frustration, and climbs back into the boat.

Chapter 57

Scott's eyes slide to me. "You believe him?" he whispers urgently.

"Yes," I admit, nodding. "If it wasn't for him, I wouldn't be here. I'd probably still be in Virginia, sitting around on a military base." I gulp, remembering how far I've come and gone in the past few months. "He helped me find Riley and get home."

Fixed in place, Scott runs a hand over his chin uncertainly. His eyes shift from Aidan to me. Bowen settles into the boat, waiting for us to join him. It's clear that once we climb back in there, this meeting is over. But whatever's happening is nowhere near finished yet.

"If what you're saying is true, one of those damn things is in my son." Scott's shoulders slump. "And my daughter too."

"You got it?" Aidan's eyes flash wide as they focus on his father.

"Today. While you two were working. Kaylee and I went to the nurse's office. We had to."

At these words, Bowen fixes his full attention on us, which prompts Aidan's dad to continue.

"I'm sure you already know Quinn and Riley got it too." This time, Aidan's eyes dart to mine. His dad thinks I have a tracker in me. I glance at the sergeant, but he doesn't flinch. Fixed in place, he's awaiting the words he came to hear. He's not going to waste time on needless details or clarifications.

"But why would our government do that? It doesn't make sense." Scott's eyes search the distance, seeking answers his mind can't comprehend. "What proof do you have? Other than someone you trust told you? I can't buy into this without some solid proof."

So far, our relationship with the sergeant has been a partnership based on trust. Riley and I never asked for proof of anything he told us. I guess we just assumed someone in his position wouldn't misrepresent himself and take advantage of us.

Actually, now that I consider it, he took an enormous risk on us. He provided weapons, a satellite phone, a car, and a ticket out of Langley just before it went into lockdown. If we had ignored his instructions to reach his wife and just went straight home, there's really nothing he could have done. Now, I wonder if he has an answer that will satisfy Scott's demand, because even if he doesn't, I still believe him.

With no hint of concern, the sergeant maintains a steady tone. "I located Quinn and Aidan through a military-issued tracking device. All I had to do was plug in the identification number and it led me right to them." Again, I notice he doesn't acknowledge that I don't have a tracker. There must be a reason for the omission, so I don't correct it.

"Initially, I was told that the purpose was to monitor pockets of the population and distribute food and resources as needed. But that was before the world started self-destructing. Before we finished cleaning up from the earthquake on the East Coast, Yellowstone blew its stack. And now we've got flooding. Do you know what impact all this has on food production, fresh water, and housing?

"Do you really believe resources will be distributed evenly when there's nowhere close to enough for everyone who survived? This promise of help, these safety communes... they're about control. Because when it comes down to basic survival, instincts turn animalistic. If you could eliminate your competition with the press of a button, without ever seeing their faces, without knowing their families, with almost no chance of it ever being traced back to you, what's your motivation to do the right thing?"

"Basic human decency," Scott utters, riveted in place.

"Well then, that's something we have in common," the sergeant replies. "Because I tried to stop this before it happened... but I couldn't. And now, I won't stop until I do."

Scott rubs the stubble on his chin before pressing a palm to his forehead. Aidan slices through the thick silence with an intense plea. "We have to do this. We can't move on until we know that this system is disabled."

Taking a step forward, Scott scrutinizes the sergeant's features, possibly searching for fabrication. "And you're certain you can stop this? Whatever it is?"

"Yes." Bowen utters the word with an unquestionable confidence. If he hadn't confessed to Aidan and I that he wasn't even certain how to shut down the database just yesterday, I'd believe him.

"So what's your plan?" Scott asks. "And just how dangerous is it?"

The intensity level drops a few degrees as we listen to the sergeant's proposal, injecting questions here and there. Although he's no longer an officer in good standing, he's still got contacts on the inside. And he's confirmed that people he worked closely with have been transferred to Fort Detrick in Maryland. On the simplest level, he wants to travel there and bring his former coworkers together to derail the database. He's convinced they're capable and willing, with a little convincing.

The discussion simmers when it's time to decide who's going. Scott insists that he and Bowen can do this, while the rest of us wait at the school. Although the sergeant doesn't want an army, he would prefer to have more than just two people on the mission. He wants Aidan and I to accompany him and Rossana. If we were stopped along the way for any reason, his plan would be to claim we're a family on our way to check on some elderly relatives. He believes this would draw less suspicion than two grown men approaching a military base.

"This guy's a trained soldier." Aidan attempts to bolster the sergeant's credibility. "He'll get us in and out before anyone knows we were there."

"Yeah, but you'll be up against an entire base of trained soldiers. And I don't like those odds." Scott's right, but no one wants to admit that.

"You know I'm not a kid anymore." Aidan chooses his words carefully, his tone respectful rather than defiant. "I'm twenty, and old enough to decide for myself."

"That's true, son, and I can't technically stop you." Scott nods to me. "But she's still a minor and I'm not sure her sister will agree to this."

"Riley knows the sergeant. And she knows how important this is. I believe she'd agree to it." I don't mention how long it might take me to convince her.

"Besides," Aidan adds. "Kaylee will flip her lid if you or Riley try to leave. She's already ticked off at me for leaving the first time. I doubt she'd be fine staying at the school with me if you left."

Scott's eyes shift to each of us, a balled-up fist pressed to his mouth. *There's no other way. He must see it.*

"If we're done here, I can take you back to the school." The sergeant's tired of waiting, and probably tired of fighting what feels like a never-ending battle.

Blowing out a breath and shaking his head in disbelief, Scott utters, "We're in."

Chapter 58

Somehow those words spark elation inside me, as if their mere utterance has fixed all of our problems. In reality, all they've done is confirm that Aidan and I will help break into a military base brimming with armed soldiers, to take down a program we know nothing about.

Banking on an assumption that the remaining water will recede tomorrow, the plan is for the sergeant to pick us up outside the school. He'll watch Aidan's tracker to see which exit we use, but we're all assuming it will be the back dock, since the front entrance is still boarded up.

Scott suggests we leave during a shift change in the main office. He's not sure if Aidan and I have been flagged after yesterday's incident, so it might draw less attention if Aidan leaves just as one group is finishing up their work and then I leave right after a new group has taken over.

The sergeant agrees and suggests we leave after night has fallen. Besides helping to conceal our movement, he's hoping that activity on the base will be relatively quiet if we arrive overnight. Maybe we can sneak in and back out under the cloak of darkness. And, he and Rossana need the entire day to get back to the cabin, set Millie up inside with access to plenty of food and water, retrieve their vehicle, and return to the school to collect us.

After all of his visits to the office since we arrived, Scott believes 9:00 p.m. would be the most opportune time for Aidan and I to leave.

Agreeing to meet again in just over 24 hours, the sergeant returns us to the school. We bid solemn farewells, heavy with the uncertainty tomorrow evening will bring.

Nervous energy chases every minute of the next day. Part of me wants to fast forward to the evening so that we can finally face, and hopefully conquer, whatever awaits us.

Scott explained the plan to Riley and Kaylee before we went to sleep last night—or attempted to sleep. Recurring scenarios of what could go wrong stormed through my mind. Although I forced my eyes closed, I sensed Aidan's similar battle with restlessness. I didn't dare join him, knowing how that ended last time.

The day wanes, along with my patience. I lie on my cot, draping an arm over my eyes to block any hints of reality from my senses. Aidan and his dad disappear after lunch, scouring every unlocked room and unblocked entranceway to conduct visual inspections of the landscape.

As the sergeant expected, the water is mostly gone, leaving

in its wake crumbled fragments of debris entombed in sludge.

Just as the fringes of my mind retreat from any semblance of coherence, Riley bounces back to the room, apparently having satisfied her daily book fix at the library.

"Quinn!" She rushes to my side. A slight breeze trails her movement, fanning over me. My mind instantly snaps back to full consciousness.

"What is it, Riley?" Frustration brims, seeping out in my abrupt tone. My body craves sleep, a direct conflict with the tingling nerves anticipating tonight's mission. It doesn't help that Aidan's been gone for hours. Instinct tugs at me like a magnet, urging me to find him and overanalyze the situation. Or maybe it's just selfishness. It hasn't been that long, but I miss him already.

"I stopped by the office and Aunt Robin got our message! Now that the water's receded, she might be able to come here tomorrow!" Throwing my arm to the side, I sit up and face her.

"Really? She's coming here?" A smile spreads across my cheeks. We don't have to leave Aidan and his family.

"I think the less people they have to transport, the better. And she just wants to see us. She doesn't care where it is." She hitches a shoulder up. *Yeah, that makes sense.*

"Wow, so she may be here when we get back." The prospect renews my spirit, like a reward for completing our mission.

"Yes! I hope so!" Riley's eyes shine with genuine hope. For this moment, I choose to share that feeling.

Chapter 59

The five of us gather for dinner, picking at our plates and sipping our drinks in relative silence. Everything's been said, there's no need to rehash concerns or advice. When we've sufficiently pushed the last remnants of food around and declare the meal over, we wander back to the room and wait.

I can't remember when a clock's hands so stubbornly refused to budge. Anticipation surges within me, spiking irritation and discomfort. *I need to be alone, for just a moment, to calm my mind and nerves.*

Excusing myself, I dash to the restroom to splash some water on my face. As I yank a thin paper towel from the dispenser, the door swishes open. The news woman, I think her name's Amy, strides past me. She flashes a glowing smile before leaning over another rectangular white sink and twisting the knob. I return her nonverbal greeting before shuffling out the door.

The brief encounter awakens memories of Jeff's insistence on broadcasting the government's wrongdoings. To expose their refusal to warn citizens of the slew of natural disasters over the past few months.

If anyone could help us do it, it's her.

Finally, yet too soon, 8:55 p.m. arrives. With a nod and a hug for Riley, Kaylee, and his dad, Aidan shoots me one final glance before turning his back to us and disappearing out the door.

I spend the next ten minutes promising Riley that I'll be back as soon as possible, unharmed. She finally releases me from a vice-like hug when Scott announces that it's time to go. I gulp a deep breath and force my feet to carry me away from my sister. Alone.

This feels wrong. *What if Aidan makes it out, but I don't? Or what if he didn't make it out but I do? What if I can't find him?*

As panic spirals through me, I focus on burying my fears. All I can do is take this one step at a time. Literally. The first step is to get out of here as quickly as possible, despite the wave of apprehension washing over me, slowing my pace.

What if they don't believe me? What if they won't let me leave? This isn't exactly a school building anymore. It's governed by the military, and from the short time I spent at Langley, I would expect some sort of procedure for everything. Including a process to keep track of who comes and goes.

Crap. What if they try to stop me from leaving? This isn't a prison, and the sergeant said I should be free to go. Even though I'm technically a minor. Leaving at night, the moment the water recedes. Not at all suspicious.

I paint a calm facade over my features, though I'll be surprised if no one hears my thudding heart. It's clearly attempting to rocket right out of my chest. Memories of when Riley and I were leaving Langley flicker through my mind. The base was about to go on lockdown and Sergeant Bowen told us we had to leave immediately, or we'd be stuck inside. Like him.

We were worried the guards at the gate would stop us, so the sergeant gave us some code words to say if we were challenged. Was it an "Alpha Beta?" I try to replay the words Bowen told us in my mind. I was even the one who repeated them to the soldier who questioned us. "There's an Alpha Beta in it for you if you don't let us go!" *No, that's not quite right.*

Slinking down the hallway, I mimic a cat burglar. Hairs along the back of my neck stand on end as the sensation of being watched chases each step. I swiftly turn in place, attempting to catch any potential stalker off guard. No one's there, though. It's just me, the shiny floor, and a nearly endless wall bedecked with colorful posters of inspirational messages. My imagination works overtime, fueled by anxiety.

Facing forward, I continue my slow progression. How appropriate that our keepers are in the principal's office. That familiar pang of anxiety washes over me, as if I'm being summoned to a trial that I've already lost. Not that I was called to the office much in school, but I'd trade just about anything to answer for skipping class or missing a homework assignment right about now. Or even stealing a boat. At least I know what to expect as punishment for that crime.

It feels like anything would be easier than convincing a bunch of uniformed soldiers that I need to leave. Immediately. And alone.

Thoughts drift to our car ride out of Langley. Riley drove at a snail's pace, so slow that I thought we'd draw attention to ourselves. When we reached the exit, I told the soldier who stopped us that there was an…Alpha…CHARLIE! It was an Alpha Charlie that was waiting for him if he didn't let us go!

That's it! That's all I have to say. My momentary elation deflates just as quickly as it ballooned. This time there's no one to follow-through with the threat. My hands join, twisting around each other like Riley's nervous tic. I focus on drawing in deep, calming breaths.

When I reach the office, there are only two soldiers on duty. They both look young, probably in their twenties. At least I've got that going for me—maybe they're inexperienced and will just open the door and wish me luck?

I push through the steel-framed glass door, a nervous smile tugging at my cheeks. Both of the office's inhabitants regard me with mild disinterest. The dark-haired soldier with olive skin clutches a stack of papers and plops down in a chair, busying himself with data entry. It's like a silent, motionless game of rock-paper-scissors and the loser has to deal with me.

Breathing out a sigh, the other soldier approaches the desk across from where I wait. He adjusts the black-framed glasses that rest on the bridge of his freckled nose. Deep green eyes meet mine as he asks what we both know is an obligatory question.

"Miss, can we help you with something?" My eyes shift to his name badge. Killorn. He eyes me curiously, maybe suspecting that I'm not here to ask a simple question. The anticipation nearly chokes me. I force the words out before I tuck tail and sprint back to my cot.

"Yes, I'd like to check out." Oh my gosh. *Did I really just say that?* This isn't a hotel. Now I sound like an idiot. I cough, trying to clear out the stupidity. "I mean, I'm leaving." I stop before something incoherent spills out of my lips.

"Miss, we highly discourage that. You're in a safe place right now and, with the way things are going, there is no guarantee of anything beyond those doors." He points toward the entrance that's still barricaded, although about a third of the sandbags have been cleared away. They rest in a lumpy, haphazard pile off to the side.

"It's more than just what's happening right here." His words are memorized, delivered with a blend of obligation and boredom. "We're not too far from Three Mile Island. If that reactor was damaged from the storm, it could create a whole new set of issues."

He mumbles something about radioactive material under his breath. But it doesn't matter. Right now, I have one mission, and that's catching up to Aidan. Considering he's nowhere in sight, I'm hoping his exit went according to plan.

There's no time to contemplate lingering questions or assumptions. *If this impacts other power plants across the country, what happens to electricity? How long will it take to get back to some semblance of normal?*

"I've got to go. I understand that it's at my own risk." *Just please hurry this up. My eyes shift to the clock: 9:12.*

"As the water recedes, the land erodes." This guy won't let

up. "We've been instructed to monitor the surrounding ground for sinkholes. I can't guarantee there aren't any out there right now."

I get it. It's not safe out there, but no one can guarantee my safety anywhere. We were driving along a highway to the beach when an earthquake ripped the road apart and tossed us into a pile of wreckage. Inhaling a deep breath, I try again.

"I promise I'll be really careful." My foot twitches as I tamp down frustration.

"It's pretty dark out there." He glances at the black-and-white clock hanging on the wall. Fixing narrowed eyes at me, he further questions, "Wouldn't you rather wait for morning?"

"Oh, this is as good a time as any." My tone borders between false sweetness and acidic. "Besides, I have to meet up with a family member and she's waiting for me." I don't need to justify myself to these people. I'm not a criminal seeking parole. Nervousness slowly shifts into an indignant determination. *9:17. Come on, already!*

The soldiers share a glance. Killorn blows out a frustrated sigh and asks me to have a seat. Moving before the bank of laptops lined up along the counter where I imagine parents once signed their kids in and out from dentist and doctor appointments, his fingers fly over the keyboard.

"Last name?" At least that's easy. *I can do this.*

"Whelan. W-h-e-l-a-n." His eyes slide along the screen, reviewing details of every occupant who shares my last name. The simple action injects an ingenious thought into my mind. Quinn Whelan is a minor, who wasn't vaccinated at Langley but may or may not have record of a false vaccination. That's two potential strikes against me. This guy seems bent on finding a reason for me to stay and I don't want to give him any.

"First name?" He looks up expectantly. I fight the urge to bite my lower lip and push the word out before I can second-guess this decision.

"Riley."

Chapter 60

Killorn asks for a photo ID. I politely explain that I lost my wallet, along with my driver's license, on the way here, so I have nothing to show. Apparently, their database doesn't have a photo to compare me to, but even if they did, I'm sure I could pass for my older sister. Our features are similar enough that they'd never notice the difference.

"Miss, we need to verify your identity. That way we can account for you, especially if anything else goes wrong out there." He motions toward the main entrance. Just beyond those doors and windows is an unpredictable world, proven by the past few months.

"I told you, I lost *everything* before I got here." My voice cracks on the word everything. That part is true. Who cares about a stupid piece of plastic that proves who I am. It's meaningless in the whole scheme of what's happened.

Sympathy flashes in Killorn's eyes, along with a hint of fear. This man's probably trained to handle combat weaponry and hostile enemies, but I sense the threat of a teenage girl on the verge of a cry-fest is enough to refocus his resolve.

He punches a few keys on the keyboard and quizzes me on every detail of information they've collected on Riley Whelan. Luckily, I'm able to verify all of it. Either I've proven myself correct or he's run out of options.

A few minutes later, I'm presented with a pass and cleared to leave. Striding out of the office, my feet gain momentum once I reach the hallway, just past the soldiers' field of vision. Rushing to the boat dock, I allow myself one moment of satisfaction. I've accomplished the first step of this plan. *Never mind how long it took.*

Just as quickly, success seeps away as I consider what I'm leaving—those I've grown attached to as family, along with the safety of the brick building housing them. When I reach the dock, I push into the night. A shiver slinks down my spine as two headlights, at ground level, cut through the solitude of darkness.

I cautiously approach, but easily recognize Rossana's face peering out the front passenger window. She offers a smile that doesn't reach her eyes. This isn't a social call, but I welcome the gesture. From the back seat, Aidan's eyes scour my every movement, searching for any sign of trouble.

I tug the door open and slide into the back, next to him. The sergeant's gaze fixes on me in the rearview mirror.

"Did everything go okay?" he asks.

"Yeah, they just kept trying to talk me into staying, but they finally let me go." I glance at Aidan, wondering if he had the same issue. I'm guessing not, since he was gone before I arrived at the office.

"Glad you made it." Aidan shuffles across the seat and wraps an arm around my shoulders. "We worried you wouldn't get out."

"Well done, both of you." The sergeant starts the car and slowly swerves toward the front of the building. "Now let's hope that's the most challenging part of this mission."

Rossana turns in her seat, facing us. "It should take about two hours to get there. You two could try to sleep if you want."

Aidan reaches across me and clicks the seat belt into place. He nudges his nose into my hair and whispers, "She's right. You try to rest."

"What about you?" I whisper back.

"I will, but for now I'm just gonna stay right here." I can't argue with that. "Hey," I whisper. "Is it safe driving right after a flood? I mean, should we be worried about mudslides or something?"

He hitches a shoulder up. "There's definitely erosion, and all that water just sitting over land can trigger sinkholes. Technically, we should have waited until officials cleared it for use, but try telling it to *that* guy." He tosses his chin up, gesturing toward Bowen. *That sounds exactly like what the soldier in the office just said.*

Flashbacks of the sinkhole that swallowed our car on the way to Langley pulse in my periphery. Over the course of one night, the asphalt we parked it on weakened. When our group climbed in the next morning to continue our journey, it collapsed, attempting to launch us directly to the center of the Earth.

"Don't worry about that right now. We'll be on the lookout." His warmth, combined with the engine's gentle hum, lull me into a calm I shouldn't be capable of feeling. Within minutes, my eyelids drift closed.

A kink in my neck wrenches me from sleep even as warmth envelops me. The source—Aidan—still cradles my shoulder with an extended arm that'll be numb soon, if it's not already. His back slouches into the seat, and his head droops against his shoulder, bobbing with the car's every movement. Those etched features are completely relaxed.

Turning my groggy eyes to the digital clock on the dashboard, I blink away the daze and stare at the black block numbers with confusion. *12:37 a.m. Why are we still driving?*

Rossana senses stirring and twists in her seat.

"Where are we?" I keep my voice calm and low, so as not to disturb Aidan.

She explains that we had to reroute a few times, stretching the expected two-hour drive well into three. The water left behind damaged roadways and fallen debris. And that's just what we can see in the headlights' narrow beam.

Whipping my head toward the window, I scan the passing landscape, searching for any indication the ground is one blink away from crumbling into oblivion. But darkness prevails, rendering the scenery to vague shadows.

I have no idea what long-term damage a flood can do. And I'd rather not find out.

Chapter 61

As the car slows, Aidan stirs, wiping the sleep from his eyes and stretching his cramped muscles. The sergeant turns down a narrow road, which looks more like a neglected alley, and shifts into park.

"We walk from here. It's about a mile."

As the rest of us stretch and twist, sparking circulation through our bodies, the sergeant pops open the trunk and slips a backpack over his shoulders. He clicks weapons into place, strapped to hiding places along his waist and legs.

After twenty minutes of traipsing through a sparsely wooded path, he raises a hand and stops. We're still cradled in night, but lights bloom ahead, confirming that activity awaits at the base.

"Wait here, all of you." The soldier I met at Langley sparks to life. "Just stay low and quiet. I'm going to check the perimeter, try to see where guards are stationed, and monitor the entrances and exits."

"What?" He didn't mention this before. *We're just supposed to stand here, waiting?* We're completely exposed, and completely clueless about what to tell anyone who might find us.

"We don't stand a chance of making it through the main entrance," the sergeant cautions. "My status is AWOL and I'm fairly certain they won't swing a welcome gate open for me."

"How long do we wait?" I'm already shivering, the sweeping chill in the air blending perfectly with my frayed nerves. *What happens if the military catches you trying to sneak onto a base? Will they shoot you on sight? I don't want to find out.* And I don't want the only person who knows what to expect to abandon us here.

"I'll go as fast as possible, but it would draw too much attention for all four of us to go. The closer we get, the quieter we have to be." He scans our faces and flashes a quick nod before turning and sprinting away from us.

My thighs burn in protest as the three of us crouch in a perpetual hold. I focus all my energy on studying our destination. From this distance, signs of life dot the base. Figures cloaked in shadow stride with purpose from one building to another. Warm lights bloom inside windows. Quiet settles amidst the life within the fencing.

When a soft crunch resonates from the tree line, all three of us swivel, searching for the source. A lone figure materializes, dashing directly toward us. The sergeant's voice reaches us just as his face comes into focus.

"I found a way in. About half a mile east there's a tree down, took out a segment of fence. It'll make an easy way in and an easy way out." He smiles with genuine sincerity. *I want to believe this will be easy, but why would anything start being easy now?*

We follow our leader, striving to match each step he takes. He and Rossana traverse the path both swiftly and quietly, while Aidan and I struggle to move with a smidge less noise than a sasquatch.

One at a time, we scramble over the downed tree. What was once an intact fence lies trapped beneath the massive trunk. Once we've all crossed, we huddle beside it, awaiting our next command. For a second, I almost laugh. *Just this one time, Mother Nature helped us out.*

"So here's the plan. As soon as we meet my contacts, we part ways. You three explain to them that this is our only chance to shut down that tracking system and that it has to be done quickly. I'll set up some motion-triggered snares in another area of the base, just a little something to catch attention and kill time. As soon as we've done what we need to do, we meet at the car." The sergeant slides the backpack off his shoulders and whips it around, setting it on the ground in front of him.

"What if you get caught? Or what if we get caught?" Aidan asks, anxiety chasing his questions.

"Actually, it would be better if *you* stayed here, kept watch, and had that car ready to roll the second our feet hit the ground." His words are directed to Aidan, who's nowhere near ready to accept that role.

"What do you mean? I'm not waiting at the car while you all do the heavy lifting!"

Raising his hands, the sergeant hisses in frustration, "Keep your voice down! You've got a tracker in you, it's like you're one more blaring spotlight announcing we're here."

"So that's why you're okay sending Quinn and Rossana

inside…" Aidan's eyes trail from me to the sergeant's wife as realization washes over us at the same time. "They don't have trackers in them."

He's right. Aidan and the sergeant are in the most danger because of their trackers. *Someone could be watching their movement right now.* The thought sends a shiver down my spine.

"They're the fail-safes." The words slip out of Eric's mouth as a low murmur. The others pause, confusion marring their features. It's a term the sergeant used when he was helping Riley and I leave Langley. He said to always have a backup plan. I straighten my spine and allow the fire flickering in my chest to speak.

"I'm fine being a fail-safe. If I can come and go without being noticed and keep others safe, I'll do it."

Aidan shakes his head firmly. "No. Quinn, you have no idea what you're doing. You shouldn't go in there." *I can't believe he's bringing this up again. Now.*

"We have no choice. How can any of us go on as if there isn't something inside you that could blow at any moment? You may not see it, but we have no future with that threat hanging over us."

I step toward Bowen, moving quickly. I'm certain reality will sink in at any moment and promptly dissolve the surge of bravery shooting through me. Before I can chicken out, I force the words past my lips.

"I'm ready."

Rossana eyes me intently. "Let's get this done."

Chapter 62

Aidan shakes his head in continued disapproval. "Quinn, you're really sure about this?"

I nod. His blue irises fix on me, pleading for this whole situation to evaporate. But he knows as well as I do that if someone doesn't stop this, some trigger-happy psychopath could end our remaining loved ones with the push of a button. I will do everything I can to preserve the lives of the people I care about most.

I understand the sergeant's intense drive. He's got a tracker too, but I doubt that's motivating his actions. Although he hasn't voiced it, he seems to carry a weight beyond the stress that radiated off him at Langley. The soldier I met there was laser-focused on sending Riley and I on our way. Now that focus is amplified and aimed at destroying our government's ability to take lives at will.

Eric pinches the bridge of his nose. With his eyes plastered shut, he responds. "Alright, we'll stick with the original plan. All three of you will talk to my contacts while I cause the distraction. Follow me and stay quiet. We're going into the devil's den."

He speaks quietly as he repositions his backpack, preparing to maneuver through the shadows.

"And call me Eric," he says. "No need for formality, especially here, where my title isn't exactly going to help us." He glances around our small group and unloads the information he's been safeguarding. "These things were deployed across the country, mostly to civilians, but some military personnel have also been injected. Not many people know that the vaccine contains a nano-tech device. To my knowledge, there were only three of us who knew at Langley. Now, there could have been a few more, but I know that the project was kept under tight wraps."

I'm not sure if this makes our mission easier or harder. Maybe easier if those who don't know about it would support our efforts to stop it. But maybe harder if they don't believe us. He breathes out a sigh and continues.

"This base is the new hub for the project. I confirmed that at least." He runs a hand over his short, brown hair.

"I believe our best bet is to kill it at the source. As the vaccines were being developed, so was the database to track each device. It's all fairly new and, if I know the man in charge, constantly changing. There must be some back-end command to disable the system or scramble the identification sequences to disrupt the tracking ability."

Aidan nods. "Yeah, that all makes sense. So we'll just tell your friends all this. Got it."

"Yes," Eric says. "I'm hoping you won't even have to explain all that. These people already know most of it. They should just need a push to act upon it."

"Don't worry, we got this." Rossana nods toward me and Aidan. "You just focus on getting yourself out of there safely."

Eric rubs the scruff on his chin as his cheeks tug into a cringing smile. "You should know, one of my colleagues, I worked with him when I was at Langley. We didn't exactly part on the best terms, but I'd bet he'd come through if he knew what was really happening."

We watch him intently, awaiting his next words. He nods, more to himself than any of us.

"I know he can do this. We find him and convince him to help us. It's that simple."

Somehow, I think if it was *that* simple, he wouldn't have needed our help to make it happen.

Chapter 63

"Like I said, there weren't too many people involved in this project. We'll start with the one I worked the closest with and ask her to track down the person who designed the database."

"I know it doesn't sound that hard," Aidan says, "Just remember that we've never been on any sort of spy mission or have any type of military training or experience." He grasps my hand and squeezes. "But I'll be there to watch your back."

My heart shudders as I suppress a smile. *He just wants to protect me.*

"Because you know," he continues, raking a hand through his tumbling brown waves. "She's not the most graceful girl I've met. No offense, Quinn, but you'd probably trip walking down a hallway and end up grabbing a fire alarm to break your fall."

The warm wisps of affection fluttering through me evaporate before I can reply.

"I'm not some gargantuan klutz, you know!" I jab an elbow into his side with unleashed vigor.

He keels away from me momentarily, choking out a low cough. "Okay, okay, sorry!"

"Let's all stay focused on the mission, okay?" Eric releases a frustrated sigh.

"Agreed," Rossana says confidently. "As long as we could convince this database contact of yours to believe us, it all sounds pretty easy. I mean, as long as we can sneak onto the base without getting caught. That sounds like the hardest part."

Raising the device I recognize as a satellite phone, he says, "Somehow I think sneaking off the base will be the hardest part. But we'll cross that bridge when we come to it. I've been waiting until the last second and it's time. I just need to know which door to use and we'll go."

His voice barely registers above a whisper when he exchanges a few quick words I can't make out. The call ends a tense minute later. Eric tucks the phone in his backpack and motions for us to follow him.

Scurrying from one shadowed structure to the next, we slink our way along darkened paths leading to the building where we should find our contact. My pulse races as we tiptoe inside the building and locate LAB 2.

Pressing his ear to the door, Eric whispers to us, "I don't hear anything." Let's hope he's right.

Tension mounting, he twists the handle slowly. As he creaks the door open, I hold my breath, expecting an alarm to squeal or the barrel of a cold weapon to be waiting on the other side. We push through and come face-to-face with a female soldier.

"Glad to see you made it." Her deep mocha eyes sweep over each of us. Something about her clipped tone seems familiar. Her warm features strike a balance with perfectly straight strands of dark hair pulled into a tight bun. I can't place her though. Not that it matters. All that matters now is that she helps us, or at least doesn't report us for being here.

"So far. Thanks for helping us, Safiya," he breathes. He quickly introduces her to us as a doctor he worked with at Langley.

"You should go. I can take your comrades to Chara." Her eyes convey more than her words. They shift nervously from each of us to the door we entered.

"Wait," Aidan interrupts. "What if we can't get this Chara to do it? Or what if he turns us in? Maybe the sergeant should come with us to help convince this person."

I tug his hand. "What are you doing? We have a plan. We can't change it now."

"Quinn, what if it doesn't work?" Aidan's eyes shift back and forth. The panic rising within him is palpable. My own heart rate skyrockets. *What if he's right?*

"There's no time to argue. The general is on base." Safiya's eyes bore into Eric's. "I know what to do and we must separate as soon as possible."

"She's right. We stick to the plan."

"Follow me to the lab. I'll give you a sense of the layout before I take them to Chara." As we trail behind her and Eric, she quietly fills him in on how she ended up at this base. "Do you know why he brought us to Detrick?"

"I'm guessing the on-site biological research facilities, but

I was hoping there was another reason." I scan Rossana's and Aidan's faces. While all this is crystal clear to Eric and the doctor, the civilians among us wear questioning looks.

"The general wishes to make further enhancements to the trackers, and he felt this location was best equipped to yield results quickly," the doctor explains. "I was pulled back into the project since I have the most in-depth knowledge of the clinical aspects. After you left, he seemed determined to strengthen the initiative. I don't believe he will ever be satisfied."

Rossana seizes a brief pause in the conversation to interject a question. "What's so special about this place? What can you do here that you couldn't do in Virginia?"

The doctor's lips purse as if she doesn't want to speak the words out loud. "This base is home to the National Interagency Confederation for Biological Research and the National Interagency Biodefense Campus. Basically, it's the center of U.S. military biomedical research and development."

She raises a delicate hand in the air as if she's introducing us to the facility. "What better place to test more enhancements to a nano-tech device than here?"

Chapter 64

As soon as we reach the relative safety of the medical lab, sound resonates from the hallway.

A sharp clacking reaches my ears, a perfectly alternating pace. Shoes. It's shoes traversing the tile floor. Too soon, the cadence spikes louder, echoing just outside the door. Silence descends, amplifying my ragged breaths.

The sergeant raises a thick finger to his lips, an unspoken warning. It's unnecessary. No one dares utter a sound. We all hover in inertia, awaiting whatever comes. Panic launches through me, a warning. My fight-or-flight instinct begs me to run and hide, but dread cements me in place.

In a barreling run, Eric tackles the three of us, shoving us behind a counter loaded with glass beakers, scales, and droppers like I've seen in the chemistry lab at school. The doctor remains rooted in place since she's not among our huddled group.

I press a fist to my mouth, squelching the roiling emotion that threatens to spill from my mouth and tear ducts. The door swishes open and clacking footfalls grow louder before they halt.

"Well, it looks like my dream team has reunited," a deep voice booms. "Too bad one of you is on the wrong side."

Eric clamps a hand over his forehead and squeezes his temples. Rossana wraps a palm around his bicep, holding on tight.

"It's over, Sergeant, Dr. Noori," the man continues, an edge of danger lacing each syllable. "I'd appreciate it if you'd join me of your own volition."

My heart thunders as the air rushes out of my lungs. *They know we're here.*

Gently peeling Rossana's hand off his arm, Eric presses his forehead to hers. A silent message passes between them before he rises and strides around the counter. She sinks lower on her knees, withering in worry. We share an anxious glance before I turn toward Aidan.

He was right beside me when we landed but has since shifted to the far bottom edge of the counter. His head nearly brushes the floor. *He's watching.* I quickly slide along the tile and join him, wedging my face next to his. Eyes wide, we observe the scene.

"Bowen." The man's eyes dance with cruel amusement. There's not an ounce of kindness radiating from him. Tension soars and fear throttles my heart as we approach an inevitable standoff. And this guy's amused? I sense he's taking in the scene peripherally, although his gaze remains fixed on the sergeant.

"How dare you show your face here," he says with such fury that tiny drops of spittle punctuate his words. "You deserted your country, dishonored your oath, and betrayed your superior."

The man's demeanor dominates the room, but Eric doesn't flinch. The sergeant's posture transforms as he responds—his back straightens and his chin rises. "Sir, as I see it, the only way to truly serve my country required that I leave my post."

"Well, that sounds rather noble. But if that's truly the case, then what brings you back here?" Arrogance oozes from this guy in his every syllable. No wonder the sergeant jumped ship. If I had to listen to this guy, and his obvious air of superiority, every day, I'd be endlessly scrubbing toilets with a toothbrush or something. I'm guessing that would be the punishment for telling someone like that what he can do with his enormous ego.

"I've returned to uphold my oath. I swore to protect my country against all enemies. And this operation, while domestic, is a threat to both survival and freedom."

"That's quite a surprise, Bowen," the man sneers. "Especially considering how much of a hand you had in the project."

Bile rises in my throat as I anticipate their next exchange. Instead, a subtle click echoes through the space. My ears perk and tension swells just before a sharp, solid bang, immediately followed by another, slices the silence. Instinctively, I drop my head and wrap my arms around it, like it's a school drill.

Rossana presses two shaky hands to her face as she rocks back and forth, unsure what to do. Aidan lunges toward her and whispers something not meant for my ears. Turning back to me, he whispers, "Stay here."

I watch as he rises and stealthily slinks from our hiding place. Even though my bones are probably rattling in terror, I have no intention of taking orders from anyone here. Two steps behind, I shadow his every move.

He turns, casting a disapproving look my way. As far as I'm concerned, there's no explanation or discussion necessary, so I motion for him to keep going. Begrudgingly, he does.

Labored breathing swirls, blocking out any other sounds. My eyes trail from one side of the room to the other in muddled time. What is probably seconds feels like several minutes.

The sergeant lies on his back, with the other man directly across from him, in the same prone position. My hands clench into fists as I consider he is the one who caused this. They shot each other, just seconds apart, but even without seeing, I'm certain the sergeant acted in self-defense.

The doctor rushes to the other man's side first. I think she's going to inspect the welt spilling dark liquid from his chest, but her first instinct is to kick away the weapon near his hand. I should feel worried or sadness that this man's hurt, but all my concern is diverted to the person who brought us here.

My eyes trail the doctor as she darts to the sergeant and hovers over him, asking him questions as she inspects his wound. That deep voice cuts through the air, this time radiating disappointment and disbelief.

"You blew it, *Sergeant*," he coughs out the last word, a thin line of crimson trickling down the side of his mouth. "If you could have just completed the job you were given, you'd be among those who were ensured a lifetime of never having to worry about food or shelter. You would have been rewarded for the service you provided. But you just couldn't do it." He coughs again, his body twitching with effort.

"No one…should decide who gets to live and…who dies…I won't be a part of it…and I won't let it happen." The sergeant's words are stronger than his body. He shudders with the effort of speaking.

Aidan and I still, awaiting a response that doesn't come.

Chapter 65

Rossana sprints around us, apparently awakened from her initial shock. She drops to her knees beside her husband and pleads with the doctor. Aidan and I helplessly watch. Tears flood my eyes. Not so much for the man obviously behind the tracking system, but for the one who tried to stop it.

"Can you help him? Can you stop the bleeding?" Her questions materialize as uneven shrieks.

Rising slowly, the doctor's eyes cloud with regret. "I don't know. But this lab is not equipped for a medical emergency. I've got to transport him to the medical facility."

Rossana shudders. Tears race down her cheeks and her shoulders quake.

"I will call for assistance. I need help to move him, and he needs to be treated now." The doctor strides to a nearby desk and picks up the phone. Almost immediately she launches into discussion, outlining exactly what she needs and where we're located.

Aidan grasps my hand as misery sweeps over him. Rossana leans over Eric, one breath away from collapsing at her husband's side.

Before the phone even clicks back into its cradle, the doctor turns her attention to us. "I don't want to intrude upon their time together, but if you need any information from him, I suggest you ask it now. He needs immediate treatment. And I'm staying with him until he's stable."

I rub my eyes and chew my bottom lip. But minor physical distractions can't stem the flow of tears eager to release like a burst dam. Aidan drops my hand, wrapping his arm around my shoulders, the instant warmth fueling a budding strength that I need more than anything right now.

Pressing his lips to my ear, he whispers through my tangled hair. "We're all that's left. We have to do it for him." Staring straight ahead, I nod. He tugs my hand into his and leads me over to the sergeant.

The doctor scurries in the opposite direction, toward the man she kicked the gun away from just moments ago. She wraps her slender fingers around his wrist, checking for a pulse, while leaning down to hover an ear just over his open mouth. Her eyes watch for the slightest rise and fall of his chest. Pushing back on her haunches, she sighs and shakes her head.

A soft murmur reaches my ears as we reach the fallen soldier. Rossana hovers over her husband, sharing words only meant for him. I turn to Aidan, his pained expression must match mine. *I hate to interrupt, but we have no choice.*

Aidan takes a deep gulp and squats beside Rossana. She slides back on her knees and nods quickly, awkwardly, scooting backward to make room for us. Swiping at her cheeks and runny nose, she closes her eyes and appears to concentrate on taking slow, deep breaths.

I drop beside Aidan as he leans forward, his face just inches from the sergeant's.

"Sir, the doctor's going to take care of you," he barely chokes out. "You have to go with her, but Quinn and I can do whatever needs to be done. Just tell us and we'll do it." His lower lip trembles, and I know it's my turn. *This is not goodbye. We can't lose him now, like this.*

I rest a palm on Eric's shoulder. He bears a crimson welt much like the other man's, but higher, closer to his shoulder than his heart. Blood streams from the wound, a viscous flow puddling beneath his shuddering frame.

Calmness permeates my soul, and I hope it's contagious. His eyes track to whoever is speaking, but his jaw remains square and tightly closed. He's probably biting back the pain.

"Sergeant Bowen, you helped us when we needed it most and I'll never forget that. Without you, I never would have gotten my sister back. You didn't deserve this." My heart seizes, a physical reminder that time is not a luxury we can afford. "You've done your part. You got us here. Now let us finish what we came to do."

He lifts his head and motions for us to lean closer. "Find… Chara. Brandon Chara. He can…help you…disable…the database."

"We accept this mission," Aidan says dutifully. I lean close to his ear and whisper, "Rossana and I are supposed to go, not you. Maybe you should stay and help the doctor take care of him."

"We can't ask her to leave his side right now," he counters. "If that was your husband on the ground bleeding, would you walk away, not knowing if he would take his last breath before you got back?"

It's too much to process at once, but he's right. Our plan was blown to smithereens. We have to adapt. My breathing hitches as a chill sweeps through my core. I remember the promise I made to myself when Riley, Aidan, and I sealed the entrance to our underground shelter. *I'll do whatever it takes to keep the people I care about safe and by my side.*

"You're right," I agree. "She should stay."

Aidan turns to the doctor. "Can you help us find Brandon Chara?"

She purses her lips. "I'll find out where Chara is and get you to him…somehow." She darts toward a desk, pushing aside the chair to tap away on the keyboard. While she tries to track down the database guy, we turn our attention back to the sergeant.

"What if we can't convince him to help us?" I ask, suddenly feeling like an insecure 17-year-old. *In fairness, how many other teenagers are trying to save the world right now?* I should be worried if my lip gloss matches my outfit, not how to convince some military guy to help us deprogram a death chip.

"You have to," he says, attempting a weak smile. "If he won't listen, you tell him he…will never…be…my…towel boy again… if he doesn't do this."

"What?" Aidan barks. *Did Eric lose too much blood? Is he hallucinating?*

"He'll understand."

I have very little knowledge of what happens behind the scenes on a military base and this conversation confirms that it's best if I stay in the dark.

"Located him!" The doctor calls. Aidan dashes to her side as her hands scramble across the desk in search of paper and a pen. He hovers over her, watching intently as she hurriedly sketches our current location in relation to our destination.

Facing Eric again, my stomach churns. Against all instinct, I push a promise past my lips and pray that we can fulfill it. "We'll find him, and we'll finish this!"

He silently raises a shaky hand to his forehead. After a moment of hovering just above his eyebrow, he slices it through the air until it lands on his hip. *Please don't let this be his last salute.* As a fat tear rolls down my cheek, I return the gesture.

Chapter 66

When I rise, Rossana rushes to take my place. She sinks to the floor and wraps her husband in warmth and soft-spoken words.

The doctor shoots a nervous glance toward Eric and pushes the hand-drawn map into Aidan's hands. "If you follow this outline, it will take you to Division Information Officer Chara's temporary office. You must tell him to disable the 'End' command immediately. Until he does that, the lives of every single person we injected with the vaccine…serum…are threatened."

We both listen intently, nodding to convey our understanding.

"Tell him that the general is dead," she says flatly, her eyes drifting to the prone figure. "And the only way to stop his legacy, the genocide of innocent citizens and soldiers, is to remove the 'End' command permanently."

Her features tighten and her tone turns harsh when she mentions the general. I sense her mind is replaying previous interactions with the man when she snaps her attention back to us. "Do you have any questions? I've got to tend to the sergeant's wounds."

Aidan opens his mouth to respond, but before one syllable can cross his lips, the room erupts in chaos.

My vision blurs as the door flies open and camouflage-clad bodies burst through, their weapons scanning the room in unison with their eyes. "Stand down!" Guns, very big guns, track our movement as we clumsily cower in startled panic.

My heart hammers as I struggle to breathe. *What if they shoot?* We're harmless, but the only thing they know about us is that we're trespassing on government property. They probably won't look favorably upon that detail.

My limbs tremble as if I'm one giant leaf fluttering in a breeze, with no ability to contain my skyrocketing fear. Aidan cloaks me in his arms, swiftly guiding me into the chair the doctor just vacated. Just as my bottom brushes the seat, he spins, blocking my view and likely the intruders' view of me. Peeking around Aidan's back, I count five of them trained on our every move. "Everyone, stay calm!"

I stifle a sob. Maybe because being commanded to, "Stay calm!" by heavily-armed soldiers does not invoke any calm feelings.

"Thank you for coming. I am the one who requested assistance." The doctor cautiously steps toward them, hands raised in the air, demonstrating that her approach is non-threatening.

The one barking out commands lowers his gun and swirls a finger in the air, a silent command to the others. Immediately, they buzz around the room as if it's a hive. One drops to the floor, leaning over the motionless man, scanning for signs of life. The others swiftly glide from one end of the room to the other, searching for hidden threats.

"Dr. Noori. I'm glad to see you're okay. Due to the nature of your request, we had to treat this as a potential hostage situation. All looks to be under control. We've got two stretchers outside."

She relaxes slightly. "Thank you so much. I need him," she motions toward Eric, "brought to the medical ward immediately. The other…he should remain in place until a commanding officer arrives."

Another soldier steps forward, having finished her sweep of the room. Her gaze laser-focused on me and Aidan. "Civilians shouldn't be here. This operation has specific security clearances and—." The doctor cuts her off.

"Their presence is necessary, and I accept responsibility for them," she asserts. "There is someone on base that they must speak with. Immediately."

Aidan and I stand back, observing the conversation, well-aware that one wrong interjection could spike suspicion to an irreversible level. In hushed tones, the doctor exchanges tense words with the soldier who appears to lead this group.

After a few minutes, they reach a strained agreement. In unison, they turn toward us. The doctor speaks first.

"Corporal Subban here will escort you to see our colleague." This guy looks anything but thrilled to be our babysitter. "He has graciously agreed to pass along a message from me that I hope will convince Division Information Officer Chara to assist you." Her eyes slide to this Subban guy, but his steely gaze remains focused on us. Through gritted teeth, he asks if we're ready.

My head bobs in an awkward nod, but Aidan verbalizes a clear, "Yes!"

The doctor reaches out, resting a hand on Aidan's shoulder as her eyes volley between us. "After you speak with Chara, ask him to bring you to the med ward. That's where we'll be." Before turning on her heel and rushing back to her current patient, she leaves us with two parting words. "Good luck."

Chapter 67

We trail behind Corporal Subban, who maintains a solid five strides ahead of us. His head turns from side to side, scanning our surroundings. It feels like our way cooler older brother is doing everything he can to avoid being seen with us in public. Distrust tingles in the back of my mind. If confronted, would he turn us over as trespassers, or would he argue we had a valid reason for being on base? His demeanor, which oozes annoyance, doesn't exactly project confidence in the latter.

I guess it's like everything else with this mission—he's all we've got. Just like Aidan and I are the only ones left to fulfill the sergeant's goal. It's become an operation of last resorts.

My thoughts wander the entire time we trek to our destination. When we arrive at the small, windowless office, Subban raps his knuckles on the door. A deep voice promptly answers, "Yes? Come in."

Subban swings the door open and steps through, leaving just enough space for the two of us to crowd inside. The man behind the desk rises cautiously, watching us closely, as if he's evaluating if we present any danger. Which is ridiculous because the guy's got to be about six-and-a-half-feet tall. His size alone is intimidating. As Aidan and I shift uncomfortably under the weight of his gaze, our escort offers an explanation.

"Sir, I've been asked to deliver these two visitors so they could speak with you. Dr. Noori made the request, as a favor. She would have brought them to you herself, but she had a medical emergency."

Subban's words register, but they only raise more questions.

"I'm sorry, do I know you?" Chara asks, his squinting eyes dart back and forth between us. His demeanor isn't exactly welcoming. Clear distrust charges the air.

My discomfort fuels a need to fill the silence. "So we met Sergeant Bowen at Langley Air Force Base. He helped me find my sister and…anyway, he came here to—" before I can continue, he rushes around the desk and stands before me.

"He's here? Bowen's on base?" His words are half-shock, half-incredulity. The reaction freezes me in place. I can't tell if he would be glad to see the sergeant or if he wishes harm upon the man. Aidan brushes up against my shoulder and responds.

"Yes, we came here with him." He stops at that, possibly awaiting Chara's reaction before sharing more information.

Momentarily dropping his guard, the giant man slides his gaze to the ground. "Where is he? I need to talk to him."

Interjecting a cough, Subban indiscreetly excuses himself. "If my presence is no longer needed, I'll be on my way."

"Yes, that's fine, thank you," Chara says dismissively before returning an intent focus on us. Subban slips out the door, effectively leaving us with a comfortable amount of personal space as we all reposition.

"He can't talk…that's why he sent us," I explain, rather ineloquently.

"Is he…?" Panic flashes through the man's green eyes. *That's a good sign if he's concerned that the sergeant's hurt.* Aidan drags a hand through his brown waves and answers.

"He was talking to the doctor, and some guy came in all 'My team's back together' and all hell broke loose. Shots were fired back and forth. The other guy went down, but so did the sergeant. The doctor's trying to save him right now."

"When we left, he was bleeding pretty bad." A shudder runs through me, and I wrap my arms around myself to stifle it.

"The man who came in, was his name General Kuraly?" Chara asks, his eyes locked on mine intently.

I hitch a shoulder up. "The doctor said to tell you the general is dead. I guess it's the same guy. And the sergeant definitely recognized him."

"Where is he now? I need to speak with him immediately." Chara grows more agitated by the second. Energy courses through him, stretching all the way to his long limbs. He raises his hands in the air as he speaks, and his legs tense, as if he's on the verge of bolting out the door.

"We're supposed to ask you to do something before we meet up with the doctor again," Aidan explains.

"What?"

"There's a command in the database, the one for the tracking devices." His eyes narrow at my words, but I keep going. "He said it needs to be removed or disabled."

"You know about the 'End' command *and* the tracking devices?" His eyes search us curiously as his words spill incredulously.

"Look, we don't know much," Aidan admits. "But the sergeant needed our help and…well, he wasn't even sure if you'd help him."

Like he's just taken a punch to the gut, Chara deflates. He runs a palm over his face. "The last time I saw him, I had been… misinformed about him."

Aidan and I glance at each other, wearing identical looks of confusion and uncertainty. *Is this guy going to help us or not?*

Rounding the desk, he plops in the chair, yanking our attention back. Plunking his elbows on the thick desk, he drops his head into his hands as if our mere presence sparks a need to confess what severed their relationship.

Chapter 68

"We worked together to create this database. I didn't really know him well, but we got along good...at first." He inhales a deep breath. "Then suddenly the general told me some things about him that...I don't believe were true. But I didn't realize it at the time. The general warned me that Bowen was showing signs of treason, that he might bail on his duties. And then just like that, he disappeared."

Aidan shakes his head. "That doesn't sound like him. Maybe he was a traitor to the project because he didn't support programming technology to control and kill people. The way he talks about it, he's willing to risk his life to stop this whole thing. Hell, he did risk his life, and we don't even know if he's still breathing right now."

Chara rubs his temples. "I know that now. But I didn't figure it out right away. I heard he went AWOL, and everything changed. The general became…angrier—as if intent on using these things like remote controls, keeping tabs on people and, if necessary, 'eliminating' any problems with minimal effort."

"How?" Aidan asks, his voice hovering just above a whisper.

"I don't understand all the medical aspects, but we're able to send a signal to the tracking technology. It sparks a pulse that zeroes in on the heart. It kind of short circuits, and…" He doesn't need to finish that sentence, and thankfully, he doesn't.

My heart lurches as my head snaps toward Aidan. He pales as if he's just had the wind knocked out of him.

He's got one of those things in him. And so does Riley. And at any moment, someone could decide to just push a button that will stop their hearts from beating. Urgency swells through me, defiant of the haze invading my mind.

"How could something like this even happen?" Although that's the only question passing my lips, a flood of others await. *Who came up with this idea? How many people does it take to put a plan like this into place? And why did they all go along with it?* Morbid curiosity morphs into unspoken accusations. We're standing before someone who had a hand in this process. Someone who helped create a 'kill code.' My eyes narrow in disbelief.

Chara physically recoils, his broad shoulders hunched, as the tender balance between morality and duty hangs between us. Lifting his chin, his eyes raise to meet ours. "When I questioned the assignment, my family was threatened. And I knew full well that the general could follow through on those threats."

"So you—" Accusations swim through my conscience but die on my lips. *If I were in that position, would I do the same thing? If someone said I could save Riley and Aidan, would I do whatever they asked?*

I have no right to judge, and we're only wasting time.

"I didn't have a choice then, but I do now." His green eyes flick back and forth between us, seeking understanding.

"We get it," Aidan says quietly.

"Yeah, we do," I nod, sliding my hand over Aidan's, resting it on top.

He flashes me a smile and we share a flicker of solidarity before he adds, "Now can we get this thing done, because I'm freaking the hell out knowing one of those things is inside me right now."

Chara straightens, leaning forward on his elbows. "Yes, of course. Look, I know everything I told you isn't your concern, but I thought you should know." Before we can ask why, he answers the unspoken question. "You came to the right place. I'll help you. Hell, I owe it to Bowen. And if the general is truly out of the picture, I might not lose my head for doing this."

He raises the lid of the laptop sitting idle on the desk. "Give me a few minutes and then I'll take you to the sergeant. We can all check on him and tell him we completed this mission."

His fingers tap the keys in quick succession while his eyes bounce back and forth as if his mind works just as fast as the machine he commands. Screens of tables and menus flash as he advances toward our shared goal. My foot taps the floor nervously. *Is this really happening? Are we actually going to stop this?*

"Medical clearance requirement…vitals transfer…" he mutters random phrases under his breath as he works.

I glance over at Aidan. He hitches a shoulder before raising his eyebrows and tilting his chin toward Chara. Instead of focusing on the man's actions, I home in on his features. Tension eases out of him as he settles into a role he's obviously well qualified for. The lines along his forehead soften, and a satisfied grin tugs at his cheeks.

Despite the mountain we climbed to get to this point, Aidan and I share a relieved smile. *It's going to work!* He clasps his hand around mine and squeezes. The thrill of our impending success blends with an acute realization of his body's proximity to mine. My nerve endings dance with electricity. Those blue eyes nearly swallow me whole when Chara jolts us back to reality.

"Dammit! The password doesn't work. I set the damn thing and it won't let me in!"

Chapter 69

The man before us stares, unfocused, into the distance, slowly shaking his head. Raising his hands in defeated surrender, he explains. "This is a highly sensitive area of the database. There were always supposed to be two people who had the password. I created it and shared it with General Kuraly. So that means he figured out a way to change it without telling me—or probably anyone."

Aidan releases his grip as if my fingertips just blasted rays of scorching flame. Planting his palms on the desk, he leans forward, locking eyes with Chara. "There's got to be another way. If the guy who changed the password is dead, we have no chance of getting it."

"Status and access around here could change quickly as soon as the general's superiors learn of his…demise." He arcs his head back, squeezing his neck. "This whole thing was set up as a rush job and I didn't program a fail-safe method to prevent the password from being changed or an easy override if it were changed without my knowledge. I need that password. It's the fastest way to remove that command."

"You said the general worked closely with Sergeant Bowen." My words draw their rapt attention. "Maybe the sergeant could guess what the password would be?"

Chara blows out a deep sigh, clearly unimpressed by my suggestion. "We could try that, but we only have three chances. After three wrong guesses, we're locked out. Besides that, we don't even know if Bowen's conscious right now."

Aidan raises and slams his hands down on the desk, anger overtaking frustration. "But we have exactly no other ideas, right?" He pauses, the permeating silence answering his question. "Then we take the only chance we have left!"

Moving faster than I would expect for a man of his size, Chara urgently gathers his laptop, a notebook, and a pen. If we weren't in the middle of a dire situation, the scene might almost be humorous—an intimidating military officer basically jumping to follow two kids and their idea to save the world.

"Follow me."

He leads us through corridors and down hallways, turning right and left until I'm certain we're in a maze with no way out. We bust into what's labeled the Medical Ward, greeted by the only other person we can trust here.

"I am glad to see you. All of you." The doctor's gaze rises to Chara's height. "Were you able to complete your…mission?"

"Not exactly. We need to talk to the sergeant about that," Aidan says.

She raises her hands in a placating gesture. "Right now, he is in recovery and needs to rest. He is in no condition for an update. You can see him in a few hours."

Our escort takes a step forward, resting a hand on the doctor's shoulder. "Trust me, he'll want to see us. We can't shut down this system without him. And I don't know how much time we have. I understand General Kuraly is…"

The doctor nods solemnly.

"Then it's just a matter of time before this place is on lockdown. An immediate, full investigation is inevitable. The smartest thing we can do is eliminate this threat before someone busts in here and takes over where Kuraly left off. You know as well as I do that something this big didn't end with him. Someone else has to know, and when they find out their ringleader is gone, they're not going to just walk away and forget this happened."

Sweat beads along my forehead as we await an end to the silent standoff. After a few tense minutes, the doctor complies.

"You're right," she agrees. "This is much bigger than one man and one base. It is not best for my patient, but it is necessary. Please wait here. I need to wake him, and I'm certain he'll be groggy."

She strides down the sterile hallway, pausing at the second door. Her slim fingers wrap around the door handle, and she gently knocks before twisting the silver handle and pushing through. The three of us wait. There's nothing to say until we get that password, and I really don't want to think about what happens if we don't.

About five minutes later, the doctor pokes her head out of the room and motions us in. Chara brushes past us, clearly abandoning any semblance of manners. Aidan and I reluctantly follow, unsure of our roles.

Chapter 70

Sitting up in bed with his eyelids closed, Eric's body molds to the mattress' upright incline. It's hard to believe the doctor just woke him. He looks completely undisturbed, with no intention of talking to us anytime soon. His pale blue hospital gown reveals hints of white gauze-like bandages wrapped around his shoulder and upper arm.

Rossana balances on the edge of the bed, attentively watching over her husband. Her tear-stained cheeks have dried, but the tracks remain. She drapes a hand over his protectively as she focuses on us.

Without taking his eyes off the sergeant, Chara slides a chair next to the bed and fluidly lowers himself into it. Completely focused on the task, he doesn't even introduce himself to Rossana.

"Hey, man, it's good to see you breathing."

The deep voice startles Eric's eyes open. Focusing on the face before him, recognition relaxes his features instantly.

"It's…good to..be…breathing," the sergeant rasps. The two share a smile before their expressions turn serious. "Look—"

Chara shuts down the implication of that one word immediately. "We'll catch up later, after you've had some rest. Right now, we have an issue, and I need the full power of your brain to focus on that. Okay?"

The sergeant nods, perhaps preserving his voice. Shadows linger beneath his eyes, but he struggles to focus. Chara quickly explains that he needs a password in order to remove the 'End' function from the database. When it was created, he and the general shared a password, but at some point, the general changed it, and now we're locked out.

After allowing a moment for the sergeant to digest the information, Chara runs a thick hand through his thinning hair and states our true purpose for this visit. "I believe you worked pretty closely with the general on this project. Do you have any idea what he might have set as the password?"

Dropping his head back on the pillow, the sergeant's eyes drift across the ceiling. He pinches the bridge of his nose and exhales a sigh. "I don't know…much about him… but I know that bastard…was arrogant. Maybe…arrogant enough to use… his own name as a…password? Try Kuraly."

Chara dips his head to the side in consideration. "Yeah, I could see that." His fingers dance across the keyboard before he taps the 'Enter' button with a flourish. Eyes fixed on the screen, his chin drops and his shoulders slump. Our attempt is rejected.

"It didn't work." He shakes his head. "We have one more try."

"I thought we had three chances?" Aidan asks.

"We do," Chara confirms. "I used one in my office before I realized the password was changed."

Tapping his forehead, the sergeant scrunches his eyes closed. We wait, fearful that one erroneous blink could somehow prompt another wrong guess. His whispered mumbles string together nonsensical series of words. "Department of…assets? No… infrastructure…population…"

Aidan brushes a knuckle along my thumb. The slight touch slows some of the anxiety swirling within me. That is until I notice his clenched teeth and stiff posture. Maybe the gesture was meant to sooth his nerves, not that I'm complaining.

The sergeant's seemingly incoherent rambling grows louder. Pride washes over his face as he declares, "Department of Operational Assets under the Resources, Infrastructure, and Population arm."

Chara narrows his eyes and raises his shoulders. "That's way too long. Could it be just one of those words maybe?"

"No, not his style," the sergeant scratches the stubble on his chin before thrusting his pointer finger in the air, punctuating his words. "I know! Try the acronyms, DOA RIP!"

With a contemplative nod, Chara lowers his head and hesitantly types one letter at a time. Each momentary pause invites an alternative, any other suggestion that may bring us success. Ragged breaths fill the charged space as we all wait, balancing on a string over the chasm between hope and defeat.

With a gulp, Chara raises his pointer finger. "Last chance.

Any other ideas?"

Three heads shake as the sergeant crosses his arms, eyeing the group. He tosses his chin back, giving his former colleague the "go ahead."

Finger hovering over the "Enter" key, Chara squeezes his eyes shut and depresses the button.

Chapter 71

No one breathes. For one collective moment, fear clings to fate's impending outcome.

Chara's stone face cracks. He tosses his head back, swiping a massive palm over his mouth. Leveling his chin, his arms drop, revealing a gleaming smile. "It worked! We did it!"

Relieved exhales roll into a low rumble of laughter that bounces around the room. Our brief celebration fades as Chara returns his attention to the laptop.

"Alright, just a few more commands and we'll be done."

"Will it…the database…still show where people are?" I ask quietly. Faces flash through my mind—Benny, Rose, Chris, although they might not have trackers. And I don't even know their last names. We never asked Rose's or Chris' and I honestly can't remember the exact spelling of Benny's. Riley would probably know, but he's always just been Benny to me.

I shake my head before anyone can answer. "Forget it, it doesn't matter."

Chara's serious gaze lands on me but shifts to the others as he addresses my question.

"We can't take the whole database down. Too many people know about it. But we can remove the 'End' code. The mastermind behind that is gone, and I doubt more than a handful of others even know about it."

Sergeant Bowen sits up straighter and wraps a hand around his wife's. "You know, the system really wouldn't be all that bad if it was used to help people."

Chara slowly nods in agreement but Aidan, Rossana, and I glance at each other uncertainly.

"I'm not saying we should continue to track people without their consent, but we could use the information we already have to ensure that those who need help get it, in some form."

"That's a lot to consider right now," Rossana says. "I think you should just focus on healing for the moment."

"Yes," Chara agrees. "One thing at a time." Turning his focus back to the screen, he retreats to the technical aspects of our mission.

Dr. Noori sweeps into the room, eager to check on her patient. She strides past the rest of us and pauses at the sergeant's bedside. While she speaks to him and Rossana, I take a step closer to Aidan and arc my neck toward his ear. He instinctively leans nearer, as if gravity effortlessly draws us together.

"What now?" I whisper.

He hitches a shoulder up and faces me. Instinctively, my eyes drop to his lips, which are dangerously close to mine. "We did what we came here to do. We should get back to our families."

"What about the sergeant? I wonder when it's okay to leave him."

"You know Rossana wants to check on Millie, so she's probably eager to leave now that the sergeant's doing much better. I bet it'll be soon."

He's right, of course, yet I can't get used to the parade of people, no matter how few it involves, that cross our path only to leave just as quickly as they appeared. Maybe all the losses these past months have fueled a need for some gains. Maybe saying goodbye these days feels too permanent.

"Yeah, and they can take care of themselves," I agree. "So, how do we do this without sounding like we don't care what happens to him?" *Because I do, I truly do.*

Chara folds the laptop and rises. "Finished. It's done." Smiles around the room greet his announcement.

The background chatter fades and Dr. Noori turns on her heel to face us. Clasping her hands together, she addresses the room. "Congratulations on pulling off your mission. So many people will never know what you have done for them. And I thank you on their behalf, as well as my own."

She swivels to meet Rossana's eyes.

"Your husband is stable, and I have no doubt he'll fully recover. Ideally, he would recuperate here for a few days, but given the circumstances, it's best if he is not discovered on base. A major investigation will be forthcoming, sooner rather than later."

Rossana nods in understanding but before she can speak, the sergeant speaks for himself.

"No," Eric half-coughs, half-barks. "None of this should have ever happened. It's stopping with Kuraly. I'm not spending the rest of my life running away."

We all share a startled look. He talked about disappearing into the sunset when this was all over. I guess that plan has changed.

"Take Quinn and Aidan back to their families. Then get Millie and come back here. We'll find a way to get you inside. I'll stay here and deal with whatever the government wants to throw at me. But I'll be damned if anyone expects me to sneak out of here with my tail between my legs."

"If you're sure," Rossana answers, half-question half-statement. "I'll be back as soon as I can."

She shakes the doctor's hand. "I can't thank you enough. And Eric's right, he's stable but he needs more rest. I'll go get our dog and then I'll be back. Once he's strong enough, we'll leave, but for now we can't risk it. He needs medical care."

Relief relaxes the lines cresting the doctor's forehead and she releases an audible sigh. Stealing a glance at the sergeant confirms her statement—he hasn't shifted an inch. His body is at complete rest, sinking into the bed. His eyes flutter beneath closed lids, stationary arms rest at his sides.

"I'll find a way to get you back in after you tend to your business," the doctor agrees. "But it is best if the three of you are gone before any officials arrive. If others find out you were here when the general died you will be pulled into an investigation. You will not be allowed to leave, and we will have to explain what you were doing here in the first place."

"Alright, you two ready?" The conversation breaks and Rossana faces us.

With one last glance at the sergeant, Aidan and I nod. We are most definitely ready to go *home*.

"I can escort you out," Chara volunteers. "We'll take the least conspicuous route." *Ah, the irony in that statement. The tallest man I've ever met is going to sneak us out of a military base unnoticed.*

The doctor nods and Chara steps toward the door, waiting. *This is it. Goodbye.*

"I know we shouldn't wake the sergeant, so please thank him," Aidan starts. "I mean, really…thank all of you for everything. I'm glad we were able to help."

I direct my question to Rossana as a heaviness clamps my chest. "How will we know that he makes it out of here, okay?" We have no connection to these people other than a chance meeting at the end of the world. Once again, the others who've crossed our path flash through my mind—Rose, Chris, Jasmine. In reality, we've lost them because we have no way to find them. *Why would this be any different?*

Rossana clasps a hand around mine as a shaky smile tugs her cheeks. "As soon as Eric's better, we'll figure out a way to get word to you. Somehow."

Although I have no idea how that will be possible in a world without cell phones in every palm, I believe every word she says.

With nothing more to discuss, Chara shuttles us through dark hallways and empty corridors before depositing us outside. The base is eerily quiet. I imagine it's the calm before a buzzing hive is shaken, and officials swarm in search of answers.

Chapter 72

The ride north is quiet, each of us lost in our own thoughts. Rossana drives while Aidan serves as my personal pillow in the back seat. Minutes into the drive, my eyes drift closed. The next time they open, the sun's announcing a new day and we're nearly back at the school.

When I stir, Aidan squeezes my shoulder, whispering, "We did it! We actually did it!"

I nod as a groggy smile slides across my lips, prompting a yawn. "We did. I just wish all four of us were coming back."

"I know, but he's gonna be okay." I settle into the crook of his shoulder and watch the scenery blur beyond the window.

The car slows as Rossana steers it to the back loading dock. We bid quick farewells and hustle to the building. A soldier stops us just inside the door, noting that this entryway will be closed, and the main entrance is open as of today. We thank her and continue to the classroom where our family awaits.

7:14 a.m. It's been less than 12 hours, but it might as well have been a week. Somehow, we crammed just about every emotion into one mission. Now that we're back, it feels like a dream I'm hoping to never repeat.

Kaylee shifts as we tiptoe into the room. Her blinking eyes fly open when she spots our slinking figures. Aidan presses a finger to his lips, unsuccessfully encouraging her to stifle any excitement. Instead, she throws the flimsy blanket to the floor and jumps out of her cot, squealing.

She launches herself into Aidan's arms. I can't help but smile. *At least she's forgotten how angry she was with her brother.*

Scott rouses, sitting up on his cot and rubbing his eyes. He stands and pulls his two kids in for a hug. Of course, Riley doesn't move. That girl could sleep through fireworks on the Fourth of July.

As I step toward my sister, a gentle hand tugs me back. With a broad smile, Kaylee pulls me into the group hug. As arms and emotion envelop me, I know that this is where I'm meant to be in this exact moment.

After everything that's happened, hope still exists. I may not have my whole family anymore, and my childhood home may be swirling in the hazardous aftermath of the tropical storm. But even Mother Nature can't break the bonds forged by loss and survival.

We wake Riley and fill all three of them in on our adventure, answering questions they toss out along the way. While the others just woke, Aidan and I crave rest. Once everyone's ready, we meander to the cafeteria for breakfast.

Fueled by success, we gulp down waffles and fruit chunks.

It's the best food I've tasted in what feels like forever. Just as we dump our trash and clear our trays, the news woman enters the cafeteria. Her eyes scan the waning line as she takes her place at its end.

I tangle my fingers with Aidan's as we pass through the open doors to the hallway. "Hey, you guys go on ahead. We'll catch up with you."

They all turn toward me as if I've just announced that we should steal another boat.

"Everything okay, Quinn?" Riley's chin drops as she pins me with her doe-like gaze.

"Everything's fine." My confident smile dissolves her concern. She nods and hesitantly turns away, wandering back to the classroom. Scott and Kaylee follow her, throwing questioning glances over their shoulders.

Aidan twists his head toward me and narrows his eyes. "What plans do you have for me exactly?"

"I think there's someone we need to talk to."

By mid-morning, Aidan and I snuggle in the cocoon of his gym mats. Scott was okay with it because he said we both looked too exhausted for any "funny business" and, since it's daytime, he, Riley, and Kaylee would be coming and going, so we wouldn't truly have privacy.

Not that it mattered, because within minutes of my head touching down on the pillow, my mind sank into oblivion. Dreamless sleep recharged my body and refreshed my mind. The others let us sleep through lunch.

By mid-afternoon, we slowly return to consciousness. This

time, Scott and Riley have updates for us. Now that the water's gone, transfers between communes have begun. Our aunt's been scheduled for the evening transport arriving here sometime after dinner. That was the good news.

Scott was finally able to get information about our missing party. Jeff's mom is alive. She was found by a rescue boat, unconscious. They brought her to an area hospital, where she spent days in a noncommunicative state. She just started talking yesterday and provided names of those she was with before she ended up there.

She doesn't believe that any of the others survived. Their boat capsized and, in a frantic fight with the elements, they lost sight of each other. They were all scrambling to help Jeff but couldn't coordinate. The pounding rain and swirling water carried them away in different directions. That's all she remembers before she blacked out.

The hospital was able to track down her other son, Matt. He's in the process of being reassigned to support local rebuilding efforts. Her plan is to stay at the hospital until Matt arrives and together, they'll figure out a future.

Confirmation of his worst fear renders Scott despondent. Dark circles ring his eyes and his complexion pales. Any hope for his wife and other daughter to stroll through the door and join us in our makeshift-shelter classroom plummets. I imagine he'll paint a brave front across his features for his son and daughter, but for the moment he exudes raw pain.

Once again, sadness dampers what would otherwise be a celebration. I'm thankful that we'll reunite with our aunt, but it doesn't eclipse the pain I feel for Aidan's loss. We may have suspected the worst, but expectation doesn't soften reality.

As we ready for dinner, the loudspeaker buzzes. An echo through the hallway confirms that it's not just our classroom preparing for the announcement. A moment later, a voice delivers a message to all temporary residents, both civilian and soldier.

Chapter 73

"Attention everyone, following is a message we've been instructed to share with you. Note that it is being broadcast in every safety commune and military facility throughout the United States this evening."

We all freeze in place, concentrating every ounce of energy on our sense of hearing. There's a low crackle before the familiar buzz, then a new voice.

"Good evening. This is Lieutenant Colonel Christopher Morris of the United States Armed Forces, speaking to you from Fort Meade, Maryland, on behalf of the National Security Agency. This nation is facing challenges like never before. We have lost many loved ones, friends, and neighbors over the past few weeks. Additionally, we have lost leaders, soldiers, and public service responders.

"What we do now will determine who we are as a nation. Although it may feel like forces beyond our control are set on separating us, if we come together, we will prevail.

"You may be wondering why President Taves isn't giving this address. He and several members of his administration are at an undisclosed location. The current state of our infrastructure exposes us to risk for a foreign attack. We must be vigilant in protecting our interests. Thus, I cannot share any further details at this time. But know that your government is at work and will guide all efforts to rebuild this great country.

"Finally, I'd like to acknowledge all those who have sacrificed and worked tirelessly to help our nation recover from the tragedies of the past several weeks. Our first responders, police force, military, and healthcare workers have all worked non-stop to save as many lives and heal as many injuries as possible.

"There's one member of my team that I'd like to publicly thank for his resolute service and dedication. Sergeant Eric Bowen has overcome unimaginable odds to save hundreds of thousands of American lives. I won't go into detail, as this address is long enough. But know that if you are walking this great Earth, living and breathing freedom in this great country, this man may have had a hand in it.

"I will provide an update again tomorrow, and the day after that, and the day after that. You will hear from a leader of your government every day until we have secured safety within our borders for every American. Together, we will rise from the tragedies and united we will stand strong. Until the next update, I bid you a good evening."

Scott swipes a palm over his chin. "Well, I know what

everyone'll be talking about at dinner tonight. I'm surprised we didn't get a message like that sooner. Maybe they were waiting until the flooding cleared out."

I rush to Aidan's side. For a moment, the room and the others fade to a distant background. He's all that I see.

"You guys go ahead. We'll catch up to you." He doesn't take his eyes off me as he effectively dismisses our family.

Scott and Kaylee trudge through the door, their steps slowed by the weight of their losses. I think we've all adapted to the continuous flow of loss, expectation, and disappointment. It's made each of us stronger, if only so that we can move forward, better prepared for tomorrow's challenges.

The second we're alone, Aidan grasps my shoulders, leaning forward slightly so that we're eye to eye.

"Did you hear that? Bowen's fine! And they even acknowledged him. Must mean that general is the only one who wanted him dead." Aidan's genuine smile reflects my own. "Even if he's still recovering, he's in good hands."

"Why didn't he say anything about the trackers?" I wonder out loud.

Silence looms as our brains kick into overdrive, analyzing what we heard as well as what wasn't said. Aidan waggles a finger in the air. "There was no reason. What we did worked...we stopped the trackers from backfiring on us all..."

I nod slowly. "Yeah...if they were neutralized, or whatever it would be, then why tell everyone? People have enough to worry about right now."

"What do you think is up with Taves?" Aidan asks. "You think he's dead but they don't want to say?"

"I think it's either that or he's hurt…bad," I agree. "He gave those other announcements until right before this latest storm. I don't think the president would just step away unless it wasn't by choice."

"Well, let's just hope this Morris guy is better than Taves," Aidan adds. "Although he did call out the sergeant, so that must mean something. He didn't sound anything like that guy who pulled the gun at Detrick."

"I guess it's over. Like, really over. And we're supposed to move forward, somehow."

Our temporary relief over the sergeant's presumed safety is shuddered by reality. We're meant to start living again, even though more than a few faces are missing from our vision of the future.

Aidan runs his fingers through my hair. Pausing at my neck, he traces my jawline as his crystal blue eyes follow the movement. Drawing our bodies closer, he presses his forehead to mine. Sadness radiates as he trembles beneath my touch. I wrap my arms around him and squeeze as if I can release him from the pain.

With no clear picture of what our future will hold, I'm certain of at least one thing. Aidan and I will be together. We'll live for those whose hearts no longer beat. Whose lungs no longer breathe. Whose eyes no longer blink.

My own eyes pool with tears as Aidan takes a step back. His subtle nod confirms that no words need pass between us.

We will remember those we lost and honor them by rebuilding a society that respects nature and values civility and kindness. Perhaps we can avoid the consequences of Mother

Nature's fury by building a world where its inhabitants revere the environment that supports all forms of life.

Shuffling feet announce the return of Scott and Kaylee. They silently embrace Aidan in comfort as a soft hand tugs at my elbow. I turn to face my sister. She's been by my side through a brutal cycle of loss, love, and the continuation of life.

It doesn't matter where we live, as long as we have shelter. Home will never again be a structure with four walls and a roof. Home is wherever my loved ones are, as long as we're together.

As Riley squeezes my hand and flashes a solemn yet reassuring smile, hope emerges.

Epilogue

A shrill cry pierces the night. My body stills, freezing in an unnatural position that was cozily comfortable while asleep. Instantly, I'm hyperaware of the feathery tickle itching my nose, begging to be scratched. My muscles threaten to revolt by cramping if I'm forced to maintain this position much longer.

The room is veiled in darkness, as is typical for the middle of the night. A cough echoes seconds before another scream erupts. This one louder and angrier. The mattress shifts as Aidan flops toward me. When a wail sounds, demanding immediate attention, he jerks upright.

Even with my eyelids gently pressed together in feigned sleep, I can envision it when he scratches the scruff on his chin and tosses the covers aside. "I'll get her, honey. You sleep," he whispers, leaning down to kiss my cheek.

"Mmmmmm," I mumble in the groggiest tone I can muster.

He chuckles. "You can't fool me! Maybe if you were Riley you'd sleep through the baby's cries, but I know you heard." His bare feet pad toward the door. "It's okay, it's my turn to check on her anyway."

"I love you!" I call as he passes through the door and rushes to the nursery. He always says it's his turn, even when it's most definitely mine.

With the whole bed to myself, I stretch across both my side and Aidan's so that I know when he returns. Snuggling under the covers, a smile tugs at my cheeks as my relaxed mind dreamily catalogs the people and circumstances responsible for my happiness.

After Mother Nature's season of destruction, people came together to rebuild. It was slow and painful, with constant reminders of the loved ones we lost, as well as the many modern conveniences that disappeared in an instant.

We never heard from President Taves again. He must not have survived what basically became a rebirth of the environment—what started with a great earthquake along the East Coast continued with Yellowstone's eruption in the West and concluded with a massive tropical storm that washed the ash away. We survived being shaken, scorched, and soaked.

Leaders came together to create order from chaos and restore civility where fear reigned. The country was carved into sections and governed locally to rebuild. Teams of experienced first responders conducted recovery efforts, clearing structures and deeming them safe for habitation.

Although the home Riley and I grew up in remained standing, it was severely damaged by flooding. Given the memories that we preferred to seal away with the house, we started over with authority-issued housing.

Thankfully, we could request placement near Aidan's family. Initially, Riley and I shared a modest home with our Aunt Robin while Aidan, Kaylee, and their dad lived nearby in the small village we were assigned. The bonds we formed only grew stronger with time. Kaylee became like a younger sister to me. Scott was a tremendous asset to our small community—always at the ready to help others, but he stayed single, never fully recovering from the loss of his wife and other daughter. He preferred to spend his nights alone, often disappearing after a hard rain, I suspect, to the caves, somewhere within himself, still hoping.

Once I turned eighteen, Aidan and I requested our own home and announced our plans to build a future together. It took about six months for our request to be approved, and we happily accepted the simple two-bedroom cottage we were granted.

Status dwindled in importance as survivors learned to trust each other, salvaging supplies and reusing anything that endured nature's wrath. So while technological advances and structures may have regressed, civilization prevailed.

Just as the edges of my conscious slip into a hazy dream-like place, a gentle humming drifts to my ears. Bare feet slap the floor as Aidan attempts to tiptoe back to bed. A gentle coo awakens my senses and my eyes flutter open.

"Sorry," he whispers. "Someone *really* wanted Mommy."

"That's okay," I half-yawn, spreading my arms to welcome the two loves of my life. Placing Hope between us, Aidan climbs back into bed. She quickly settles into a relaxed state, nestled in warmth and safety.

In comfortable calm, our breathing grows slower and thoughts drift to all those who were part of the journey that led us here.

We never found out what happened to Rose and Emily. The last time we saw them, Emily was moving her mother out of the house where Aidan and I took shelter during a tornado. We spent the night in Rose's basement with her. We'll never forget the place where we first met. Our paths crossed when Aidan was *borrowing* water from an outside spigot, and I diverted from a run to pet some of Rose's feline entourage. Sometimes we tell Hope stories about those times, even though she can't understand yet. Someday we'll tell her everything that happened during the summer that Nature fought back.

Scott says that any lessons learned from these disasters will be forgotten too soon and that history is bound to repeat itself. Humans are resourceful and inventive, but that innate determination to survive generally guides their actions. The common good can quietly fade into the background when the individual's needs take priority over all else.

But for now, we'll focus on what we've gained instead of what we lost. On how we're all starting over, on even ground, in a society that hinges on cooperation and community.

Aidan and I still visit Couturier Caverns. It was strong enough to withstand the storm. Somehow my Northern Lights still shine. We flip the switch sparingly, just long enough for a glimpse every few visits. Then we settle in with a lantern and reminisce about the summer we lived down here.

Sharing smiles, we relive sneaking away from the others to flirt. We chuckle about Scott's seamless planning, accounting for every crumb of food down to each person's bathroom breaks. Someday we'll bring Hope here and tell her about her parents' underground adventures.

When the laughter subsides, sobering memories creep from the shadows. We talk to Aidan's mom and sister, and even Jeff, in case they can hear us, somehow. We recollect the message Dr. Noori recorded, with a little help from local TV show host Amy Kehm. She and a crew member traveled down to Detrick. With minimal equipment—and a boost from her station's generator— once basic communication channels were restored, she was able to capture and share a message from a credible source.

The goal was to spread understanding of what happened and how we can prevent it from happening again. That message still plays through my mind sometimes.

"I am Doctor Safiya Noori, a physician serving in the United States military. I want to talk to you about the crossroads we have reached, and what we as a nation can do to take the best path forward.

"If you are hearing this message, you have seen it for yourselves. We've been hit with one natural disaster after another. Besides that, you may have witnessed species of insects growing more aggressive, including cases where they've caused grave injury to those they've bitten or stung. Maybe you've noticed trees and plant life dying, withering for no clear reason. Animals scarce, as if hiding.

"Whether you want to believe it or not, nature turned against us. Maybe we destroyed one too many forests or let one too many oil spills ravage the ocean. Maybe climate change paved the way for an environmental collapse. I don't know why the world went wrong, but it did.

"Obviously, it's too late to stop the chain of events that have occurred, but if there's anything we can do to honor those we lost through tragedy after tragedy, it is to live for them. We can't make careless choices now and assume the effects will never make an impact.

"Right now, every single one of us must come together to create a sustainable community. Not just for today, but for many years to come. I believe we've been given a clean slate, and if we can put our differences aside and focus not on each individual's wants, but on the community as a whole, then perhaps we can build a better world, one small square at a time."

AUTHOR NOTE

Dear Reader,

Thanks for sticking with Quinn, Riley, and Aidan! I hope you enjoyed reading about their struggles and triumphs. I'd like to envision that they spend a long, healthy life together in a society that values environmental sustainability and embodies peaceful coexistence.

Although this is the last book of the *Nature's Fury* series, I'm uncertain if any of the characters will demand to be heard again. In the spirit of "never say never," who knows if the opportunity to revisit the story will present itself. If it does, I'll be ready to weave it into another book or short story.

As always, if you enjoyed *Hope Emerges*, please share a review on Goodreads and/or the retailer site where you purchased it. Reviews help both authors and readers!

Until the next time, stay in touch through social media and my website. I'll announce future projects there. And sign up for my newsletter to get the latest updates right in your inbox!

ACKNOWLEDGEMENTS

Michelle Preast of Indie Book Cover Designs, that's a wrap, for now, on the series. I honestly don't know which book's cover I like best because I love them all so much! Thank you for creating amazing depictions of each book's contents. Your designs invite readers and make me giddy! ☺

Emily Angeline, Robin Asick & Beth Suit, thank you for serving as beta readers for every book in this series! You scrutinized my drafts and made the final stories better than I could have ever imagined. Beta reading takes an incredible amount of time because it's not just reading, it's truly processing every word choice while weighing believability, character motivations, and so much more. Yet you all gave your time and energy freely. I can't express how much I appreciate all of you – and the time and talent you shared with me, Quinn, Riley, and the gang!

Vanessa Anderson at Night Owl Freelance, phew – we did it! A whole series. Thank you for everything – the cheering, the challenging, the cheekiness. ☺ Absolutely all of it boosted every book in the series and improved the overall story arc. I greatly appreciate your input and expertise, especially when I was trying to figure out how this whole process worked!

Friends & family members, thank you for your ongoing support! A simple text, email, or even your familiar faces at signing events went a long way in boosting my confidence and I truly appreciate every effort you made!

ACKNOWLEDGEMENTS

Scott, Landon & Aidan, this book's dedicated to you! Your encouragement helped me stay on track to finish this series and your input helped me fix a few plot holes and story details! Thanks for always being there when I needed to talk about the story, or talk about anything but the story! ♥

ABOUT THE AUTHOR

A. E. Faulkner was born and raised in Pennsylvania. When she's not lost in a book, she loves spending time with her husband and two sons, especially while hiking, biking, or exploring nature. She loves *almost* everything about nature—ticks excluded, and one of her biggest fears is the repercussions we will face when nature can no longer tolerate human destruction. As such, she never tires of reading dystopian-themed tales. Stories about the end of the world absolutely fascinate her.

FOLLOW HER WORK

To learn more visit:
AuthorAEFaulkner.com

She can also be found:

Tweeting @AuthAEFaulkner

on Facebook @authaefaulkner

& on Instagram @authoraefaulkner

To leave a Goodreads review, please visit
Goodreads.com and search for
Hope Emerges by A. E. Faulkner.

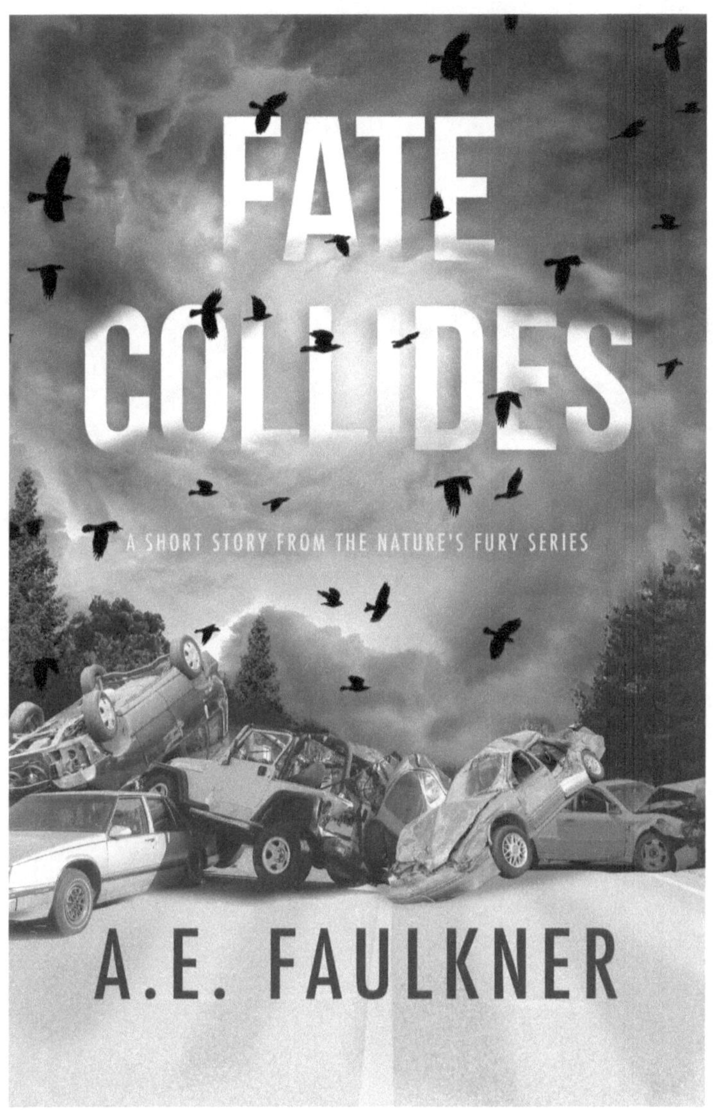

FATE
COLLIDES
A SHORT STORY FROM THE NATURE'S FURY SERIES
A.E. FAULKNER